Far Wychwood mysteries by Patricia Harwin:

Arson and Old Lace
Slaying Is Such Sweet Sorrow

Available from Pocket Books

SLAYING IS SUCH SWEET SORROW

TRICIA HARWIN

POCKET BOOKS
New York   London   Toronto   Sydney

This book is a work of fiction. Names, characters, places and incidents are products of the author's imagination or are used fictitiously. Any resemblance to actual events or locales or persons, living or dead, is entirely coincidental.

An *Original* Publication of POCKET BOOKS

 POCKET BOOKS, a division of Simon & Schuster, Inc.
1230 Avenue of the Americas, New York, NY 10020

ISBN: 0-7434-8225-5

First Pocket Books printing March 2005

10 9 8 7 6 5 4 3 2 1

POCKET and colophon are registered trademarks of Simon & Schuster, Inc.

Cover designed by Julienne Ha

Manufactured in the United States of America

For information regarding special discounts for bulk purchases, please contact Simon & Schuster Special Sales at 1-800-456-6798 or business@simonandschuster.com

For Mother and Dad,
who would have loved
all this.

ACKNOWLEDGMENTS

I want to acknowledge the help of all the people in Oxford who gave me directions, information, and good cheer, and whose names I didn't take down; my hard-working, imaginative agent, Pam Strickler; and my creative, conscientious editor, Christina Boys.

CHAPTER ONE

Since there's no help, come let us kiss and part.
Nay, I have done, you get no more of me,
And I am glad, yea, glad with all my heart,
That thus so cleanly I myself can free.
Shake hands forever, cancel all our vows,
And when we meet at any time again,
Be it not seen in either of our brows
That we one jot of former love retain.
　　　　　　　　　　　　—Michael Drayton

It was no use lying to myself, the baby was not in the house. I had searched every nook a sixteen-month-old boy could fit in, and Rowan Cottage had far more nooks than most houses. He was gone.

And it was my fault. What kind of grandmother leaves a toddler sleeping on the sofa and goes out to dig a damn perennial border, just because a sunny April day is a rarity in England? Although Archie had never shown any ability to reach, let alone turn, a doorknob, I knew how determined he was to figure things out. Emily was right, I wasn't fit to watch him. This time she would cut us apart.

When I had moved to this Gloucestershire village almost two months before, the plan had been for me to take care of him almost every day while my daughter practiced psychotherapy at the hospital in Oxford. But when I unwittingly put him in mortal danger not once, but twice, she had revised it to a visit or two a week. Not that I'd ever intended to put him in harm's way, but Archie, at barely a year and a half, and I, at sixty, were so alike in our impulsiveness—our need to pull back veils had caused us to stumble through one where a murderer waited.

I went to the front door and grabbed hold of the lintel, weak with apprehension, looking out at the one road through Far Wychwood, a two-lane that connected with a main route to Oxford a mile beyond the village. People went down our little road pretty fast, although there was a four-lane several miles away that got most of the traffic.

The scruffy black cat that had adopted me peered around the door of the potting shed by the stone wall. It was his favorite place of refuge when Archie visited, though I had also known him to simply disappear for days. He was so easily spooked that I hadn't yet been permitted to touch him. I had no doubt he deeply resented that I gained his trust with tuna fish and then brought in a toddler on him.

"Where's he gone, Muzzle?" I murmured.

That ridiculous name was the one he had come with, given by the old man who had lived across the road when I first moved to Far Wychwood, the only person the cat had ever completely trusted. I glanced over at the piece of ground where his cottage had stood, just an empty rectangle of tall weeds under the April sun. The ruins of the burned-out building had been cleanly removed, as if George Crocker's long life there had never been. "Muzzle" was the old man's country pronunciation of "mouse hole," the cat's field of operations in that ancient cottage.

I stepped out into my front garden, and he came toward me warily, tail in the air. The scar on my right arm throbbed dully as the sight of the old man's property raised subconscious memories of the day I'd been caught in the blaze that destroyed the cottage.

A few seconds later a shock went through my whole body at a screech of brakes and a shout off to my right. I ran into the road, my heart knocking the breath out of my chest, knowing what I would see.

A tiny shape lay unmoving on the shoulder of the road by the waist-high stone wall in front of the old village schoolhouse. I knew it was Archie by the overalls and the ringlets of yellow hair, and despair slumped like a sinkhole into my brain.

Running toward him, I was vaguely aware of some kind of car sitting slantwise across the road and a male figure with something red about him, standing there looking down at Archie.

I stopped a few feet from the man and screamed, "Stupid, stupid— Couldn't slow down, could you? You've killed my baby!"

"No, no, I didn't, I swear!" he stuttered. "I *didn't* hit him, he fell—"

I sank to my knees beside Archie. His quicksilver presence, incessantly searching and questioning, seemed utterly stilled. He was sprawled on his stomach with his blue eyes closed, his soft pink lips open, even the curls seeming to lie lifeless against his head. My faithless husband, my brilliant Emily—it seemed to me at that moment I'd never loved them or anyone except this child lying like a piece of refuse beside the road.

I heard the man babbling on, "I was driving along, at the speed limit, I assure you, and I saw the little boy standing on the wall there, and then as I reached it I saw him lose balance and fall. He hit his head against that large rock, do you see? I stopped to help him . . ."

Then, incredibly, Archie made a little moaning sound and turned on his side. His features puckered into a frown, his eyes still shut.

Relief flooded through me. The man exclaimed, "There, he's not— He's knocked himself out, that's all! Best to take him round to your local GP. Let me carry him for you."

"There's no doctor here anymore," I answered breathlessly. "The one we had's been gone ever since the murder."

"Murder?" he repeated, startled.

"But somebody has to examine him," I went on. "Look where his poor little head's starting to swell, behind his ear. Concussion, it must be, oh, Archie, oh, God—"

"Oxford's less than half an hour away," he said. "We'll take him to the main hospital." He slipped his arms under Archie and lifted him from the ground. "If you'll just hold the door," he began, stepping toward his car. I scrambled up and jerked the passenger-side door open. "No, best let him lie on the rear seat—" he began, but I broke in.

"I'm going to hold him, don't try to stop me."

"Very well, get in and I'll give him to you." We accomplished this, and I sat cradling Archie while the man got in beside us and started the car. He glanced over and said reassuringly, "There, his color's coming back, isn't it?"

"Just drive!" I snapped.

But as we headed through the village I had to admit that Archie's cheeks were pinker now, and he had started making mewing noises, scowling, closing his fingers around the bottom of my cardigan. After a few minutes he tried to sit up, pulling on the sweater. His eyes popped open as he got nearly vertical. He grabbed the right side of his head, where the swelling was increasing rapidly, stared at me indignantly, and said, "Ow!"

"Just be quiet, baby," I said. "I know it hurts, but we're going to make it all better."

His face scrunched up and he wept in soft whimpers, knowing another outcry would hurt just as that one had.

My panic had begun to subside and now I felt sorry for my rudeness. It hadn't, after all, been the man's fault. I glanced at him for the first time. He was, at a guess, in his early twenties, thin and lanky, dressed in jeans and a red sweater under a tweed jacket. His straight brown hair kept flopping over his forehead, so he had to push it back every few minutes. If I were his mother I'd make him get a decent haircut, I thought fleetingly.

"Sorry," I said. "I shouldn't have jumped to conclusions, but I tend to do that."

"Not at all," he said with that embarrassed air the English get when accepting an apology. "Quite understandable. I'm Tom Ivey," he added shyly.

"Catherine Penny. And Archie Tyler." I nodded toward my grandson.

"Oh, I say, is *that* who—" His amiable young face was filled with amazement. "Peter Tyler's son! Of course, and you're the American mother-in-law. Peter has often mentioned you, said you lived in Far Wychwood, but somehow I never connected—I'm Peter's colleague, well, that's to say, I'm only a postgraduate student, a junior research fellow, while Peter of course is a lecturer and, we're all sure, will be named to the headship tonight, as our current head's retiring at the end of this term. If anyone at Mercy College would be an excellent head of faculty, he would. And of course you'll be there to see the presentation, I mean to say, I'm sure the little chap will be completely recovered well beforehand—"

"I'm not going," I said brusquely. "Can't you drive any faster, Mr. Ivey?"

"Call me Tom. 'I hold he loves me best that calls me Tom.' Sorry, couldn't resist, that's from Thomas Heywood, one of the minor Elizabethans. But you probably don't know of him. Frightfully irritating habit we all have, coming up with these quotations, but our heads are simply stuffed with them. Did you say you're not coming to the ceremony? Oh, do reconsider. Peter thinks the world and all of you, he'll be—"

"Before you go any further, I'm telling you I *won't* be at the ceremony, and before you ask why, I'll tell you it's nothing to do with Peter, who I'm crazy about. I'd have to be in the same room with my ex-husband, Emily's father, and his—dolly-bird, isn't that the expression? The woman he left me for a year and a half ago, in America. They're visiting Peter and Emily for a couple of weeks, and I'm not going near Oxford during that time, not for anything. Well, except an emergency, like this."

"Oh, I do apologize for prying," he said, in an agony of embarrassment. "Peter hadn't told me—I didn't mean—" He fell silent.

We were soon climbing a steep hill to the enormous white rectangle of John Radcliffe Hospital, in the suburbs of Oxford. Then down a driveway to a door labeled ACCI-DENT AND EMERGENCY. Inside, about half a dozen people in various stages of misery occupied a row of uncomfortable chairs in a narrow hallway near the reception desk.

"Yes, may I help you, Madame?" inquired a young black woman behind the desk, in a crisp Oxbridge accent.

"The baby fell and hit his head on a rock," I told her breathlessly. "He's got a big swollen place on the side of his head there—"

"He's on our records, is he?" she asked, turning to her computer.

"Yes, Archie Tyler. Can't somebody see him right now?" I begged. "Just look at that swelling!"

"Must follow proper procedure, mustn't we?" she said coolly, typing.

Another woman, dressed in nurse white, came through

a set of swinging double doors, consulted the list of names, and shouted, "Thatcher!" An old man got up and limped after her through the doors.

"While you wait," Tom Ivey said behind me, "mightn't I ring Peter up and let him know what's happened? He said he'd be at home today."

I nodded distractedly, and he set off for a bank of phones down the hall.

"Do you know Emily Tyler?" I asked the guardian of the gates. "She's on the psychiatric staff here."

She smiled for the first time. "Oh, I know Emily very well indeed."

"Well, this is her boy. She should be here this afternoon, seeing a private patient. I've really got to go and tell her about this."

"You'd be best advised to remain here, Madame," she replied. "They might call you and you'd miss your turn. But I'll ring her consultation room if you like."

"No, no, I have to see her face-to-face to explain how I let it happen. Somebody else told her the last time, and it was awful."

"Very well. You can take any of the chairs in the corridor."

I gave up and carried Archie to a chair. During the ten or fifteen minutes we waited, his weeping subsided and he succeeded first in sitting up, then in scrambling to the floor, uttering an absentminded "Ow!" every few minutes. When he crawled down the line of chairs to start untying the shoes of a woman too sunk in discomfort to notice, I dragged him back.

"Feeling better, I'd wager!" said Tom, beside us again, and I had to admit the boy was recovering at a rate I'd never expected when I'd seen him lying by the road.

When my name was finally called the nurse took Archie from me, assuring me firmly that I'd be allowed in after the doctor had finished his examination. So I went back to the reception desk and got the directions I needed, took the stairs to the next level two at a time, and burst into my daughter's consulting room. She was sitting in a leather wing chair, dressed severely, as she always at work, in a plain black pantsuit with her long blonde hair pulled tightly back in a chignon, horn-rimmed glasses perched on her nose. Despite her best efforts, she still looked like a teenager, although she was a licensed psychotherapist as well as a wife and mother.

My lingering apprehension must have showed, because as soon as she saw me she jumped up from the chair and her face went white.

"Oh, God, what's happened to him now?" she cried.

There was another woman in the room, sitting opposite Emily, but I hardly noticed her as I stuttered out an account of the accident.

"Now, it's *okay!*" I finished. "He's conscious, he's crawling around and causing trouble already. And the swelling will go down, I'm sure, bad as it looks—"

Emily was already headed for the door. The other woman came after her, protesting in a voice stretched taut as a bowstring, "You can't leave me now. You can't draw those terrible memories out of me and then just walk out on me!"

Emily turned to her for a second. "We will reschedule, Mrs. Stone," she said shortly. "It's my child!"

"What about *my* child?" the woman called after her as Emily went out the door. Her curiously deep voice broke with desperation. She grabbed my sleeve and stopped me as I hurried past her. I saw now that she was tall, thin, with jet-black hair piled on top of her head in a messy bun, and piercing dark eyes that held me almost as irresistibly as her fingers.

"He killed my child," she said. "That's what she has to help me deal with. He killed Simon! And I think he's planning to kill me too . . ."

A shiver went down my spine. I had never encountered any of Emily's patients before, and of course she never talked about them. This woman was speaking to me from another realm of consciousness, one I hoped I would never understand. I pulled loose and hurried down the stairs after Emily.

We went down a hallway, like the rest of the hospital all gray linoleum and white walls in need of repainting, and into a windowless cubicle furnished with an examining table, a sink, and a metal cabinet with lots of shallow drawers. Archie was on his feet now, a stethoscope hanging around his neck, pulling open one drawer after another and exploring among the sharp instruments inside. A young man in a white coat was trying frantically to pull him away from the cabinet, but Archie was small enough to dodge him and, obviously, well enough to enjoy the game.

Emily approached from behind and swiped him up

before he saw her. She looked him over and gasped at the swelling behind his ear.

"Good afternoon, Ms. Tyler," the doctor said, lifting his stethoscope off Archie.

"Dr. Barnes," she said with a distracted nod.

"I don't see any sign of concussion," he told her. "Young children easily develop these startling swellings, but they recede quickly. I think you're quite safe taking him home now. In fact, as quickly as possible."

People were suddenly crowding through the door behind us, filling the little room. I turned and saw Tom first with my son-in-law, Peter, beside him. Rose, Archie's young nanny, trailed behind them, and then I caught a glimpse of the man I had loved and trusted for thirty years. A curving, green blur was now attached to his left side, and that was all I wanted to see of the woman who had broken up my marriage. I quickly fixed my eyes on the far wall. I had never seen her, didn't even know her name. Emily and I always referred to her as "Barbie," knowing she had to be the kind of sexpot the dolls were modeled on.

Archie leaned out from his mother's arms and enumerated, "Papa-Danda-Zanny-Vofe!" He pointed at Tom and said, "Dat?"

Rose ran over to embrace him, tears running down her cheeks. He ignored her, still pointing at Tom and demanding, "Dat? Dat?" until Tom realized what was needed and said, "Oh—Tom."

"Ta," said Archie with satisfaction.

He started squirming, trying to get down from Emily's

arms. Her father stepped over and took him, raising him way up over his head. Archie shrieked with delight, Emily gave a strangled cry, and I yelled, "What do you think you're doing, he's got a head injury!"

Shock and anger forced my eyes to Quin, although I'd sworn I would never look at him again. There was the same cocky grin I knew so well, the thick, wavy hair, not yet all gray like mine, but grayer than the last time I'd seen him, the sharp blue eyes that met mine with an expression I'd never seen in them before, like a challenge he wasn't sure that he could carry off or that I would meet. He lowered the baby against his chest.

"Calm down, Kit," he said quietly. "He's okay. When Emily hit her head on that swing it swelled up just as big and it went away within an hour. Remember?"

That damned overconfident grin, the nerve of that demand that I share a memory with him, and, most of all, that blur of green attached to his side, filled me with poisonous vapors that threatened to explode and take the whole room out, until I released it in a voice that betrayed me by cracking: "Shut up!" I shrilled.

"Shup!" Archie echoed with delight.

"Archie!" Emily cried. "No, no, nice little boys don't tell people to shut up." She glanced at me indignantly.

The doctor, obviously anxious to be rid of the lot of us, broke in, "As I was saying, it will be quite safe to take him home so long as he's watched for signs of concussion. Those would be excessive drowsiness, confusion—"

"That's ridiculous," I interrupted, driven into a fury at everybody, myself included. "You haven't had him x-rayed for a fractured skull, and *something* has to be done about that swelling! How can you say people with no medical training can recognize symptoms of concussion? He needs to be here, with proper medical supervision!"

"I assure you, this child does not have a fractured skull," the doctor said with growing annoyance. "He is anything but lethargic." He gestured toward Archie, now bouncing up and down in Quin's arms, chortling, "Shup! Shup!"

"He shows no sign of dizziness or disorientation, his pupils are normal—in short, he doesn't require an X-ray and, as we do have other patients waiting to be seen, I feel quite confident in releasing him."

"What are you, an intern?" I demanded. "I want him evaluated by a specialist."

"Come along, Catherine," said Peter, obviously embarrassed. "You're making too much of a bit of a bump. I'm sure we can trust the doctor's diagnosis."

"Yes, Mother," Emily said. "He *is* our child after all, and if Peter and I are satisfied that he's not seriously hurt, that's an end to it."

"We'll be with him till it's time to go to Peter's award ceremony," Quin had to put in, "and we'll watch him all the time. And of course little Rosie will call us if there's any problem later." Rose, standing across from me, blushed and smiled shyly. "You can even come back with us, Kit, and help us watch him. How about that?"

I hadn't thought the level of anger inside me could rise any higher, but now I felt the way Krakatoa must have just before it leveled Sumatra.

I shouted, "Don't you tell me what I can do! And don't call me Kit!"

"Mother, stop it!" Emily commanded.

"I really must ask you to take your discussion to some other area," the doctor said stiffly, "as this room is needed. And *should* you require a consultant—"

Blundering out the door, I heard Emily saying earnestly, "Certainly not, Dr. Barnes, and do let me apologize—"

The woman who had been with Emily upstairs was now standing beside the reception desk, tearing a tissue to shreds as she watched the door to the examining rooms. Her hair had come loose and was falling around her face. Her black eyes kindled, looking over my shoulder, and then I heard Emily again, her voice soft and steady: "Have you been waiting all this time, Mrs. Stone? Everything's all right, we'll be able to finish our session after all."

She came around me and took the woman's arm, deftly removing the shreds of tissue from her hands and putting them on the desk. Mrs. Stone's tense face relaxed, and she clutched Emily's hand as if it were a lifeline. They moved toward the doors.

"Mrs. Tyler is such an excellent therapist," the young black woman said to me, and a smile again softened her ultracompetent manner. "She has a real gift for coping with disturbed patients. But of course you know that."

I hadn't known. Her profession had always been a bone of contention between Emily and me. I believed neurosis was just another name for self-indulgence, that a no-nonsense attitude and plenty of outdoor exercise were of far more use than complaining to a psychologist. But it was good to hear that people who worked with her thought she had "a real gift."

"Now," I heard Peter say softly, "you've got it over with, you've seen and dealt with him, so you'll be able to come to the presentation of the headship tonight, won't you?"

I turned and saw him looking down at me with genuine eagerness in his intelligent brown eyes. He was a tall, angular young man, rather good-looking once you got past his scholarly stoop and self-effacing manner. I had always been fond of him, and I was touched to see that he really did want me there at his big moment.

"Oh, Peter." I sighed. "Are you sure you want to take the chance of another scene like that one? I knew if I was forced to be in the same room with them, I'd behave badly."

"You'll not need to go anywhere near them," he assured me. "There will be nine people there besides you and them. Please say you'll come. It means a lot to me."

How could I refuse that? It was true, the first encounter had to have been the worst. I vowed silently that I'd stay on the other side of the room and prove to everybody that I *could* control my emotions.

Tom Ivey drove me home, chattering nervously, glancing over occasionally to be sure I was not going to burst into another temper tantrum.

"I *am* glad you've agreed to come tonight," he said as we pulled out of the hospital's parking lot. "I'll be able to introduce you to Gemma, my—my fiancée, even if just now things have been rather put on hold. She'll come to her senses, of course. She's also a junior fellow at Mercy. We've both worked with Peter, although of course Edgar Stone ultimately heads the area the three of us work in." He was frowning now, and his hands had tightened on the wheel.

"Stone? Wasn't that the name of that woman Emily was treating?"

"Ah, yes, she's his wife. Everyone at the college feels most awfully sorry for her—everyone except for her husband, that is." His scowl deepened. "He's a cruel bugger, always doing the poor woman down. There"— he pointed at the windshield—"we're about to pass their house."

I saw a two-story brick house, much like the others on the street leading out of Oxford, except that it was the only one with a tiny front yard encircled by an iron fence about the height of the average man. All the blinds were drawn too, creating a generally unwelcoming effect.

"So you and Peter work for this Edgar Stone?" I asked. "I didn't know they had that kind of working relationship at Oxford."

"Well, as I'm sure you know, we're part of Mercy College's staff for 'Elizabethan Dramatists Other than Shakespeare,'" he said, with a self-deprecatory laugh. "A small, select faculty, as one might say. Edgar Stone is something of an authority on an author called John Ford. Very rum fellow, Ford, and exactly right for Edgar—his plays are full of women driven mad by sadistic men," he finished bitterly.

"I knew Peter's specialty was Elizabethan authors," I said as we swung onto the four-lane road that led to Far Wychwood. "He sent me copies of the reviews for that book he published last year, from the *Times Literary Supplement* and half a dozen other illustrious places. I got the impression it made quite a splash."

"Oh, absolutely! *The Heroic Villain* was the book of the year in academic circles. It's the reason Peter is sure to get that full professorship tonight. He's the only one of our faculty who's published anything at all noteworthy in the past decade. Apart from myself and Gemma, who are really still apprentices, in a manner of speaking, the rest of our little group are in the sere, the yellow leaf, as the Other Fellow says—middle-aged, I mean," he amended with another little expiatory laugh.

" 'The Other Fellow?' "

"Oh, that's our name for Will Shakespeare. Bit of a joke, you know."

"And though Peter's made such a name for himself, he's still considered a sort of employee of this Edgar Stone fellow?"

"Well, I shouldn't put it quite like that. Makes us sound a bit like tradesmen," he said with guileless snobbery. "You see, in order of Oxford rank, we junior fellows, who are not yet through our course of studies, are hoping for eventual promotion to lecturer, a permanent teaching position. Eventually a lecturer can become a reader, with less teaching to do and more chance to concentrate on one's own research. That's the highest position most dons achieve. Only the most accomplished are appointed full professor."

"But Peter can become head of the department without being a full professor first?"

"Oh, quite. It's up to the current chair to make that decision. At present, Peter is a lecturer, so he, as well as Gemma and I, are rather expected to help one of the readers like Stone with research and the like. The other two readers on our faculty are pretty somnolent, haven't published for years, while Peter's already made a name for himself. Well, Edgar Stone is involved in this long-term project trying to prove that his chum Ford had a hand in the Other Fellow's *Titus Andronicus*. But between you and me, the rest of us think it's what I believe you Americans call a 'boondoggle'—just a way for Edgar to claim he's still working!"

We were turning off the main road, onto the two-lane that led through Far Wychwood. I felt a surge of happiness every time I came home to my village. I had lived in New York City for over thirty years and loved it, but I had never had the sense of belonging on its streets that I had among these ancient cottages of golden stone and gray tile, the dark forest of giant beeches and oaks that gave the place its name, the fields stretching out on all sides in countless shades of spring green, and the little group of friends gathered in front of my gate with anxious faces as Tom's car drew up.

"Ah, your friends have turned out," he said with a smile. "And there's my father coming to join them."

Beyond the little group of women I saw a lean, white-haired man hurrying along the road from Church Lane, his black cassock fluttering in the breeze.

"Your father—oh, of course, Ivey!" I exclaimed. "Talk about not making connections—you're the new vicar's son!"

"Yes, that's why I was here this afternoon—filial visit, you know."

He waved to the old man as I got out of the car, then drove off toward the Oxford road as my friends gathered around me with questions about Archie's condition. I hadn't seen anyone around when the accident had happened, but by now I knew the mysterious way news travels in a small village.

"He seems all right," I told them, "the intern who examined him thought so, anyway. I'd rather have had a specialist, but I was outvoted." I was still a little sore about that.

"*What* sort of person examined him?" asked Alice White, a fluttery silver-haired lady dressed in her usual lacy dress with gloves and hat. " 'Intern'—that doesn't sound like a proper doctor!"

"I believe it is the American term for a houseman," the new vicar said breathlessly as he reached us, "one taking medical training in hospital."

"Well," said my best friend, Fiona Bennett, "I'd not worry about it anymore, my dear. Emily and Peter are the last people to take any chances with that baby. Come along down to my house and we'll have a nice strong cup of tea to settle your nerves."

She was a plump, earthy woman who, like me, was amazed to be entering upon her sixties. She had lovely blue eyes and gray hair in a pair of braids wrapped round her head. She and her husband, John, a detective sergeant in the Thames Valley police, had moved right into my life like the oldest of friends during my first days in the village.

"Oh, I wish I could," I answered. "But I have to go to this party tonight, where Peter is supposed to be awarded a headship. I agreed in a weak moment, and now I can't get out of it."

"Ah, your son-in-law is to be made head?" the vicar exclaimed. "How gratifying! I read *The Hero Villain* last winter in one sitting, really quite thrilling, I could not put it down."

I couldn't help smiling at him, his pale blue eyes alight with scholarly excitement. He was so much the idea I had always had of a rural English vicar, it was almost funny. Our previous vicar had been a loudmouthed young modernist, detested by the entire village. When he was gone, after the murder, we had expected something as bad if not worse, but miraculously we got the Reverend Henry Ivey, a gentle and studious septuagenarian, and such a traditionalist in liturgical matters that some of the villagers muttered about "popishness."

"Well," said the remaining member of the group, our shopkeeper-postmistress, Enid Cobb, "I got the best thing for a blow to the head, Hawkins' Bruisin' Compound, only eighty p the bottle. I'd wager they don't know about it at that hospital. If you really want to help the little feller, you might come by the shop on your way out."

I thanked her without committing myself, and she sniffed, giving me a knowing look from her small, squinted eyes.

The sun was getting low, and I knew I needed a shower and maybe a bite to eat before heading back to Oxford. When they had left I opened the gate and went up the worn brick path. The rose vine that climbed beside the door was green now, and I stopped to check for buds among the leaves. Surely there would be some soon, and I felt certain they would be the old-fashioned, cabbagey kind, with that strong, sensuous perfume.

If only I could stay home, have a peaceful evening with my music and books as the the antique mantel clock chimed off the hours—instead of trying to make conversation with people far more intellectual than I was, and to control my temper in the presence of a pair of people I hated!

I caught sight of Muzzle, almost concealed in the uncut spring grass, just outside his favorite refuge. He must have been watching to see if Archie was still around before he ventured into the house.

"Oh, Muzzle." I sighed. "I wish I could hide in the potting shed too!"

CHAPTER TWO

'Tis not a black coat and a little band . . .
Or looking downward with your eyelids close
And saying, "Truly, an't may please Your Honour,"
Can get you any favour with great men.
You must be proud, bold, pleasant, resolute,
And now and then stab, as occasion serves.
                    —Christopher Marlowe, *Edward II*

The award ceremony was to be held in the Senior Common Room, where the dons hang out when they aren't teaching or burrowing in the library. Peter and Emily had given me a tour of Mercy College weeks ago, so I knew where to go. I parked, as Peter had told me to, at their apartment building by Folly Bridge, and walked up St. Aldate's to the college. It sits between the square, modern city police station, and the great baroque facade of Christ Church College, at the edge of Oxford's academic center, since it's an upstart only a couple of hundred years old. Its buildings, forming the usual square around a pampered lawn, are in the classical Roman style of Robert Adam, popular at the time of George III whose statue stands haughtily atop the tunnel-like entranceway.

The college porter checked a list of names and waved me through. I stopped for a moment and squeezed my eyes shut, reminding myself one more time that I had to play it cool and indifferent. I had let Quin get to me this afternoon, but I would definitely keep it together tonight.

I followed a cobbled path to a building that formed one side of the square, then up a flight of dark, rather damp-smelling stairs toward voices and light coming out an open door. I stopped on the top step, took a deep breath, and smoothed my red silk shirtwaist dress, hopelessly out of fashion but the only dressy garment I had brought from the States. I'd almost left it behind, thinking I'd have no use for it out in the country, but tonight was the second time I had needed it. I'd been nervous on the first occasion, entering a stately home to be presented to the upper crust, but that was nothing compared to the dread I felt tonight.

I stepped through the door into a beautifully proportioned room with one tall, arched window and three walls of packed bookshelves. A fireplace crackled with flames, portrtaits of nineteenth-century academics looked down at me from ornate frames, a small television set crouched shamefacedly in a corner. It was not a large room, the eleven people standing around on the softly faded Oriental rug pretty well filled it. I flashed an uncertain smile, my eyes sweeping over the group, getting a vague image of middle-aged men in dark suits, one heavyset woman, and two or three slim ones. Among the latter I recognized Mrs. Stone, Emily's patient. I nodded at her and at Tom Ivey, before my eyes came to a screeching halt and hung a sharp left as they collided with Quin and his Barbie doll.

"I can't tell you how happy I am that you decided to come," I heard my son-in-law say, at my shoulder. I turned to him gratefully and met his sympathetic gaze. "I appreciate how difficult it is, but you'll see, everything will go smoothly."

Now I noticed that Emily was with her father, engaging him in determined conversation, and I realized she and Peter had divided the job of supervising her parents this evening.

"No reason it shouldn't," I said firmly. "How's our boy getting along?"

"He was fine all day. We've stopped worrying about concussion."

"That's a relief!" My eyes scanned the crowd again, moving so quickly past Quin and his woman that Peter noticed.

"It turns out she's no Barbie, is she?" he said quizzically.

I didn't understand what he meant for a moment, and when I did I stared at him in surprise. I had called her that for so long, and thought of her, when forced to, as a sexy young babe, that I could hardly believe what he had said. My eyes turned reluctantly toward the fireplace, and I looked at her for the first time.

No, she was definitely not a Barbie. She had to be in her forties, a couple of decades older than I'd imagined her. She wore a long jacket that matched her gray woolen dress and tried its best to hide her rather too-round hips and stomach. Her face was square-jawed, and middle age had carved some furrows around her wide mouth and her best feature, a pair of large, expressive brown eyes. She knew how to wear makeup to emphasize them and play down the jaw problem, but she seemed to have given up on her hair, it just hung down straight in a Dutch bob with bangs.

So he had left me for a middle-aged, overweight woman with a bad haircut! It had hurt enough when I thought I'd lost out to youth and beauty, but this was worse. I must have been cast aside for something she had that I not only didn't have, but couldn't even perceive. A tornado of anger and confusion went whirling through me, and somewhere in the middle of it a little voice whispered, What is this? He can't hurt you anymore, remember?

They must have felt my gaze, because simultaneously they turned their heads and met it. She remained expressionless, but he threw me a nervous, tentative smile. I was so far from smiling at that moment, my facial muscles felt paralyzed. Incredibly, he nudged her, nodding toward me, and she took a step forward. I spun around and started across the room toward the window, thinking with bitter satisfaction of a phrase from some Victorian novel: "She cut them dead!"

I should have been thinking instead of where I was

going, because I walked right into one of the middle-aged men. His glass flew out of his hand, splashing both of us. I looked down at my one good dress, its skirt now decorated with a purple Rorschach puzzle of wine.

"I do beg your pardon," said the poor man earnestly, pulling out a wrinkled handkerchief and dabbing ineffectually at the skirt. "Entirely my fault! Always been renowned for my clumsiness. Out, damned spot!" he muttered abstractedly.

"Not at all," I said, "it's not your fault. If that *woman* over there hadn't—"

"My dear Catherine," said Peter, back at my side, "what an unfortunate accident, but it mustn't cause any change in your plans." He murmured so only I could hear, "Don't give her the satisfaction."

"I shall of course pay any cleaning bills," the other man went on, bleeding with contrition. He was tall and heavily built, a great bear of a man except for his open, bespectacled face and graying hair in dire need of a barber's attention.

"This is Geoffrey Pidgeon," Peter said. "He was my tutor in undergraduate days and the main force in my getting a lectureship. Geoffrey, Emily's mother, Catherine Penny."

Geoffrey squeezed my hand so hard I wanted to yelp.

"Absolute gubbins," he went on relentlessly apologizing while I tried to free my aching hand. "Ever since a boy, I've been causing these situations, don't know why unless it's that there's just too much of me." He finally let go and ran his hand through his hair, making it stand up on top like a cockscomb.

"For heaven's sake, Geoffrey, give over," someone said. "I'm sure the lady has other, no doubt equally modish raiment in her closets."

That snide remark had come from a man who contrasted with Geoffrey Pidgeon in every particular. He stood near the window with a pretty, dark-haired young woman, and when I looked at him he made a slight bow.

He was tall, slim, and startlingly handsome, with a shining head of blond hair untouched by gray although I had a feeling he was the same general age as the rest of these people. His eyes were a piercing blue, almost hypnotic. His dark suit was beautifully cut, obviously tailormade for him, and he wore a red rosebud in his lapel that picked up the small red figure in his silver tie. There was something charismatic about the man, and something unsettling too.

"Edgar Stone," Peter said shortly, "Catherine Penny."

He would have led me away, but Stone jumped in. "I once removed a wine stain like that from the leather cover of a fourteenth-century book. I wonder if I should tell you how I did it?" He cocked his head, waiting for me to bite.

"Since this dress has done duty for at least twelve years," I responded, "I think I can retire it without bothering you for help. High time I got a new one."

A few people laughed discreetly at that, but Edgar Stone said, "No trouble, I assure you. I have some expertise in restoring the old and outworn." He eyed my dress. "I collect rare and antique documents, you see."

What a puzzling man. He couldn't be flirting with an old biddy like me, but for some reason he seemed determined to get a rise out of me.

"Have you found anything exciting recently?" asked the girl, gazing up at him with a sort of awe. I had a feeling she had spoken just to get back his attention.

"As a matter of fact, I had a great piece of luck the other day," Stone answered, granting her a brief smile before turning his gaze back to Peter and me. "You might be interested in it, Tyler—a very good copy of Jonson's *Bartholomew Fair*, late seventeenth century."

"Congratulations," Peter said gruffly.

His hostility seemed to amuse Stone. "Of course, I had to take some less interesting pieces to get the price down sufficiently, a Dickens, an original volume one of Blackstone's *Commentaries*, a boring little chapbook from Westminster School."

I heard Quin's voice, from across the room. "Really, an original Blackstone? That's something I've always wanted to own. I'm a lawyer—barrister—you see."

"Ah, yes, William Blackstone—a Pembroke man."

That comment came from the heavyset woman I had noticed before, sitting in an easy chair a little away from the others. She was dressed very plainly, in a gray suit with woolen stockings and sensible, lace-up leather shoes. The thick lenses of her glasses distorted her eyes, making them appear startlingly large and wavering, as if she looked up from under water. Peter led me over to her, obviously anxious to escape from Edgar Stone.

"This is Dorothy Shipton, our resident Webster expert. Emily's mother, Catherine Penny."

"Webster, as in—?" I said as we shook hands. They both looked at me with amazement.

"John Webster," she amended. The full name meant nothing to me either. "Elizabethan playwright—*The White Devil? The Duchess of Malfi?*"

"You'll have to make allowances for my being a Yank," I said. "I'm sure every schoolchild in England knows all about John Webster, but he's not exactly a household name in the States."

"Rather strong medicine for schoolchildren," said another man, who stood nearby with an attractive woman. "I don't think he's particularly well known to the general public here, either, but you should take a look at one or the other of those plays. For beauty of language, I'd say he comes pretty close to the Other Fellow."

"Violent, however," the woman beside him put in, "simply full of murder and mutilation! George Bernard Shaw, for one, found his plays quite disgusting."

"Yes, well, Shaw's the fellow who dismissed Elizabethan dramatists generally as 'a rabble of dehumanized specialists in elementary blank verse'!" Dorothy Shipton exclaimed, firing up with indignation. "It's quite true, Ms. Penny, that Webster's plays are full of cruelty, but then so is life, isn't it? And if you appreciate strong female characters who know their own minds, you can't do better than his two great duchesses."

"We'll have to provide you with a copy of *Malfi*," Peter said to me. "I'd be most interested to hear your reaction." He indicated the man and woman who had just been speaking. "Let me introduce you to the famous head of our Elizabethan playwrights faculty, Cyril Aubrey, and Ann, his wife."

As I shook hands with them, Peter went on, "You've heard of Aubrey, I assume?"

Not very tactful, because it must have been obvious from my face that I hadn't.

"No, no, why would she?" said Cyril Aubrey. "It's not as if the *Ur-Hamlet* were even as well known as John Webster to people outside our field, Peter."

"Well, I do know *Hamlet*," I said. "That's one Americans actually read in school."

They laughed, and Peter explained, "The *Ur–Hamlet* is something no one has read, because like a great many Elizabethan works, it was never published. It's only known from references in letters and diaries. You see, while Shakespeare's *Hamlet* was first produced in 1601, another play by that name is mentioned by people who'd seen it before 1589."

"Earlier than any play by the Other Fellow," Dorothy put in.

"Quite. People used to speculate this lost *Hamlet*—the *Ur*, by the way, is a Germanic prefix meaning 'primitive'—was an early effort he later refined into the play we know, and others suggested various contemporaries as the author. But all speculation ceased eight years ago when Cyril's definitive book on Thomas Kyd came out."

"I was fortunate, that's all," said Aubrey, looking uncomfortable, as Brits so often do when they hear themselves praised. Dorothy and Ann exchanged indulgent smiles at his modesty. Edgar Stone was smiling too, in his smug way, watching us but not deigning to join the conversation.

"Aubrey found a bundle of old letters in a London antiques shop," Peter went on, "among them one by John Puckering, a government official who interrogated Kyd in prison. He mentions in passing that Kyd is the author of 'the revel called Hamlet.' When the book came out with this letter reproduced in it, you wouldn't credit the sensation it made. He's been a celebrity ever since—at any rate, in literary circles."

"Oh, come along, Peter," said Aubrey, in an agony of embarrassment. He was a brown sort of man—brown tweed jacket, friendly brown eyes, an unruly mop of graying brown hair. Why were academics so averse to good haircuts? I wondered. There was a generally rumpled look about Cyril Aubrey, and I figured he was just too immersed in Thomas Kyd and his cronies to notice when his hair needed combing or his shirt ironing. His wife was smiling at him fondly, so I presumed she had given up long ago on making him presentable.

She was beautifully groomed herself, her straight brown hair parted in the middle and falling smoothly to frame a serene, oval face, her long blue dress perfectly fitted to her tall, slender figure.

"You know quite well it was that book got you your professorship, Aubrey," said Dorothy bluntly. "When old

Morehouse retired in the year it came out, you were the only possibility."

"Dorothy is working on her own interesting theory," Peter said, "with regard to Webster."

"We all of us have our interesting theories," Tom put in.

"Quite," said Cyril Aubrey. " 'Lighting our candles from their torches,' to paraphrase the *Anatomy of Melancholy*."

"Yes," said Dorothy, " I'm seeking to prove Webster actually practiced law—his plays are notable for their trial scenes, and someone of his name *was* admitted to the Middle Temple in 1598. I'm on the trail of some trial records that may mention him, hoping my luck will prove equal to Aubrey's."

"I'm sure we're boring Mrs. Penny most awfully," he said. "It must seem extremely odd to outsiders, this devotion of ours to authors of whom most people have never heard."

"*Catherine*," I said. "And no, I don't think fame is what makes a writer worth reading."

"Tyler, don't you expect Mrs.—er, Catherine would like some refreshment?" Aubrey suggested. He had finally succeeded in changing the subject. Peter apologized and hurried off to a long table set with plates and glasses. I turned to call after him that I had eaten and would do perfectly well with a glass of ginger ale, but my voice died in my throat as I found myself face-to-face with my ex-husband. I'd had no idea he'd been standing right behind me. I stepped back quickly. Emily was watching us apprehensively, over by the fireplace.

"Listen, Kit," he said, lowering his voice, " I just want to say, whatever happened last year, we had a lot of good years together and we shouldn't forget them."

I could only stare at him, speechless. Did he actually think I'd agree with that load of bunk?

"You know it's not fair for Emily and Peter to have to divide up like this to keep us apart. They deserve a regular family, they need us to get along, to enjoy our grandchild together. Come over and meet Janet. I don't expect the two of you to be friends, but won't it be easier for the kids if you get down off your high horse and act civil to us?"

Peter stood frozen by the refreshment table, and Emily was slowly shaking her head, silently begging me to behave.

I took a deep breath and almost whispered, struggling to control my voice, "If Emily suffers, it's your fault and nobody else's—except that cheap bimbo you're dragging around. Just don't you ever dare to speak to me again!"

Now Emily was beside us, murmuring urgently, "Dad, don't keep trying. She doesn't *want* to talk to you. Please, please, both of you, don't ruin Peter's evening."

I turned and left them. Sorrow squeezed my heart as memories flashed through my mind of the three of us in our apartment on West Eighty-third, on vacations, at ballet recitals and soccer games—all those shared moments that had made us so close, as we would never be again. How could such a dreary-looking woman have been the cause of such total destruction?

I went and stood by myself near the door. The dons

had noticed that little scene, of course, and cast discreet glances toward me, but they were far too polite to show their curiosity openly. Peter started toward me with a plate and glass, but I waved him away. I didn't want to try to talk until I could get my breath back. He joined Emily and Quin, standing together in uncomfortable silence. But the other member of the group, Quin's new woman, wasn't with them.

I saw her with Edgar Stone, over by the window. He was leaning over her, his eyes fixed on hers as if she were the only person in the room, his smile wide with delight at whatever it was she was saying. And she gazed up at him with similar fascination. I noticed the dark-haired girl who had been in the same favored position before, standing apart, watching them and smoldering. Tom Ivey spoke urgently to her, turning eyes full of hatred on Stone when the girl flounced away without answering him.

"Edgar the Dreadful, Peter and Tom call him." I hadn't realized Emily had come over to me until she spoke. "He's only after Gemma because hurting Tom is his idea of fun. But the silly little thing takes him seriously, when everyone else knows she's only the latest in a long line of women he's tumbled and then dumped."

"It's no wonder his wife needs your services," I said.

We both looked over at Mrs. Stone, seated at the far end of the room, accepting a glass of sherry from Cyril Aubrey. She wore a fitted green dress that emphasized her too-thin figure, her chest as flat as a boy's, her hip bones jutting out. Her dark eyes seemed huge, like pictures I'd seen of starving third world children. They were fixed on her husband, who smiled a little private smile as Quin, frowning, led his girlfriend away.

Emily sighed. "Obvious sadomasochistic motivation on both sides. But of course she's the one who's losing their little game. Let me introduce you to her."

We went over and Emily presented us to each other. Mrs. Stone's given name was Perdita, with the accent on the first syllable. I was going to remark how lovely it was, but she spoke first, fixing those haunted dark eyes on my skirt without smiling.

"There's blood on your dress," she said, and again I was struck by the deep, dramatic timbre of her voice. "You've cut somebody, haven't you?"

"No, it's only wine," I said. "You're right, though, it does look like blood."

"Entirely my fault," I heard Geoffrey Pidgeon say. He was standing a couple of feet behind her, in the shadows, so I hadn't noticed him.

"I hate these gatherings," she went on, "but Edgar always makes me come, so he can watch me watching him. Look how happy he is! My *husband*—he enjoys flaunting his latest conquest in public while I look on."

"So does mine," I responded.

"Oh, Mother," Emily moaned. "He's not actually—"

"I think Mrs. Stone put it very well," I said.

She cocked her head and regarded me curiously, and then burst out laughing, with a slight edge of hysteria. People stopped talking and looked over uneasily.

"Have you taken your medication, Mrs. Stone?" Emily asked her in a low voice.

"No," she retorted loudly, "I haven't taken it. I've just had rather a large glass of sherry instead, and it's made me feel much better than medicine does. What do you think of that?"

Emily replied, "I think you showed good judgment in not mixing drugs and alcohol."

Perdita's defiant attitude disappeared in a second. Her eyes lighted with excitement, and she grabbed Emily's hand. "I didn't want to be all muzzy tonight. I wanted to enjoy your husband's success with you like a friend, not like a patient—"

"Yes, I'd like that too," Emily said, smiling down at her.

We heard Cyril Aubrey's diffident voice and turned to see him standing in the middle of the room, rumpling his hair nervously as he said, "I suppose it's time we fulfilled our purpose in gathering tonight."

All eyes turned to him, and people grew quiet. Emily stepped over to Peter and took hold of his arm, and they smiled at each other happily.

"It has been almost twenty years since I established the faculty of non-Shakespearean Elizabethan drama at Mercy," Cyril Aubrey began, "and very satisfying years they have been. But it's time now to hand the reins, as it were, to another. Time to start down a different path."

"You're far too young to retire," Dorothy said. "Ought to wait until you're a weary old party."

"Well, Ann would not agree," he went on, smiling at his wife. "She has all sorts of plans for us, travel, study—I'm rather vague as to the details, but she can give you the complete schedule."

"I've been waiting for years, quite like Patient Griselda," Ann said.

"The choice of successor to a headship at Mercy is traditionally the decision of the retiring head alone," he went on, getting more nervous as the big moment approached. "Once he—or, in these days, I should say she as well—has informed the college council of that decision, the office is considered conferred. Mercy is fortunate in its faculty, fortunate indeed, and so the choice has not been an easy one."

Emily was hugging Peter's arm, and he was doing his best to look as if all this was of only casual interest to him.

Aubrey fumbled with his glasses, taking them off, wiping them with his handkerchief, putting them back on and blinking at us nervously through them.

"Oh, do get on with it," Dorothy demanded. "Don't keep the poor fellow in suspense!"

"Well," he resumed, "I have finally come to the conclusion that the headship will be best bestowed upon our longtime colleague Edgar Stone, and have so informed the council."

Complete silence fell over the room. The faculty stared in astonishment as he shook Edgar's hand, and then a hoarse cry startled everyone.

"No!" Perdita Stone was on her feet, staring wide-eyed at the two men. "No, you can't do that!" she cried. "You can't reward *murder*, you can't—"

She stepped toward them, shaking her head in disbelief.

"I've told you," she said pleadingly to Aubrey, "I've written you letters telling you what he did—didn't you get my letters?"

"We've all got your letters, my dear," said Dorothy sadly.

Everyone watched her in acute discomfort, except for Edgar. His eyes glittered, and that unpleasant smile twitched his lips. He was enjoying this.

"Yes, you've done your best to humiliate me and destroy my career, sending those ridiculous missives to everyone who knows me—haven't you, *darling*?" he said mockingly. "Fortunately, they all know you're barking mad."

Emily threw him a dirty look as she and Geoffrey tried to get Perdita to sit down quietly. But she shook them off.

"You want *punishing*, for what you did to Simon—and instead you are rewarded!" She finally sank into her chair and then cried out in a voice that shook with genuine passion, " 'Justice! Oh, justice! Oh, my son, my son—my son whom naught can ransom or redeem!' "

Edgar clapped his hands three times, slowly. "Brava!" he cried, still grinning. "A bit melodramatic, perhaps, but then *The Spanish Tragedy* is that kind of play."

"Oh, I say," Cyril Aubrey exclaimed, "you make the poor woman feel—"

" 'Roscius, when once he spake a speech in Rome—' " Edgar began, gazing at him steadily. Cyril broke off and turned away sadly.

"Heywood?" Dorothy ventured, but Edgar ignored her. Geoffrey threw him a glance of sheer hatred before turning his attention back to Perdita. "Come along, let me escort you home," he begged.

"Yes, Mrs. Stone," Emily joined in, kneeling beside the chair to look into her eyes. "It would be best if you went home now. I'll come with you, if you like."

Her anger had subsided into dull despair now. "It can't be allowed," she said, as if to herself, then she stood up. "Yes, I want to be out of this place, away from these people. Not one of you understands what simple justice is!" she flung at them.

She left with Geoffrey, refusing Emily's offer to go along.

Edgar looked around at the faces of his colleagues, his eyes glittering with amusement. "Well, I'm surprised too! Aubrey, dear fellow, you've staged a coup! Didn't we all expect the wunderkind, Tyler, to be chosen, just because he'd written a popular book?"

"Now, now, old fellow," Aubrey said, "we all know Tyler's book is more than just 'popular,' it's an extremely important work that casts a whole new light—"

"Important?" Stone laughed aloud. "It's a sensationalist hodgepodge of unsubstantiated guesswork. It's the kind of vulgar popularization these young fellows coming up call 'scholarship' because they're too lazy to do proper research."

"Unfair, Edgar!" Dorothy snorted angrily.

Cyril Aubrey, increasingly woebegone, exclaimed, "Oh, I say, there's no call to insult Tyler's work." He turned to Peter and begged, "I was sure you'd understand, Tyler, age and experience, you know . . ."

Peter, although he had become paler as Edgar Stone went on, controlled what he must have been feeling and said in a steady voice, "Quite right. I'll say nothing, Stone, except for 'Congratulations.'"

"What noble restraint!" Stone sneered.

"Indeed," said Dorothy indignantly, " 'Calumnies are answered best with silence.'" She looked around with fire in her blurry eyes. "Jonson, *Volpone!*"

"By God, if no one else will say it, I shall," Tom Ivey burst out. "Edgar Stone isn't fit to be head of college! He'll discourage every sign of original thinking and run the place like a petty dictatorship."

"Come along, Tom," Aubrey pleaded, "I know Edgar better than any of you, and I know you're wrong about him. I hate to say it, but I fear you are letting personal animus over—well, romantic matters affect your judgment. Peter, who could just as well do the same, is able to keep his feelings subordinate to his judgment, and you might—"

"What do you mean," Peter interrupted, his eyes narrowing, "I 'could do the same'?"

Aubrey stared at him, at first in surprise and then in dismay. "Oh—do you mean that you didn't know—Oh, my dear boy, I assure you I meant nothing whatever! It was only a slip of the tongue, I mean to say—"

Edgar Stone gave a startling bark of laughter. "That's torn it, Cyril!" he said happily. "In your usual bumbling manner, you've given away the deep dark secret little Mrs. Tyler and I have been keeping. I should never have told you about that incident, should I?"

Peter looked at Emily in amazement. She was glaring at Stone with cold scorn.

"*I* wouldn't have told anyone," she said. "If I could wipe it from my memory I would. It was the most disgusting thing that's ever happened to me."

"My God," Peter breathed. "Are you saying he tried—"

"This has got to stop!" Dorothy bellowed, rising with some difficulty from her chair. "I declare this party over. I've never witnessed such appalling behavior, and as for you and this outrageous blunder you've made, Cyril Aubrey—"

"Edgar," young Gemma broke in, her voice trembling, "you didn't really come on to Peter's wife, did you?"

"You sick sadist," Peter said, giving up the struggle for self-control. "I knew what a goat you were, but you will not insult my wife and get away with it!"

He stepped toward Stone while Emily begged, "No, Peter, don't make it worse! It was only once, and I got rid of him easily!" Quin grabbed his arm to stop him.

Edgar Stone was obviously having the time of his life.

"What a stimulating evening!" he said. "But I believe Dorothy's correct, our revels now had better be ended." He walked to a sofa loaded with coats and purses, took a bowler hat from the pile, and put it on at a jaunty angle.

"Come along, my dear fellows," Aubrey pleaded, "let bygones—I mean to say, you're going to have to work together, aren't you? Any animosity will make it most difficult. Do put all this behind you!"

Edgar turned and looked at Peter. "Do you know,

Tyler, I find it hard to see how we *can* work together, after the way you addressed me just now. Yes—when I become head at the end of term, I'm afraid I shall have to demand your resignation—for the sake of staff morale."

He gave one of his little mocking bows, and left us.

Everyone had had enough, and the gathering broke up pretty quickly. Though left alone, Gemma repulsed Tom's attempt to escort her. Poor Aubrey stood there watching us go like a child who's been sent to Coventry for misbehavior. Quin and Emily went out on either side of Peter, talking to him earnestly, and the Barbie trailed behind them.

When I reached the street I almost had another collision, this time with Dorothy Shipton. She'd started up the street, then hurried back when I emerged from the entranceway.

"I say, are you hungry?" she demanded. "I'm starving! Mercy's known for the paucity of food at its do's. Besides which, I'm a bit unnerved by all that happened—and I'd rather not go back to my empty house just yet." When I admitted to a certain hollowness, she went on, "Fancy a doner kebab, then?"

"I've no idea what that is," I admitted.

She led me quickly up St. Aldate's to a small square beside a Gothic church where several undergraduates stood around eating from Styrofoam boxes, dripping red sauce on the paving stones. A large white van stood there, humming loudly and emitting rank fumes. The top half of one side was open, and in the bright lights inside two

Arab men were cooking on a grill. I saw a column of pressed lamb turning on an upright spit, as I'd seen before in Greek restaurants in New York.

A doner kebab turned out to be the same kind of pita sandwich Americans call a gyro, only instead of yogurt sauce, the lamb strips, lettuce, and tomatoes were topped with mayonnaisy coleslaw and a thin "chili" sauce with a definite bite.

"The kebab vans are a sort of Oxford tradition," Dorothy told me as we sat on a low stone wall to eat. "They come out when the sun goes down and stay open until the wee hours of the morning."

Sitting in front of an ancient church, looking across the street at Wren's great Tom Tower looming over Christ Church College, eating a Middle-Eastern sandwich while buses roared past, I got a distinctly Alice-in-Wonderland feeling, although Dorothy didn't seem to notice the incongruities.

"Now, I do want to apologize for my colleague's appalling behavior," she said in her gruff way. "Edgar Stone has always been a difficult man, and his treatment of his wife is quite beyond the pale. His faults have increased as he's aged, until I really think he's become unbalanced. God knows what's going to happen to our little faculty." She shook her head.

"Why did Mercy College ever hire such a man?" I asked.

"Ah, well, he used to have some reputation as a scholar. And then, this Elizabethan staff has been a cohesive group for a long time. We were all undergraduates together at Magdalen, you see, although it was really the OUDS that made us such a close-knit group. Oh, I'm sorry," she went on, seeing my blank look, "that's the Oxford University Dramatic Society. We all acted in its productions." She pulled out a packet of tissues and gave me one, and we both concentrated for a minute on removing the runny red sauce from our hands and faces. Then she went on. "Perdita was actually a wonderful actress, and a brilliant scholar as well, quite different from the poor creature you've just seen. All the men were in love with her, especially Geoffrey Pidgeon, who seemed to have won her until Edgar suddenly made a dead set at her. He can be very charming, although you wouldn't guess that from tonight's exhibition. He still has great success with young women. He's been causing a ridiculous scandal with that little graduate assistant. But I only meant to say, I wish you'd seen us in more civilized form."

"I wasn't so civilized myself," I said sheepishly.

We finished our sandwiches and then she stood up, saying, "Well, I shan't keep you longer, although going home is not pleasant for me. My dear friend of thirty years died less than a year ago, and since she's been gone I don't seem able to get used to being alone." Tears filled her eyes, and she wiped them away angrily with the back of her hand. "Stupid of me!"

"Not at all. I understand," I said softly. "It takes time."

"Sorry. Behaving like a sentimental fool."

She had insisted on paying for the kebabs, so it wasn't until I had almost reached the road to Far Wychwood, my lips still tingling from the chili sauce, that I noticed my purse wasn't on the car seat beside me. I pulled over and looked on the floor and the back seat, but finally I had to admit it must still be on that sofa in the Senior Common Room.

One more memory failure, I thought as I turned the car around and headed back into Oxford—one more disquieting reminder of my age.

When I drove back past the house Tom had pointed out as the Stones', a woman was almost running down the path, and as she came through the gate I was astounded to see that it was Quin's girlfriend. She was carrying a tote bag with a picture of Big Ben on it, and she looked strangely agitated, casting glances over her shoulder at the house, where only one downstairs window showed a light.

What reason could *she* have to go to Edgar Stone's house? Not a single one came to me, unless—but that was ridiculous. Had Quin actually got himself involved with some sort of nymphomaniac, who would make an assignation with another man the first time she met him? What kind of craziness was going on here?

The porter at Mercy College unlocked the Senior Common Room and helped me to find my purse, which had fallen down beside the sofa. I was retracing my path within about half an hour from the time I'd started back.

I heard the screaming before I got to the Stones' house, and then the siren as I pulled up by the curb. There was light streaming out of the open front doorway now, and a light on upstairs as well as down. A woman was screaming inside the house, people were emerging from their houses up and down the street to see what was happening. And, most bewildering of all, I recognized my son-in-law's car parked at the curb, just ahead of mine.

The siren got so loud it hurt my ears as two black-and-white police cars swung into the street and pulled up beside my car. I was followed by three constables as I ran into the house. I saw a staircase at the end of a short hall-way and Perdita Stone, dressed only in a silky gray night-gown, backing slowly up the stairs. Her eyes were very wide, her long black hair loose and wild, her hands pressed to her mouth as if in a futile attempt to hold the screams back.

The police ran through the open door of the lighted room on my right, and I followed them. Edgar Stone was huddled on the floor in a corner, staring without blink-ing, a white telephone lying beside him, disconnected from the wall. A large, gold letter-opener stuck out of his chest, and his shirt, the flowered carpet around him, and the white telephone gleamed with his blood.

The constables had already mobbed the only other person in the room. I saw my son-in-law, Peter, standing beside the dead man. Our eyes met for a moment as the police, shouting their legal formula, pinned his arms back and began to handcuff him.

CHAPTER THREE

*In case, afterward also, in riper years he
chance to be set on fire with this coveting
of love, he ought to be good and circum-
spect, and heedful that he beguile not himself to be led willfully into the wretchedness
that in young men deserveth more to be pitied
than blamed and contrariwise in old men, more
to be blamed than pitied.*
— Thomas Hoby, "The Courtier"

I was well acquainted with the Oxford City Police
Headquarters, having been interviewed there after
one of my narrow escapes. Not only that, I was acquainted with a detective sergeant who worked there,
my friend Fiona's husband. So when Peter, Perdita
Stone, and I were ushered through the entrance by that
pack of constables, I immediately started throwing his
name around.

"I want to see John Bennett," I told the officer behind
the reception desk. "There's been some terrible mistake,

these people have actually put handcuffs on my son-in-law! Why they'd think *he* could possibly have—"

"He's dead, isn't he?" Perdita was babbling hysterically. The officers had prevailed on her to put on some shoes and a coat, but below it her nightgown fluttered around her ankles. " I woke up because there was noise downstairs, and he was *dead*. He looked more horrible than Simon did, much more!"

Peter was the only one who said nothing at all. He stared straight ahead, pale but stoical.

"I said, I want to see John Bennett," I reiterated. The burly desk sergeant was ignoring me, talking to one of the constables who had brought us in. The calm impersonal attitude of all these uniformed people was maddening. "I *said*—"

"Yes, Madame, I did hear what you said, there's no need to shout," said the desk sergeant firmly. "D.S. Bennett's not in the building at present."

"Somebody has to tell me what we're doing here, and why my son-in-law, a respected lecturer at Mercy College, is being treated like Jack the Ripper!"

"You and the victim's wife are here as material witnesses. Mr. Peter Tyler is at present our prime suspect in a murder investigation, as I'm sure the officers informed him at the scene. That's all I can tell you, Madame. Things would go a lot easier if you'd take a seat and wait until someone's ready to interview you."

"I'm going home," Perdita cried out, "back to Tyneford. We were happy there. Let go of me," she commanded the female constable who held her arm. "I want to go home!"

"I'm going to call my daughter," I told them, "not only is she Peter's wife, she's also Mrs. Stone's therapist, and it looks like you're going to need her."

Nobody objected. Perdita had started slapping at the constable, fighting to free herself. The desk sergeant sent another officer down the corridor at a brisk trot as I went over to the public phone. When Emily answered I tried to explain, but it wasn't easy.

"I'm at the police station, darling. Your patient Mrs. Stone is giving them a hard time, and Peter—it's outrageous, and I told them so, but they think he murdered Edgar Stone!"

A gasp, a few seconds' silence, then she said, "*Murdered?*"

"Yes, somebody stabbed him, it was awful, there was blood all over! Of course there's no way Peter could have done such a thing, but they say he's their prime suspect, can you imagine? You have to come right down."

"Wait a minute—what are *you* doing there?"

I blew out my breath in exasperation. "Does it matter at this point?"

My heart sank as I heard Quin's voice in the background asking what was wrong. Now *he* would be sticking his nose in!

"I'll be right there," she said and hung up.

When I turned back I saw Perdita Stone sitting off to one side, still talking feverishly, her hand in that of a middle-aged woman wearing the same kind of power suit my daughter wore. She was listening quietly, stroking the hand, occasionally putting in a few words. I figured she must be their resident therapist, letting the poor woman ramble on to calm her down.

Peter was gone.

"Where have you taken my son-in-law?" I demanded of the desk sergeant. "I won't have him interrogated until John Bennett is here to do it!"

"Madame," he said with forbidding courtesy, "it is not police policy to offer suspects their choice of interviewers. D.S. Bennett is occupied on another investigation and is not expected in tonight."

"Do you think he's gone home by now?"

"I have absolutely no idea!"

I hurried back to the phone and called Fiona.

I explained the situation and waited while she expressed the predictable shock and disbelief. Then I asked whether John was home yet. When she said he wasn't, I implored her to send him over as soon as he got there, and she promised she would.

I turned from the phone and saw a pudgy, bald detective with a little mustache waiting for me. He identified himself as D.S. Parker and asked me to accompany him to one of the rooms down the corridor, a little larger than a walk-in closet, furnished with a metal table and two folding chairs.

"Now, then," he said when we were seated, "I'd like to hear about what brought you to Mr. Stone's house and what you saw there."

He sat back and listened intently as I told my story, nodding dismissively at my protestations about the impossibility of Peter having killed anybody.

"All right, Madame," he said when I stopped for breath, "that's very helpful. So you entered the house because you heard Mrs. Stone screaming, and you saw Mr. Tyler standing over the body, is that correct?"

"No, that is not correct," I answered snippily. "He wasn't 'standing over' him, he was at least a foot away from him. And has anybody noticed there's no blood on Peter, while everything else in the vicinity is sopping with it?"

"That can happen, depending on the angle of attack," he said. "Don't worry, Madame, our technicians will be looking into those things. Did you happen to notice a handkerchief lying on the floor beside the desk?"

"Handkerchief? No," I said, "but you have to understand, Peter is the most—"

"Or the broken lock on the door into the study?"

"No. How do you know Peter didn't just come in because of the screaming, like me? And how did your police know to come there, anyway?"

"We had a telephone message, which I can't discuss with you, I'm sure you'll understand why."

"I don't understand anything! What evidence could you possibly have?"

"Look, I understand your faith in your son-in-law and your desire to help him. Not sure my mother-in-law would react quite the same." He smiled at his little joke, but I only continued to glare at him. "We'll be needing to talk to you further, but for tonight you're free to go home. Now, come along." He stood up and opened the door. "You'll have plenty of opportunity to help us later."

I was certainly not going home. I planted myself in one of the hard metal chairs bolted to the wall in the lobby to wait for Emily. Mrs. Stone and the therapist were gone. I set myself to mulling over everything I could about that evening's events, and suddenly I remembered something crucial that had been knocked out of my mind by the shock. I jumped up and hurried over to the desk sergeant, who looked up from his papers with controlled irritation.

"I just remembered I saw someone else coming out of Edgar Stone's house this evening! Get that sergeant back, I've got to tell him. She must have done it, she's definitely capable of murder!"

"Who was that?" he asked skeptically.

"This—woman my ex-husband's traveling around with. She came out of the Stones' about half an hour before the police and I arrived. And she looked really upset!"

Before he answered, the street door opened and Emily entered with her father. She wore her usual housedress, a caftan bought on her honeymoon in Morocco. Her blonde hair flowed over her shoulders, and her face looked quite bloodless.

"It's all right, darling," I said quickly, "I think I can clear him." I turned to Quin and spoke to him, though it was like hitting myself in the chest. "Where's your girlfriend?" I demanded.

"Mother, this is not the time to start—" Emily began, but I went right on.

"Where is she? Do you know? Hiding from the police, isn't she?"

"Kit, for God's sake calm down!" he answered angrily. "What difference does it make where Janet is? Can't you get your mind off her even at a time like this?"

"Not when I saw her fleeing from the scene of the crime!"

"What are you talking about? God, you're in one of those hysterical fits of yours, I should have known—"

"Just tell us where she is right this minute," I said, deliberately keeping my voice steady to prove him wrong.

"She's at the hotel," he finally answered. "She was tired, she wanted to go to bed, and I went to Emily and Peter's to visit awhile. Peter got a phone call and had to go out, and a little while later you called to say he's been arrested! Are you going to tell us what's happened, or do I have to find a cop who'll tell me?"

"Pardon me," the desk sergeant put in, "am I to understand you're Mrs. Tyler?"

"Yes," Emily answered, stepping over to him. "Please, could you tell me what's happened, Officer?"

As he gave her the few facts they were willing to divulge, I turned back to Quin.

"I was driving past the house where the murder happened," I said in a low voice, "and I saw that woman come running out looking all upset. That was a good while before I went back by and heard Mrs. Stone screaming, and found Peter there with the body. So she's every bit as likely a suspect as poor Peter—who obviously only went in because he heard the screaming, just like me."

"Janet? Why would she go to see a guy she'd only met for the first time that evening?"

"I'm supposed to understand the motives of a person like that? But I told this policeman about it, and I'm not leaving until they bring her in and find out what she was doing there."

"Wait a minute. This is just too convenient—*you,* of all people, were the only one who happened to be passing by when she ran out?"

"Are you calling me a liar? You—the grand champion of liars?"

"Mom, Dad, stop it! Stop it!" Emily said, her voice cracking with strain. "Look, just go away, both of you—I can't *deal* with your problems right now!"

We both fell silent, shamefaced at having made things worse for her.

"There's really no reason for you to stay," the sergeant said quickly, "and it might be better for all concerned if you did go home."

"Absolutely not! I won't leave her alone in this mess," I burst out, and at the same moment Quin said firmly, "I'm here to support my daughter, and I'm going to stay."

"I'd really rather you both go," Emily said. "I'm quite capable of handling things, and you two are only complicating them."

That hurt, but I persisted. "Sergeant, didn't you hear what I told you about that woman coming out of Stone's house?"

"Yes, Madame, but we're going to be concentrating on Mr. Tyler just now. We shan't be questioning any other witnesses until tomorrow at the soonest." He still sounded skeptical.

"How can you just wait around, when she might be—"

"That's enough," Quin said, tight-lipped. "This is so like you, throwing wild accusations around, going off half-cocked and causing trouble. Man, do I remember thirty years of that!"

While struggling to contain my fury for Emily's sake, I noticed that she was gone. I looked down the corridor and saw her disappear through the door of one of the interview rooms, D.S. Parker holding it open for her and then shutting it behind himself.

"Listen," I heard Quin saying, more calmly, "I wasn't going to let things get like this. I was going to convince you we shouldn't be enemies, with all the years we've got—"

"Oh, right," I retorted, "as you just told me, thirty years of *that*!"

"But, if you'll let me finish one sentence," he snapped, "I'm not going to let you make up fantastic tales to try to get Janet in trouble. One thing I didn't think you could be was vindictive, but obviously I was wrong."

"I am *not* making this up! All right—she was carrying a tote bag with a picture of Big Ben on it, and she didn't have that at the party, so how would I know about it if I hadn't seen her when I said I did?"

Doubt crossed his face for the first time. "You might have seen her somewhere else."

"I thought she was in bed at the inn. If I saw her at all, she must have lied to you about where she was going."

He frowned, unable to refute that. "I'm going back to our room and ask her about it," he finally said. "She'll be able to explain everything."

"Darn right she will, after you've coached her! I'll just come along, and see how she explains everything with me there listening."

He only shrugged, but I followed when he went out the door, staying a few steps behind so there was no question of my being *with* him. His considerably longer legs strode so fast up St. Aldate's that by the time we reached St. Giles Street, six long blocks on, I was pretty winded, and when we walked into a very large and obviously expensive hotel a few doors beyond, I had to stop for breath. He didn't glance back until he reached the staircase, and then he waited, tapping his fingers on the banister, while I glared at him across the luxuriously appointed lobby, holding my side and heaving with each exhalation. After a couple of minutes I crossed to the stairs with what dignity I could and climbed behind him to the next floor.

She obviously had him living pretty extravagantly these days. I knew, vaguely, that his clients paid him well, but we'd never been big spenders. That was how we'd discovered Far Wychwood. It had a great old inn, The Longbow, which didn't cost nearly as much as one like this, in the heart of Oxford. We had stayed there when Emily was married, and again when Archie was born, and I'd loved the village so much that when Quin told me he was leaving, I'd gone back there to lick my wounds in rural peace.

He put a key into the lock of a door, and stood back to let me precede him into the room.

She was sitting at a small desk near the window, writing a postcard. She looked up, then turned in her chair, the brown eyes widening in astonishment when she saw me. Without makeup, her square jaw and rather rough complexion were more noticeable. She had a bathrobe on over a satiny beige slip, and travelers' fold-up terry cloth slippers. She got to her feet, smiling uncertainly.

I wasn't going to put up with any "civilized" behavior, if that was what she had in mind. I started barking at her, "I'm only here because I know you were—"

But Quin, taking advantage of his louder voice as he had his longer legs, drowned me out. "Something awful's happened, honey. That guy we met at the college this evening, that Edgar Stone? Somebody's killed him, and they've arrested Peter for it."

"My God." She sat down again. Her voice was low-pitched, throaty, probably sexy if you happened to be male. "But, Tib, why would Peter do such a thing?"

Tib? I stared at Quin, unable to believe he'd let anyone give him such a nickname. He did have the grace to look embarrassed. I turned back to her.

"Peter didn't," I said in a voice dripping with scorn. "*You* did."

"Me?" She looked bewildered. "I didn't even know him!"

"Then what were you doing in his house this evening?" I shot back before Quin could interfere. "I drove past around nine o'clock, and I saw you running out of the place. You were the guiltiest-looking slut I've ever seen."

"That's enough, Kit!" Quin ordered. "Why can't you—" He broke off and went over to the girlfriend. His face was furrowed in an uneasy frown as he looked down at her. "She says she saw that tote bag you got in London, so I guess she's not making it up." I snorted derisively. "*Was* that where she saw you?"

She didn't turn a hair. In her place, I would have been giving as good as I got, either blustering to cover my guilt or loudly indignant at being accused of something I hadn't done. I'd wondered what he saw in her, and now my triumph at having caught her out was dulled by the realization that he must like her because she was nothing like me.

"You were talking to him at the party," Quin went on, as she sat there staring at me without speaking. "I wondered at the time what that was about."

Now she looked up at him adoringly, took hold of one edge of his Windbreaker, and slowly ran her hand down it.

"It was about *you*," she said. "I wanted to surprise you, but now—"

She went to the closet, lifted the Big Ben tote bag from a hook, and pulled a large leather-bound book from it. She held it out to Quin.

"I saw how excited you were when you heard about it,"

she said, "so I asked the man if he would sell it to me. That's what we were talking about."

As he took the book his frown changed to an expression of amazement.

"It's the Blackstone!" he exclaimed. "The first volume of the original edition—my God, Janet, this must have cost you a mint!"

"No, I was surprised at the reasonable price he offered me. He said anytime I wanted to come to his house I could have it, and he gave me directions. When you were going to your daughter's after the party I thought it was a good chance, so I said I was coming back here, and instead I went to buy your book. I was going to keep it for your birthday, but . . ." She glanced over at me, and Quin turned to look at me too.

"There you are," he said with satisfaction. "It was nothing like you thought. Just the latest example of you jumping to conclusions from inadequate evidence."

"When I saw her," I said stubbornly, "she was practically running out of the place, looking back over her shoulder. Why would buying a book make anybody that upset?"

"All right, I told you his price was low," she said, still imperturbable. "Well, I found out why. After I had the book he kept talking, not wanting me to leave, and finally he made a crude pass at me. He—put his hands on me, and tried to make me do the same to him. I had to hit him to get away. That's why I was hurrying, and a little upset."

"Maybe you had to do more than hit him," I said

doggedly, knowing my case had pretty much collapsed.

She threw me a pitying smile. "It wasn't my first experience of something like that. You don't have to kill them to get them off you." She turned back to Quin, dismissing me. "Tib, I tried to read some of that book but I couldn't understand it, not even the first page! And you know I have a pretty good legal vocabulary. You are so *brilliant*, to want to read a book like that! I mean, I knew you were, but it's not your mind I think of first anymore . . ."

She gave him a little secret smile and then dropped her gaze, as if modesty prevented her from elaborating on that, in front of an outsider. The big brown eyes flickered to his face again for a second, then down to his hand, now caught in hers. Damn, she was good.

I could see by his besotted little smile that he was eating it up. Much as the performance turned my stomach, I had to admit I believed her story. Being felt up was not a credible motive for murder, especially for somebody as unflappable as this one.

She looked at me again, savoring her triumph.

"That was a really malicious thing to say," she murmured. "Wasn't it, Tib?"

He smiled ruefully. "Not the classiest thing you've ever done, Kit," he said.

"I was just trying to help Peter!" I retorted, and that was as close to an apology as I would go. "And I'm going back to the police station now to try some more."

"Wait," he said as I started toward the door. "I'll come too."

"Oh, Tib," she pouted, "don't go! It's late."

"Honey, you can see I have to help Emily and Peter, can't you?"

"You're *always* with them. We've hardly been alone since we got here. And you know she doesn't like me. Can't we go home before we get involved in all this—unpleasantness?"

"I know it's not much fun for you, but I love my daughter too."

I left, disgusted to hear him practically begging her for permission to go. I figured she'd have him in bed in a matter of minutes, and probably on the train to the airport by tomorrow morning.

So I was surprised, after I'd been at the police station for ten minutes or so, to see him come through the door. We looked at each other warily, like a couple of boxers reentering the ring.

The desk sergeant had told me, with his usual reluctance, that John Bennett had arrived. A minute or so later he emerged from one of the corridor rooms, smiling in his solemn way, and came and pressed my hand between his.

"I'm terribly sorry, Catherine," he said, looking down at me mournfully from his six feet plus. He was my age, lean and shrewd, with silvery hair and an air of quiet strength. I felt more hopeful as soon as I saw him. "The whole thing seems incredible. I want to let you in on what they've told me since I got here, it probably won't make it easier, but at least you'll know why they've taken Peter into custody."

"Quin Freeman," I heard behind me, and his large, square hand appeared, thrust out so that civility forced John to let go of my hand and shake his. "Mrs. Tyler's father. You're in charge of this case, are you?"

"Well, no," John said. "I'm actually a friend of Catherine's from Far Wychwood. She called my wife and asked for my help, and I'm of course only too glad to offer it. Very pleased to meet you. I knew, of course, that you were visiting Emily. She's waiting for us in incident room B, perhaps we could all adjourn there where we'll have more privacy."

We were both on our way as soon as we heard Emily's whereabouts. She was sitting in a folding chair at a metal table, in a room a little larger but just as forbidding as the one where I'd been interviewed earlier. Her caftan's bright African colors were startling in the gray bleakness of the place. She was keeping herself firmly under control, sitting up very straight, her jaw clenched.

I leaned over and hugged her.

"It's like a bad dream," she said in a tight little voice. "Peter doesn't understand what's going on any more than we do."

"They let you see him?" Quin asked.

"Yes, for a few minutes."

"I was going to insist on that, if they hadn't."

"I assure you, Mr. Freeman, we shan't deny Peter anything he's legally entitled to," said John. "Please have a seat. I hate to say this, but there is some rather strong evidence against him. First, as your daughter has told us, and I'm sure you'll confirm, we know a call came through to Peter at their apartment at quarter past nine this evening. It was from Edgar Stone, and we've verified that it was made from his house. Apparently he asked Peter to come there, as he had something to tell him that couldn't wait, something that would affect the two of them and nobody else, and in a profound way. Peter went over immediately, and when he reached the house he says he found the front door open as well as the door to Stone's study, where we've determined the lock was violently broken.

"He claims to have found Stone already dead. As he stood looking on in disbelief, he says, the victim's wife appeared in the doorway, saw the body, and began screaming. Apparently she made her way to the stairs and was backing up them when the police, and Catherine, arrived."

"Why all the 'he says' and 'he claims'?" I demanded. "That's a perfectly believable story and I don't see why you would doubt it. Somebody else got there earlier and killed him, that's all!"

"Except for this." He lifted a tape player from the floor and set it on the table. "This call came in to the 999 emergency operator at nine-thirty-six precisely."

He pressed a button, and Edgar Stone's voice filled the room, a panicky near-whisper.

"Send the police to 225 St. Crispin's Road. I've locked myself in the study. A man named Peter Tyler is outside the door, threatening me with a knife—he'll kill me if he gets through the door. Send the police. Hurry!"

"Stay on the line, sir," the 999 operator's calm voice

said. "I'm dispatching police. Are you in immediate danger of your life, sir?"

"Yes, damn it!" Stone's voice growled. "He'll break the lock at any minute. I tell you, he snatched up this knife, this letter opener, from my desk, and tried to stab me with it. I managed to elude him and lock the door, but he says he's going to kill me!"

"And this is someone you know? Don't hang up, sir!"

"Yes, yes, a colleague of mine, Peter Tyler—"

The line went dead. We sat in stunned silence, staring at the tape machine as John turned it off.

After a few minutes Quin blew out a heavy breath and said quietly, "Deathbed statement."

"Exactly," John replied. He looked at Emily and me. "The statement of a victim as to his killer's identity, given on the verge of death, is very powerful evidence. Mrs. Stone has identified the voice on the tape as her husband's. She also said something about an altercation of sorts between Peter and Stone, earlier in the evening?"

We didn't answer, but I knew seven other people could testify to the way the man had goaded Peter and how furious he'd been, especially when he learned what had happened to Emily.

"We'll have nothing to say about that at present," Quin said decisively. "Emily, I'm going to find the best lawyer around, and we're going to beat this."

"Okay, what about fingerprints?" I broke in. "Peter wasn't wearing gloves. If he'd broken in the door, if he'd used that knife, his fingerprints would be all over them."

"Actually, that turns out to be another point against him," John said, almost apologetically. "The knife and the door handle had been wiped clean of prints. A man's pocket handkerchief was found lying on the floor. Our lab has already performed an iodine vapor test on it. I'm afraid it is full of Peter's prints. His only explanation is that he did not wipe the objects and has no idea how his handkerchief came to be there."

He stood up. "I know this has been a great blow to all of you. There is nothing more you can do here tonight. Why don't you go home and get a little rest?"

I reached for Emily, but Quin somehow got there first and had hold of her left arm before I could get the right.

"Come on, baby, I'm taking you home," he said. "I'll be over first thing in the morning and we'll straighten this out."

"I'll come and spend the night with you," I began, but she waved me away.

"Just let Dad drive me home, I'll take a sleeping pill. I know you want to help, Mom, but it'll be best if you get some sleep too." She kissed me, and her lips felt cold against my cheek. "We're going to have a lot to get through."

So I let her go with her father, smothering the selfish little voice inside me whispering that he didn't deserve to be the one she turned to. They had always been close, even more as she'd emerged from childhood and it had become clear she was more like him than me. They shared this careful, analytical attitude toward life, a disapproval of impulse and a distrust of emotion, and since I was the embodiment of both, she and I couldn't understand each other the same way she and her father did. Hurt feelings aside, I was glad he could be with her at a time like this. He would know better than I would when to offer love and when to step back.

When I walked into the parking lot it seemed like a hundred years since I'd left it. That was the thing, I went on musing as I got into my car, that logical, lawyer's mind-set Quin had, that had made his collapse before the power of love so incredible. All our friends, his colleagues at the law firm, everybody we knew back in New York had told me he was the last man they'd have expected to do such a thing. And I had trusted him completely for thirty years, ever since I'd met him at the foot of the Washington Monument, surrounded by cherry blossoms and hippies, at the big anti–Vietnam War march of 1971.

I had come to New York from Cincinnati just in time for what everyone calls the sixties even though much of it, my part anyway, took place in the early seventies. I never got into the wilder aspects, the drugs and promiscuity, but the idealism, the faith in people's underlying goodness, the abhorrence of war, were part of me before I ever got to New York. I had my master's in library science and easily got a job in the public library system, made some friends, and positively wallowed in the city's cultural riches. I hadn't been looking for a man at all, so it was amazing to realize, a few months after we got back to New York from the march, that I was falling in

love with this young public defender with shoulder-
length hair and a passion for helping the poor. It was
even more amazing to realize that he was falling in love
with me.

We had married and found a Manhattan apartment
that we shared first with a stray dog called Charley, and
then with our little girl. Quin had worked his way up,
over the years, from the public defender's office through
bigger and better law firms, and finally into the high-
powered one where I assumed he still worked. I had
gone on in the library system and never risen above my
original position, because I hadn't anything like his am-
bition. I'd thought my life was pretty close to perfect,
and though I missed Emily when she left us, I was
proud of her Rhodes scholarship, happy when she
found the right man, and quite prepared to move on
into old age right there on West Eighty-third, beside
Quin.

I pulled up in front of my cottage, turned off the headlights, and sat there for a few minutes just looking at the
place. It had taken me sixty years to learn that you can't
really plan the future, especially when it involves other
people. There was no way I could have imagined, two or
three years ago, that Manhattan by now would be only a
memory, the library's budget problems and the city's
scandals no longer on my radar, that I would be living
alone in a seventeenth-century cottage in England. I
couldn't even have imagined owning a cat, I thought, as I
caught sight of Muzzle slinking warily across the yard
toward me. I'd never liked cats, but here I was catering to

an old black tom that wouldn't even give me the satisfaction of an occasional petting and purring session.

I heard him slurping water from the bathroom faucet while I got into my nightgown and slippers. He had started doing that soon after he moved in with me, and after lifting him out of the sink a few times, I'd given up and now left it dripping for him. Since he spent most of his time wandering outside, picking up who knew what organisms, I didn't feel like sharing a faucet with him, so I'd begun drinking and brushing my teeth in the kitchen. The bathroom sink had become Muzzle's property pretty quickly, and I only wondered what he would claim next.

I had formed the habit of listening to *Book at Bedtime* on the BBC every night. A very good reader was currently making her way through Mrs. Gaskell's *Cranford*, and it was wonderfully comforting that night to curl up in the green baize wing chair in the parlor and listen, sipping a hot cup of Horlicks.

When I got into bed I heard Muzzle settling himself in a corner of the bedroom, on a cushion I'd put down for him. He'd only go there after the light was out, and if it went on again he would be gone in a second.

I was thinking about Peter as I settled into my pillows. Poor boy, spending this night in a jail bed! They couldn't be very comfortable, and even if they were, the knowledge of what was happening to him would be enough to keep him awake. I tried hard to think of another way to clear him, since my first try had been such a spectacular failure, but my weary brain refused to cooperate, and soon I was asleep.

CHAPTER FOUR

The cloudy day my discontents records,
Early begins to register my dreams
And drives me forth to seek the murderer.
                    —Thomas Kyd, *The Spanish Tragedy*

You can never trust English weather for long. We'd had a three-day spell of beautiful spring days, so I wasn't surprised to wake the next morning to the patter of rain on my slate roof. I looked at the clock on the nightstand and swore when I saw 6:00. It would have been lovely to turn over and fall asleep for another hour, but I had been wakened, as I always was these days, by Muzzle's plaintive meowing from the floor beside my bed. I knew if I didn't give him breakfast and let him out, it would just go on and on. Really, I should put his cushion downstairs somewhere and shut my bedroom door, I thought as I emerged from the covers into the damp, chilly air. But I knew I wouldn't do that. There was something comforting about having a living creature in the room with me at night.

He shut up once he had me on my way to the kitchen, and followed at my heels, even brushing quickly across my legs for encouragement while I opened the cat food can. Once he was settled to his bowl I could start boiling the water for my steel-cut oatmeal and for instant coffee. I would still have to let him out before I carried my breakfast into the dining room, or I'd be eating it to another chorus of meowing. Even on rainy days he had to do a quick patrol of the area, but I'd have to remember to let him in again before I went to Oxford. As he stepped warily onto the doorstep, I brought in the pint of milk the roundsman left every morning, and the *Oxford Times* that lay beside it.

The murder of Edgar Stone dominated the front page, with a mercifully blurry photograph of Peter being led, handcuffed, into the police station. I argued with the newpaper story while I ate breakfast, furious at its neutral tone. People reading it might actually think he was guilty! Which was absurd—although that phone call to 999 *was* a problem. If it weren't for that, I would have no trouble coming up with other suspects, because everybody who knew him seemed at least to dislike Edgar Stone.

I washed up my few dishes, took a shower, and got into slacks and a sweater, trying all the time to figure out why Stone would have fingered Peter instead of the real killer. By the time I was into my raincoat Muzzle had had enough of the wet outdoors and was back on the doorstep, reaching up to paw at the doorknob ineffectually.

"It's never going to work," I told him as he scooted through the door. "Not without an opposable thumb."

I turned the heat up a little, to keep him comfortable, and hurried out to the car. Driving into Oxford I heard the radio weatherman cheerily predicting a full day of rain, not even offering the hope of "sunny intervals," as they sometimes did. I passed Stone's house, closed and dark, and wondered how his poor wife was coping. She was well rid of her sadistic husband, but such a shock couldn't have done her mental condition any good.

Emily had given me a key to their apartment, and I used it in case she was sleeping, although it was almost eight-thirty now. As soon as the door swung open I realized how dumb it had been not to call first. Quin and his woman were already there.

Archie jumped up from the sofa where he'd been sitting between them, ran to me, and threw his arms around my legs, immobilizing me in the doorway.

"Nana," he said happily.

I knew better than to confine him in a hug. I just rubbed his curls and said, "Archie." He responded, "Ow!" and backed away, and I realized his head was still tender from the bump yesterday.

Emily came across and gave me a kiss, murmuring, "I should have called you when they came. I just didn't think."

"Neither did I," I whispered back. "Don't worry, I'll be good this time."

Her face was pale and strained, her eyes pink-rimmed. I put my arms around her and for a moment we stood there in a three-way hug, before Archie bounced back to Quin.

"Nana, taypay!" he announced, waving his arms at Quin, so I was forced to look at him. He was holding a small portable tape player on his lap.

"Hi, Kit," he said, smiling. Of course I didn't answer. I glanced at the girlfriend and saw with satisfaction that she looked sulky and was obviously, as he had said, not having much fun.

Archie started punching every button on the little machine at once.

"No, no," Quin said, taking hold of his hand. "You don't get any music that way. This is what you do," and he set one small finger on a button and pressed it down. A shrill, saccharine voice came from it, singing, "Oranges and lemons, Say the bells of St. Clemens, You owe me four farthings, Say the bells of St. Martin's—"

Archie's eyes got bigger, and he stared at the player as if it were magic. When the singer paused at the end of the song he breathed reverently, "Taypay!"

"It's yours," Quin said, putting Archie's hand around the machine's handle. "When the music stops I'll show you how to hear the other side."

The girlfriend grimaced when Archie leaned against her leg, examining the tape player. She moved a little away, out of contact with him, and didn't see Quin's brief frown as he noticed her distaste for his grandson.

Archie ran over to Rose, his shy young nanny, making herself as inconspicuous as she could in a straight chair at one end of the room. "Vofe, taypay!" he informed her.

"Ooh, isn't it lovely?" she said, glancing furtively at Quin. Rose, I knew from past experience, was highly susceptible to older men with dominant personalities, and she appeared to have developed a crush on her employer's father. "Isn't your granda kind to give you such a nice gift?"

Archie plopped down on the floor with his new toy. That irritating voice was now singing about the Duke of York's pointless sortie up the hill.

"We've got a CD player now, of course," Quin said, "so I brought the old tape player for the kid. More fun for him than CDs, with all the buttons to push. It ought to keep him out of your hair, Em, with all that's going on."

"Either that, or drive me round the bend," she answered, a little irritably. "But thanks, Dad. It does seem to be a hit."

"I wish you'd tell me something I can do to help too," I said. "Maybe cook dinner? Or run some errands for you?"

"I can't eat," she answered shortly. "Rose will look after Archie's meals. I can't think of anything just now, Mom. Dad and I have an appointment in about an hour with this solicitor he found who's supposed to be really good. Maybe he'll represent Peter." She was twisting a strand of her blonde hair around her finger, tighter and tighter, as she used to do at tense moments when she was a child.

"I could go too," I said and was annoyed to catch a glance exchanged between her and Quin. "I will *not* get excited, or insult the man, or—any of the other things you're thinking. I might even come up with some questions that wouldn't occur to you."

"I'd be willing to bet you would," Quin said. He laughed, and Emily even smiled a little. "I think I know what to ask another lawyer, Kit, even over here. It's going to go better if Emily and I handle it."

That familiar condescending tone was more than I could take.

"Listen, mister," I burst out, "I had thirty years of that superior attitude, the same amount of time you had of my jumping to conclusions, and I thank God I don't have to put up with it anymore! Save it for Big-eyes there."

That actually got a rise out of her. "Are you going to let her go on calling me names?" she demanded of Quin in a voice that was still quiet and steady, but a few octaves higher than I remembered. "I told you I didn't want to come to England. You said we'd all be friends, but she won't let us be, and I knew she wouldn't."

"So why *did* you bring her?" I joined in. "Just to rub our noses in it? Just to humiliate me and make life a little harder for Emily and Peter?"

"Mother, don't say another word!" Emily cried out. "You promised me only minutes ago you wouldn't do this!"

Archie ran over and threw his arms around my legs again. "Shup, Mummy!" he piped at Emily.

She stared at him, and then, as if the last straw had been laid on her back, she gave way and burst out crying.

Quin got up and enfolded her in his arms, and Janet went into the powder room and slammed the door.

Archie looked on in amazement at the effect his newly acquired word had created, and I whispered to him, "You see, matey, that word's bad news, just like we told you. You'd better go give Mummy a kiss and tell her you're sorry."

He trotted over and did his leg-hug, and she picked him up. He patted her wet cheeks, saying unhappily, "No, no!"

"Don't worry, darling. Remember what I told you? It's okay to cry."

Archie shook his head, not buying the psychological jargon, while she tried to pull herself together. In the background the tape player shrilled, "Bobby Shafto's gone to sea, Silver buckles on his knee—"

"I'm sorry, Mom—" Emily started to say, but I interrupted.

"No, you're quite right, I just can't be in the same room with those two peacefully and I won't try it again. I'll check every time to be sure they aren't here." I heard Quin give a big, exasperated sigh, but I didn't rise to the bait. "You interview your lawyer, and I'll go down and talk to Peter. I haven't heard his side of it yet, and if nothing else, he'd probably like to see a friendly face."

"Tell him I love him," I heard her say as I opened the door, and I knew she was still crying because I heard Archie scold, in a scared little voice, "No, no—bad Mummy!"

* * *

"How is Emily?" were the first words Peter said to me when we faced each other on either side of a plastic mesh barrier. He looked as haggard as I'd expected. I'd had to wait until noon for visiting hours, so I'd had a long walk, and when I returned they told me a couple of visitors had beaten me to him. About half past, two of the men I'd met last night came out, nodding to me as they passed. I'd forgotten their names already, but I recognized their faces, solemn now and worried.

"She's doing very well," I answered, doing my best to keep my feelings out of my voice. "She and Quin are interviewing a lawyer this morning. He's supposed to be really good. And she wanted me to tell you she loves you."

A momentary spasm of anguish crossed his face. "Tell her the same when you see her again. I keep thinking what this must be doing to her, and that's as hard to bear as imprisonment."

"Tell me what happened, Peter. Maybe there's something I can grab hold of, something that will point a way out of this nightmare. What about the other people who were in the Senior Common Room last night?"

"Yes, Cyril's been here this morning," he answered, misunderstanding my meaning, "waiting outside when they opened the place, he and Geoffrey. They can't understand this any better than I can."

"Right, Cyril Aubrey's the chair of the department, isn't he, and Geoffrey was your mentor?"

"Yes." He brushed his hair back with a trembling

hand. "I keep wondering why Stone would stage his own death like that? Calling me, calling the police—"

"Is *that* what you think happened? Do the police think it could have been suicide?"

"No, they say that's unlikely, from the way the knife—" He broke off, shuddering. "When I saw him, Catherine, all that blood, the look on his face— Do you know, I wasn't even aware of the police until they were pinioning my arms? I hardly knew where I was."

"Okay, we've got a new possibility," I said, grasping at straws. "However unlikely, he could have killed himself and schemed to lay the blame on you."

"It's hard to credit. He always disliked me, disliked all the younger scholars who were coming up and displacing his generation. Claimed we were degrading the science of literary research, and when my book was so successful I came to symbolize all that to him. But isn't it pretty ridiculous to think he'd have gone to the length of killing himself, just to destroy me?"

"Maybe he had a fatal incurable disease. Did you ever see *Rebecca?*"

He rubbed his forehead in distraction. "*Rebecca?* That Hitchcock film—oh, yes, I see what you mean. But that's only fiction, Catherine."

"You can learn a lot from old movies. It's the only reason I can think of to stage it himself. Well, if it's true, it will come out. They'll surely do an autopsy."

"An—Oh, a postmortem. I've no idea how these investigations work, but it seems logical that they would."

"I'll find out. I'd been thinking of other possible suspects, but this is a more likely scenario, if they're sure it's his voice on the 999 tape."

"They say Perdita swears to it, and Geoffrey said they've asked him and Cyril to listen to it while they're here and give their opinions too. I certainly had no doubt it was him when I got that call asking me to come to his house."

"Tell me about that. Tell me everything that happened."

"Emily and I went home, Quin came with us, as it was still early and he wanted to spend time with her. Janet was tired and went back to the hotel."

I sighed, remembering what a rush it had been, thinking that in one fell swoop I was both going to save Peter and give that woman what she deserved.

"About an hour and a half later I answered the telephone and heard Stone asking me, almost ordering me, to come to his house immediately. He said he had received news that would be of great benefit to both of us, and to us alone. He sounded quite excited. It was certainly out of character for him, as I said he'd never showed interest in anything that might benefit me before. I must come alone, he said, and immediately. He would be waiting for me."

"What on earth could it have been? Do you have any idea?"

"No, not one. At any rate, I went, and when I got there I found the doors standing open, both the front door and the entrance to his study. I stood in the hall for a minute and called his name. Then I went into the study and saw him. The shock froze me in place. I couldn't take my eyes from him. I heard screaming, I've been told it was Perdita when she came down and saw us, but I don't remember her. I only remember your face suddenly appearing at the door, and then the police were dragging me away."

He had broken out in a sweat, remembering it. My indignation had grown as I'd watched and listened to him—it was outrageous to think of this gentle scholar, dedicated to his poetry, his wife and child, on the way to trial for a violent killing. I had never even seen him lose his temper—well, only once, last night when Edgar Stone had bragged about trying to force himself on Emily. I stood up quickly, pushing that memory away.

"Peter," I said, holding his gaze with mine, "one way or another, we're going to get you out of here, and I mean without going through a trial. When somebody is innocent there's evidence of it somewhere, and all that's needed is somebody who cares enough to find it."

He gave me a melancholy smile. "I hope you're right, my dear. It's some consolation, at least, to know I shan't be broken on the rack like Thomas Kyd, or thrown into water to prove my innocence by floating. I've good friends, and sufficient money, and I live in a relatively civilized period of history. It's possible I'll sleep in my own bed again."

But he didn't look as if he believed it.

Later I walked up Magdalen Street to the point where it changes from a typical narrow, medieval Oxford street to a broad, tree-lined boulevard in the continental style, called St. Giles. If not for the Gothic shapes and gold Cotswold stone of the buildings lining it, you might think you were in Paris or Rome. A few yards along, I ducked out of the rain into my favorite pub, The Eagle and Child, for lunch.

Even in my preoccupied state I felt the thrill I always got at sitting in the pub where C. S. Lewis and his pals the "Inklings" used to meet, where Tolkien first read *The Lord of the Rings* aloud to them. I always ate in the big, open room where they had met every morning, rather than one of the two small, more private rooms off the entrance hall, or the addition built on behind in recent years, all glass and pale wood. Old photographs of the Inklings hung above the dark wainscoting, one of them including Lewis's doomed American wife leaning on her cane. Despite the success of the filmed versions of Tolkien's epic, the "Bird and Baby," as the regulars call it, has never been turned into a tourist trap. I did hear the accents of a few American pilgrims, but basically it is still an unassuming little "local" for those who want a warm, cozy place to eat classic pub food and drink good ale.

I was lingering over my cheese and chutney sandwich and half pint of "Old Hooky" when a couple stopped beside my table and a familiar voice said, "I say, what's happening to Peter? Have you seen him?"

It was Tom Ivey, with the pretty dark-haired girl who had snubbed him at the gathering last night. She looked as if she had been crying for hours, with washed-out eyes and a red nose.

"This is Gemma, my fiancée," he told me. I thought I detected a certain determined emphasis on the last word. I invited them to sit with me.

"Peter's pretty glum, but he's hanging in there," I told them.

"How could Peter have hurt Edgar?" Gemma burst out bitterly. "He could upset people sometimes, but it was just his way, he didn't mean anything by it, underneath he was—" Tears welled in her eyes, and she choked off, biting her lip.

"Underneath he was a bastard!" Tom finished, going pink with anger. She turned to him indignantly, and he backed right down. "Please don't be angry, darling. I know you can't see it the way I do—not yet. Edgar could be very charming. I understand why you left me for him, really I do. And I'm sorry you're grieving. I can wait until it gets easier for you, however long it takes."

"I'm sorry," she said to me, mopping her cheeks with his handkerchief. "Edgar and I were— I just can't understand how Peter could do that to him!"

"He didn't," I said firmly. "You worked with him, didn't you? How can you believe he could do such a thing?"

"But the police have arrested him." She stared at me in surprise. Her eyes were really beautiful, an unusual gray-green shade with long, luxuriant lashes.

"It's all a big mistake. We think he may have committed suicide and staged it so Peter would be blamed."

Swept away by incredulity, she actually laughed through her tears. "What do you mean, suicide? Edgar would never have done that! He had too much to live for. He and I were going to—Well, it doesn't matter anymore, does it?" She sniffed back more tears. "I've heard him ridicule people who'd killed themselves—cowards, he called them. He always said that was the way his wife would choose one day, and he had nothing but contempt for his wife." She leaned back, shaking her head scornfully. "No, Edgar was far too brave to go that way."

"And Peter is far too good a person to have killed him," Tom put in, "which leaves us with the famous person or persons unknown, whose voice somehow sounds enough like Stone's to fool his own wife." He looked over at me and shook his head. "I don't see how *that* could be."

He got up to give their order at the bar. She insisted she could not eat, he begged her to take just a little something to keep her strength up, and I got ready to leave. I liked Tom, but somebody needed to tell him a girl who had been so infatuated with a bully like Edgar Stone was not going to be won by servile adoration.

I went back home for the afternoon and busied myself with household chores. When Muzzle began his plaintive serenade, I opened the back door and awaited his decision. He looked out at the steady rain for a few minutes, then shook his paw as if it were wet, glared up at me, and stalked back to the hearth rug. He always blamed me for bad weather.

At about five o'clock I rang Emily. "Hi, is the coast clear?" I said.

"Oh yes, they're going out for the evening, to some

posh French restaurant and then to a nightclub called Midtown Manhattan. I guess that's as close as she can get to going home."

"A nightclub! He never liked that sort of thing, any more than I did."

"Well, it wasn't *his* idea. But it will give us a chance to talk, if you want to come over."

"Right, I'm on my way. I'm going to make us some Cincinnati chili, and we'll have a nice evening together with no interference from them."

She was sure she couldn't eat anything, but I gathered up a box of spaghetti, cans of beans and tomatoes, some chocolate, cinnamon, cloves, cardamom, turmeric, and cumin, an onion, and a block of cheddar cheese, the bizarre ingredients of a type of chili made only in my Ohio hometown. I stopped by Enid Cobb's shop for half a pound of fresh ground sirloin on my way out of the village.

"Don't look good for Emily's man," she said gloomily as she made change. "Seemed a nice young chap too, who'd of thought he'd break out like that?" I didn't let myself be drawn into an argument about it.

The first sound I heard when I came into the apartment was that sugary voice singing about how she loved sixpence, jolly jolly sixpence. Archie didn't even notice me for a minute, he was so absorbed in finding the right buttons to interrupt that song and rewind into the middle of "Oranges and Lemons." When I called to him he looked up in surprise, threw his new treasure to the floor, and ran to hug me. He whooped, "Taypay, Nana!" and ran back to fast-forward into "Bobby Shafto." "See?" he said to me, beaming.

"Rose!" Emily called raggedly from the kitchen. She came into the living room as Rose emerged timidly from her bedroom. "Archie, why don't you go to the nursery and show *Rose* how the tape player works?" Emily said. She had obviously had all the interrupted nursery rhymes she could take.

He shook his head. "No. See, Nana?" And off went the singer into the middle of another song.

"Archie," I said, "if you take the tape player in the other room for a while, I'll give you candy." I pulled out a little bag of what the English call boiled sweets, left in my jacket pocket from the last babysitting day. He grabbed for it, but I held it out to Rose, over his head.

"Mother!" Emily exclaimed. "You can't *bribe* children!"

"Sure you can," I said as he trotted eagerly after Rose to the nursery. "Works every time. Now," I went on quickly while she continued to sputter, "come back in the kitchen and let's visit while I fix us some comfort food. Remember how I used to make the chili for you when things were going wrong—when Charley the Dog died, when you lost the part in the school play? It was one dish you never turned down, however upset you were."

"This is a lot worse than those times," she said sadly as we adjourned to their small kitchen. "This is the worst thing that's ever happened to me. It's even worse than when you and Dad split up."

"I know, darling." I got out a big pot and started crumbling the meat into it. "I'm so glad I get to spend an evening with you, but I'm surprised your father would want to go out dancing at a time like this!"

"I told you, he didn't," she said, jumping to his defense. "*She* did. She went along with us to see Mr. Billingsley, and she just—"

"Oh, yes, the solicitor," I interrupted eagerly. "How did that go?"

"He seems very knowledgeable," she said, frowning briefly at the interruption. "And I was relieved Dad was with me. He knew just how to talk about technical points of law, and he could evaluate Mr. Billingsley much better than I could have done."

"So is he going to defend Peter?"

"Well, we engaged him, but he's a solicitor, Mom, he only handles the out-of-court work. He'll provide Peter with a barrister who'll represent him at—at the trial."

"There doesn't need to be a trial," I said firmly. "This Mr. Billingsley should be able to find evidence that Peter's innocent, before it comes to that."

"Oh, Mom, he doesn't do that sort of thing," she said wearily. "He's a lawyer, not a detective."

"Then maybe we need a detective too!"

"Let's just wait and see what the police uncover. They want to find the real murderer, you know, not just prosecute Peter." As I started to argue she went on doggedly, "What I was about to say was, Barbie just sat there pouting while we talked to him. It's so obvious she wants Dad all to herself, she resents it when he pays attention to me instead of her. So when we got back here, she drew him off in a corner and they started having a pretty intense conversation. I took Archie into the nursery and spent a little time with him, and when I came out they were standing there kissing, looking as if they were glued together. He actually had his hands on her bum. I'm sorry, Mom—you'd probably rather not hear about that."

"Well, I didn't think they confined themselves to handshakes," I answered, attacking the onion with a butcher knife.

"I went back into the nursery, and cleared my throat and made some other noises so they'd know I was coming out, and when I did they were sitting on the sofa, holding hands like high school steadies. Mom, I thought the onion was supposed to be diced, not totally shredded like that."

"You're right." I shoved it into the pan. "Plays him like a violin, doesn't she?"

"Poor Dad." I was proud of the way I kept my mouth shut at that. "So he told me they were going to have this evening out, and they left soon after. He was so apologetic about it. But I've been frustrated at not being able to talk with you about Peter, so I was going to grab the opportunity and ask you to come over, if you hadn't rung me first."

"This is so unfair to you!" I said. "It would be better if they did go home, then you wouldn't have to play this musical-chairs game with us on top of everything else."

She shook her head sadly. "I don't want him to go home yet. I've missed him, you know, and I believe him when he says he's missed me—and you too."

"Oh, please!" I erupted. "Missed me! That's unforgivable—to try to get your sympathy with a lie like *that*! I thought I detested him before, but—"

"All right, calm down," she ordered, wearily. "I shouldn't have mentioned it. I do understand how you feel. Let's not even mention Dad and Barbie for the rest of the evening."

Cincinnati chili is served over spaghetti and under a mound of cheddar cheese. It's not to everyone's taste, and Rose only sipped at it gingerly and then went to make herself an omelet. Archie ran around waving strands of spaghetti, yelling, "Fwag!" I didn't see him eat anything except a fistful of cheese. But Emily almost finished her plateful and said she felt better for it. I could see Archie's racket was setting her already raw nerves on edge, so while we put the dishes and utensils in the dishwasher I proposed taking him off her hands for a while.

"He can come home with me for the night and stay all day tomorrow."

"Oh, God, Mother, I can't deal with another accident now!" was her reaction.

"I swear I'll keep my eyes on him every minute. Please, darling, give me another chance. It will make me feel like I'm doing something to help you. I can't talk legalese with solicitors, but I can give you a little peace and quiet."

For a few minutes she watched Archie, who had climbed onto the back of the sofa and now launched himself into the air, laughing at poor Rose's admonitions.

"That girl's bound to give notice when he hits the terrible twos," she mused gloomily.

"She needs a day off in the worst way," I agreed.

"All right, Mom, you take him, then Rose can have a bit of a breather. I don't blame you any more for the scary things that have happened when he's been with you, I know there's only so much anyone can do to keep a boy like Archie out of trouble. But please—"

"I know, best beloved, and I swear nothing will happen this time. Only one thing—let's lose the 'taypay' temporarily. I can't take a whole day of 'Oranges and Lemons,' et cetera."

He didn't notice its absence in the excitement of getting ready to visit Muzzle and the apple tree and my big backyard. While Emily packed his overnight bag I said, "By the way, how's your patient, Mrs. Stone, getting through this?"

"Well, I don't really know, because she's not my patient anymore. I sat down with her at the police station last night, but she said she no longer needed counseling, now Peter had given Edgar the punishment he'd deserved all these years."

"Wow. She did hate him, didn't she? What did she mean, the other night, accusing Edgar of murdering her son? He didn't really do that, did he?"

She shook her head. "I can't discuss her case with you, Mom. It would be unethical. But whether or not her most extreme accusations had any basis in reality, he did abuse her emotionally for much of their marriage."

"So do you think she'll be okay, now she's free from the abuse?"

"Of course not. The woman has a Major Depressive

Disorder, an Intermittent Explosive Disorder, and bereavement issues that will probably never be resolved. She still needs help, but if she refuses to accept it there's nothing I can do. I urged her in the strongest possible terms to take her medication faithfully, but she's in such a manic state right now that she probably won't. I'm trying not to think about it—I can only cope with so much at one time."

It was past Archie's usual bedtime when we got home to Rowan Cottage. He was so tired, it wasn't hard to get him directly from the front door to the staircase. Muzzle was at full alert in the sitting room, ready to run for cover if Archie so much as looked at him, and I didn't want a confrontation that would force me to let the poor cat out in the rain. He would keep me awake meowing about it until I did, if he got really spooked.

I bedded Archie down in my second bedroom, and he fell asleep pretty quickly, clutching the stuffed Peter Rabbit I'd bought him when I first moved to England. Love had not improved its appearance. Rose had had to sew its left ear back on, and the plush fur had been hugged and washed until it had turned some indeterminate color. I stood for a little while watching Archie sleep, listening to the cat lapping from the bathroom faucet.

How could I let him grow up fatherless, seeing Peter only four days a month, and in prison clothes, wondering as he got older whether the terrible things the state said about him were true? *Somebody* had to prevent that. Maybe the police and the very knowledgeable Mr. Billingsley would find the answer, but I had a feeling they were working on the assumption of Peter's guilt. The only alternative so far was the suicide theory, and that depended on the autopsy results. If they didn't give Edgar a motive, then unlikely as it seemed, person-or-persons-unknown must have somehow killed him and implicated Peter.

Bending to kiss my grandson's cheek, I made a silent promise that nobody was going to take his father from him if I could help it.

CHAPTER FIVE

Spring, the sweet spring, is the year's pleasant king,
Then blooms each thing, then maids dance in a ring,
Cold doth not sting, the pretty birds do sing:
Cuckoo, jug-jug, pu-we, to-witta-woo!
                              —Thomas Nashe

I was woken by a bloodcurdling squawl and sat straight up in the dark, fumbling at the bedside lamp. The clock said 5:20. Over in the corner Archie and Muzzle crouched facing each other, the cat pressed against the wall, his back humped and his fur standing on end like a Halloween cat. Archie reached for him, and before I could get to them Muzzle let out another yowl and swiped his claws across the baby's arm.

Archie's reaction sounded a lot like the cat's. He sat back staring at the scratches in amazement as Muzzle darted out the bedroom door. When I reached him he had started howling in earnest, and three shallow channels on his arm were welling blood. I carried him into the bathroom, bypassing Muzzle's sink and setting him in the bathtub to wash the scratches and cover them with antiseptic and a Band-Aid. Once he couldn't see them, he made a lot less noise about them.

"Well, I wouldn't have let it happen," I said, "but it's one way to learn you don't corner cats." At least it wasn't as bad as knocking himself out.

I changed his diaper and got him into the clothes Emily had packed, a pair of pull-up jeans and a long-sleeved shirt with OXFORD UNIVERSITY on the front. When we got downstairs I found Muzzle at the door, meowing desperately, and when I opened it he shot out and disappeared in the vegetation while I picked up the milk and the paper.

Archie looked after him and said sadly, "Cat."

"You have to be slow and gentle with animals, matey," I said. "But you'll learn."

He began his explorations while I cooked my oatmeal and made instant coffee. I knew from experience it was hopeless to tell him to stay in a chair, so I toasted him a slice of whole wheat bread and spread it with Marmite, a salty brown yeast paste universally fed to English babies. Having tasted it once, I was amazed that Archie could eat the stuff. He chomped at it steadily while removing all the pots and pans from under the sink, dumping out the wastepaper basket, and struggling mightily to open the back door, which I'd been careful to lock. I had to have my breakfast orange juice, outrageously expensive though it is in England, and I'd poured him a glass too. Every time he wandered near the table I held it out and he took a sip before toddling off again.

Breakfast accomplished, I'd started washing the dishes when the phone gave its double ring. I went into the sitting room to answer it, calling to Archie to follow me. He came in and set to work pulling the books off my wall of shelves.

Fiona Bennett was on the phone. "I wondered how you're coping with this awful Peter-thing. Nobody can believe he could commit a violent act of any kind!"

"Of course he couldn't," I answered. "I'm doing my bit right now by taking Archie off Emily's hands. I was going to call you later, to see if John knows anything more since last night. He was the only one at the station who'd tell us a thing."

"You know about the phone calls, of course? That's the worst of it. No, he went off this morning without telling me any more. It's not his case, of course, so I shan't be able to pump him as I did about our local murder."

Suddenly I noticed Archie had decamped, leaving a pile of books behind.

"Listen, will you ask him what they learned from the autopsy—I mean, postmortem?" I said quickly.

"Oh, I know what *autopsy* means. I've heard the results of any number of them on the American police shows. I was a tremendous fan of one a few years ago, about this police surgeon who solved all the murders instead of the detectives—I can't recall the name. Of course, I'll ask him. What are you looking for?"

"There's just a possibility Stone could have committed suicide, so I want to know if there was any evidence of his facing death soon, you know, cancer or something."

"Suicide? Oh, surely not, John says the angle of the knife was downward, so it must have been someone standing over him. I can't imagine killing oneself by lifting a knife above one's head and bringing it down into one's chest. It *would* be quite a dramatic sight, but unlikely, wouldn't you think?"

"I guess so." I sighed. " Sorry, I've got to run and see what Archie's doing. It's awfully quiet in the kitchen."

"Oh, dear. Well, perhaps I'll look in later. I'm off to A Bit of Old England now." That was her antique shop in the touristy village of Broadway.

Archie had climbed up my kitchen step stool onto the countertop, where he stood investigating the previously unknown wonders of the wall cabinets. I was beginning to realize that climbing was currently his favorite activity. I managed to lift him down without any dishes getting broken, and whirled him round a couple of times to turn his indignant howls into laughter. Then we went upstairs so I could put on slacks and a sweater and get us both into shoes. The rain had stopped during the night and the sun was showing itself intermittently. I planned a nice long walk, staying on pavement until the ground and foliage dried.

Archie refused to ride in a stroller anymore, so I had to suit my pace to his short legs and his need to keep stopping to pursue his investigations. Emily and I agreed he was just like the Elephant's Child in *Just So Stories*, full of " 'satiable curiosity," which he had to satisfy, "with the world so new and all." The countryside was a treasury of strange and nameless things. "Dat?" he kept demanding, solemnly repeating each word I supplied, committing it to memory so, I knew from experience, he would be able to repeat it immediately the next time he saw the thing.

I turned us left up the main road and we mosied along the grassy shoulder, taking about a quarter of an hour to cover the hundred yards or so to Church Lane. There we hung another left and proceeded between high hedgerows full of wildflowers and dripping shrubs, toward the village church. St. Etheldreda's is a square, stone building in the Norman style, without ornament except for rows of sharp-pointed zigzags around the front door, like teeth ready to eat you if you try to come in. From what I knew about the Normans, they were more inclined to the military than the artistic, and their churches always seem to have a defensive air. But St. Etheldreda's is beautiful in its own blunt way. I even like the squatty tower with crenellations around the top like castle battlements, none of that poetic stuff about reaching toward heaven with a spire.

There were cows in the field on the other side of the lane, which delayed Archie for quite a while. As I stood waiting for him, uttering an occasional "uh-huh" to his commentary on these amazing beasts, I looked all the way down the lane, at the manor house. Built, like the church, by the Norman lord who received this area after the Conquest, it was now a mixture of styles as his descendants, the Damerels, had torn down and rebuilt sections of it in the styles of their own eras. I'd been inside on a couple of memorable occasions, but I knew I'd never be invited there again. I felt a momentary sadness, thinking how violent death and desertion had decimated the family that had occupied that house for centuries. Only one of them was left behind, living there now in self-imposed isolation from the village.

"Come on, let's go find the cat," I finally said to Archie, with perfect confidence that Muzzle would never let that happen. It got him toddling again, though, and I guided our expedition through the medieval lych-gate, into the churchyard.

The enormous beeches and oaks were in full leaf now, rustling in the chilly breeze, shading the graves of Far Wychwoodians from the time of the Plantagenets to the most recent, a numbered plate in the ground where Muzzle's old friend George Crocker lay unmemorialized. Some of us had talked about buying a headstone for him, but nothing had been done yet.

Archie's main interest was the low, mossy stone wall that surrounded the churchyard. I stood close by while he pulled himself from stone to stone until he stood precariously on top. At that point I wrapped the bottom band of his sweatshirt around my hand, behind where he wouldn't see, and kept a tight hold while he teetered along to the inevitable fall. This time he hung suspended from my fist instead of hitting the ground. When I set him down and let go of his shirt, he started right back up the wall.

"Because it's there, I guess." I sighed, spotting him again.

"Ah, Mrs. Penny! You've brought your grandson to see the church—what a good thought!"

Mr. Ivey, the vicar, was coming toward us in a flutter of black, his fine-boned face lighted by a smile.

"*Catherine*, please," I said for the umpteenth time. "My married name was *not* Penny, and anyway I'm divorced now."

"Oh, I do beg your pardon." The smile drooped into a concerned frown. "What a great shame! I can't begin to understand the marriages and divorces and remarriages that seem quite normal to people nowadays. The comfort of a long-lasting partnership with one person is life's most consoling gift, at least I found it so. Constantly adapting to the ways of someone new must be extremely stressful."

"I'm not going to remarry," I said shortly.

"I'm very sorry—Catherine," he went on. "I didn't mean to sound judgmental, that is of course one of the main things a clergyman has to guard against! It's only that my marriage was such a source of happiness to me, I wonder how— Well, there I go again! As I started to say, it's never too early to introduce a child to— Oh, dear! Is he all right?"

Archie was again dangling from my grip on the sweatshirt, laughing as he swung back and forth in the air.

"Yes, as long as I watch him like a hawk."

"Very good—'watch him like a hawk'! They do watch the ground very intently, don't they? I might use that in a sermon. One could say that's the way God watches over us."

"You were very lucky to have such a good marriage," I said, setting Archie on his feet and trying to herd him away from the wall. "How long has it been since you lost your wife?"

"Ten years," he answered sadly. "People told me it was a blessed release, but do you know, even in the last stages of her illness, when she was unconscious all the time, I was unwilling to let her go. Selfish of me, I daresay, but just to know she was still on this earth was important to me. Tom didn't understand that. I'm not sure I do myself."

"I think I do," I said as the three of us finally started moving toward the church. "I was only twelve when my mother died, and she died suddenly, not like your wife. But I remember feeling that the world was a different place, a foreign place, if she wasn't in it anymore. It passes, though, that feeling."

"Oh, yes. I've learnt to live without her, of course. God doesn't leave us without consolation. I had Tom to raise, as well as my work."

"Tom's a fine young man."

"He is, although these days—" He broke off as we passed through the forbidding doorway into the serene, flower-scented little church with its heavy round pillars, low ceiling, and age-worn oaken pews. Archie went for the pews, crawling under and over them, talking to himself.

"Is Tom having problems?" I asked.

"Well—I must admit to being rather worried about this engagement of his. The young woman—Gemma—seemed at first very suitable, academically minded, well mannered—They became engaged last winter, but after only a few months she became infatuated with the man who was so unfortunately murdered the other night, Mr. Stone. She broke off the engagement and Tom was devastated. Now Stone is dead, he tells me the ring is back on her finger—the one she'd returned to him when this fellow took up with her! Doesn't that seem to you very flighty behavior? Hardly auspicious for a successful marriage."

"Well, yes, it does," I had to admit. "And my own experience tells me any attempt to talk to him about it just results in a quarrel?"

"Quite." He sighed deeply. "He is far too much in love, I'm afraid."

I was touched by his openness, so untypical of the English, telling a near-stranger like me such personal things. There was a naïveté about him that was very appealing. I was about to confide how immovable Emily could be when she'd formed an opinion, to show him he wasn't the only parent with that problem, when I heard a ringing crash at the front of the church. We both started and looked toward the sanctuary. Someone had left the celebrant's chair close beside the altar, and Archie was in the process of climbing from the one to the other while a gold candlestick rolled back and forth on the floor.

He made it onto the altar before I could reach him and stood up on the embroidered white cloth that covered the stone top, beaming at his accomplishment. I heard the vicar oh-dearing and tut-tutting behind me as I put my hands under Archie's arms and lifted him to the floor, complimenting him enthusiastically on his jumping ability.

"Do you think this would be a good chance to speak to him about the sanctity of the altar?" he asked.

"Oh, Vicar, he's much too young," I said, unable to repress a laugh, "and his vocabulary's very limited. I don't think he's anywhere near ready for theology!"

Archie was now squatting on the floor, rolling the candlestick around, and I could see the white candle it held had split down one side.

"You must let me pay for a new candle," I said to Mr. Ivey, "and I'll take the altar cloth home and wash those muddy shoeprints out of it."

"No, no, we have quite a supply of candles, I shouldn't think of taking money for it. The cloth, now—I'll accept your kind offer there. Mrs. Watkins won't be coming for the laundry until Tuesday, and we shall need this cloth for Sunday services." He fingered it rather wistfully. "Some of the parishioners disapprove of these things, you know—candles, altar cloths, even the use of the old Prayer Book. I've been told my services come perilously close to papistry!" He smiled ruefully. "I have tried to explain that these things were the norm in our church until about thirty years ago, but of course people have forgotten."

"I think most of us like your way of doing things," I assured him. "It's a tremendous relief after Ian Larribee!"

"Ah yes, my predecessor of scandalous memory. Shocking to hear of a priest doing the things he was accused of! Oh, I believe you are correct, it's only a small group of people who disapprove. But I hate to think I keep anyone from finding satisfaction in worship. I wonder who left that chair so near the altar? It ought to be at the back of the sanctuary."

The last remark came as I followed his gaze and saw Archie starting up onto the chair again. This time I lifted him down without any games and answered his protesting howl with "Not going to happen, matey" as I carried him struggling down the aisle. Once in the churchyard he was quickly distracted and only grumbled a bit as he followed Mr. Ivey and me to the gate.

"I'll have the cloth back to you before Sunday," I promised. "I do apologize for Archie. You won't have to do a bell-book-and-candle to restore the altar's holiness, I hope?"

Not a very tasteful joke, I realized, as he thought seriously for a moment before answering, "Oh, no, not even I should go that far, Catherine."

Archie and I resumed our meandering walk, heading down the lane and then the main road past Rowan Cottage. I caught a glimpse of Muzzle's worried face peering around the doorway of the potting shed, but Archie was chasing a butterfly and didn't see him. The sun had gone in, and it looked as if it might rain again as we went into the Cobbs' small combination village shop–post office. Enid's habitually narrowed eyes became slits and her mouth set in a hard line when she saw Archie. I knew she was envisioning a floor littered with cans and broken bottles. But her husband, Henry, up a ladder stocking shelves, looked down at us with his customary sunny smile.

Archie headed right for the ladder, but three young girls immediately converged on him as he passed the cosmetics, and the one with the blonde dreadlocks scooped him up and bounced him enthusiastically.

"Hello then, Archie!" she sang out, planting a big kiss on his cheek. "Remember me—Jilly? You've grown quite a bit since I last seen you, han't he, Audrey?"

Audrey, Jilly's inseparable friend, stood holding her own baby, a plump little girl about a year old dressed in a conventional pink knitted baby suit, in contrast to her mother who had recently dyed her spiked hair bright orange, and wore studded black leather pants, boots, and jacket. She had acquired a little silver nose stud since the last time I'd seen her.

"He's getting a big boy, i'n he?" she joined in. "Now then, Archie, don't you remember Diana? Say, 'yes, I played with her down at the petrol station last month.' "

Archie of course said nothing of the kind, but he and Diana gazed at each other with the avid amazement small children always show when they spot a contemporary.

"Ooh, I think there's something going on there," said the third girl, a rather silly redhead named Patty Jenkins.

"How are things going with the new baby, Audrey?" I asked.

She patted her stomach, with a contented smile on her bright purple lips.

"Going a treat, Cath. It's what I do best. See, I don't just like getting preggers, I like *being* preggers too!"

Enid Cobb's bullhorn voice broke in, heavy with disapproval. "Was you three planning to buy any of that face muck, or are you just using me shop like your local?"

Archie was struggling to be released, so Jilly set him down, and the three of them started toward the door. Before they went out Audrey turned back to me and said, "We was all sorry to hear about Archie's dad being had up for that killing." The other two murmured agreement. "Poor Emily! Fancy finding out your man's a killer."

"He's nothing of the kind!" I responded indignantly. "Don't you go around saying such a thing, any of you. Peter wouldn't hurt a fly."

"But how's he going to get round that phone call from the bloke, saying he was killing him?" asked Patty.

I was dumfounded. "How do you know about that?" I demanded. The village's jungle telegraph system always amazed me, but this was something only the police and Peter's immediate family were supposed to know about.

"Molly Harper's got a friend at the station," Jilly explained.

"She's shagging a constable," Audrey elaborated, "and he told her, and she told Patty, so now everybody knows."

I blew out a deep breath in frustration as they left, calling good-byes to Archie. Henry Cobb had him well in hand, murmuring encouragement as he helped him to climb the ladder, holding him carefully by the arms and showing him how to back down when he'd gone high enough.

"Them girls is running wild," Enid announced as I turned to the counter. "Disgraceful how their mothers lets them dress and talk! That Audrey's dead lucky young Harry Ames was willing to marry her, though I still say, as I said from the start, he'll rue the day."

Audrey had produced Diana without revealing the father's name, although the village was sure it had been a young man who'd left for parts unknown when she started to show. But Harry Ames was a decent fellow, if several degrees less cool than Audrey, and seemed happy to be a father to Diana as well as his own expected son. Audrey had announced she was naming this one Elton.

"Oh well, maybe things will work out for them," I said. She answered with a scornful snort. "She's not such a bad sort, Enid. You must admit she's a really devoted mother."

"Mark my words," was her only answer.

"Oh, all right. I'll have a loaf of brown bread, a package of chipolatas, and, let's see, a packet of Twiglets, please. And a can—I mean, a tin of those little raviolis."

While Archie was otherwise occupied, I paid for a bag of boiled sweets too and slipped them into my pocket for occasions when only bribery would work.

"Did you hear the news about old George Crocker's place, then?" Enid asked as she rang up my purchases. When I said I hadn't, she went on with relish, "It's been sold! Mind you, I don't know no more, not yet. But I do hear there's a building firm from Chipping Campden been out to measure the ground and that."

So, I was to have a new neighbor. As Archie and I

made our slow way back to Rowan Cottage, I felt a tingle of excitement at the possibility of making friends with somebody even newer to the village than I was. I hoped they wouldn't turn out to be like the London couple who had bought our former doctor's house, at the other end of the village. They had no interest in living among us but descended on Saturdays with groups of friends in pricey sports cars, partied until the small hours, and then lay around the next day recuperating until they left in the late afternoon. It would be dreadful to have people like that across the road.

Archie was tired out by now. I warmed up some of the canned ravioli, one of his favorite foods, and he ate about half of them and drank a few sips of milk, then lay down on the hearth rug in the sitting room and fell asleep. I lifted him onto the sofa and covered him, then settled myself in the wing chair with a cheese sandwich and my current mystery novel. I was not going to leave him alone there again, even if the door was locked this time.

I was starting to nod off over my book when the phone rang. I sprang up to answer it before it rang again and woke the baby.

"Is everything all right?" Emily asked with barely disguised apprehension.

"Yes, darling, no disasters, accidents, or mishaps this time. Didn't I promise you? He's having a nice nap. What's happening there?"

"I just got in from my adolescent group," she answered. "They were more than usually fractious, probably because I couldn't concentrate on them as I should have.

Lack of adult attention is the root of their problems, and they're always poised to say I'm just like their parents." She gave a deep sigh. "But I can't think of anything but Peter right now!"

"Of course you can't. None of us can."

"Dad and I are going to see him this afternoon, with Mr. Billingsley. Of course *she* has to come along. I don't know why she doesn't just go shopping or something. She doesn't give a damn about Peter or me. I wonder if she even cares about Dad, except for his money. He told me she and her husband were really poor when he met her."

"She was married too? Oh, never mind, I don't want to know about it!"

"Yes, she dumped the guy as soon as she got a chance at Dad. Oh, Mom, why did everything have to turn out like this?"

"You think *I* know? Darling, you sound just about at the end of your rope. Let me take you to that Italian restaurant you like this evening, when I bring Archie back. We'll have a good dinner and talk about what we can do to get Peter cleared."

"I already promised Dad I'd go to dinner with them."

"Oh, for Pete's sake! Does he think he's helping you by making you hang out with that woman all the time?"

"Mother, he's doing his best, and I appreciate it!" Her voice cracked, and I forced myself to speak calmly.

"All right, love, I'm sorry. Listen, why don't I keep Archie tonight, then you can have the evening with your father and you and I can visit tomorrow morning? Just be sure they know to keep away, and everything will be fine."

"Oh, I don't know. I miss Archie. The place seems eerie, all quiet and orderly like this. What if they really do take Peter away from us? What if Archie never has a father to love him like Dad loved me?"

She was on the verge of tears again, so I took the decision off her shoulders. "You go ahead and have your visit with Peter and your dinner out, and I'll bring the baby back tomorrow morning. He's having a great time, and so am I. Just try to believe Peter's coming home soon, because he is! Maybe your Mr. Billingsley will come up with some new idea after he talks to him."

It hadn't rained when Archie woke, so we went out to the garden to work on the perennial bed I'd been planning ever since I moved into the cottage. I had diagrammed the drifts of compatible colors, changing through the seasons, all down the two long sides of my backyard, and now I was ready to double-dig it. This involved taking out the topsoil, breaking up the subsoil, removing weeds and big stones, adding dried manure and bonemeal, and returning the topsoil. Guaranteed to work off worry, anger, and frustration, at least temporarily!

I had bought a miniature shovel for Archie so he could "help" me, and he pitched in enthusiastically for short periods, sending dirt flying in all directions until one thing or another distracted him. After an hour or so we had a break and I sipped tea while he ran around with his Twiglets, small sticks of dough coated with that Marmite stuff he liked so much. I had just resumed digging, and he was trying unsuccessfully to climb into one of the rowan trees that had given the cottage its name, when Fiona Bennett came around the side of the house.

"My word, you're dirty!" she exclaimed. "Why you're determined to create this perennial border is beyond me. Just stick in a flowering bush here and there, much less tiring and messy."

"I've always wanted a perennial border," I answered stubbornly, sitting down on the back step beside her. "Besides, there's nothing like strenuous exercise to keep one young and flexible." But I didn't mind taking another break. I had to admit my back and arms were getting sore.

"We're too old for that sort of thing, Catherine," she insisted, not realizing that was the best way to harden my determination.

Archie wandered over, his face smeared with sticky brown Marmite, and ordered, "Dig!"

"Your gran wants a rest," Fiona said firmly. "Show me how well *you* can dig."

He went back to his shovel for a few minutes but then got a new idea and toddled around the yard calling, "Cat!"

"I spoke to John," Fiona said. "He called me at the shop, said he had a little time free and just wanted to see how my day was going. Wasn't that sweet of him?"

"I seem to be hearing about one happy marriage after another today," I said with some acerbity. "The vicar's, Audrey's, yours. What is it, a conspiracy to make me feel like a failure?" I laughed to show I didn't mean it, although I sort of did. "Did you remember to ask him about the postmortem results?"

"Yes, indeed, that's why I closed the shop a little early and came to tell you what he said. There was nothing whatever wrong with Edgar Stone. The postmortem found him a very healthy specimen, in fact more fit than average for his age."

"Damn!" I sat thinking for a few minutes, watching Archie crawl under a bush looking for Muzzle. "Oh, well, suicide did seem unlikely, the more one thought about it. Now we have to figure out how those calls were made, if Edgar didn't make them. It just had to have been the real murderer, somehow sounding so much like Edgar that his wife and two of his colleagues are certain it was his voice."

"Hardly likely, dear," Fiona said. "No thug off the street could have done that, or would have had reason to. No student with a grudge could have done it either, and again, why would they want to incriminate Peter? You must face the fact that it *was* Stone who made those calls."

"But I can't face that, Fiona! It means Peter killed him, and I know that's not true. Okay, the only people who had an obvious motive are his colleagues at Mercy. Stone was going to be the new chair of their department in a few months, with power over their careers."

"That's a motive for finding a position somewhere else, not plunging a big knife into somebody," Fiona replied.

"What if the first call was genuine, he really had some

startling news to tell Peter," I began again, "and somebody killed him to keep him from telling it?"

"More plausible," she admitted.

"How could we find out what that news was?" We fell silent for a few minutes, thinking.

"Perhaps his wife would know," Fiona offered.

"I'm sure he wouldn't have confided in her, but she could have seen or overheard something, right?" I felt a new rush of hope, almost as exciting as when I'd gone after Barbie. "You know, I think I'll go and talk to her tomorrow, Fiona! She's got some mental problems, of course, but if she does know something, I'm sure I can get it out of her."

Fiona turned down my invitation to stay for dinner, because John for once was coming home in time to eat with her. I gave up digging and joined Archie's futile cat hunt, crawling under bushes with him and ending with a grand chase around the garden. It was after five o'clock by then, his usual supper time, so I gave him a bath and got him into his pajamas, then showered and changed and started cooking.

One meal he would sit down for was a boiled egg served in an egg cup, with "soldiers," strips of whole wheat toast to dip in the yolk. I fried up the sausages the Brits call chipolatas, pretty much like American breakfast sausages instead of the big fat "bangers" they prefer, and he ate one with his egg and toast, and drank some apple juice. I had the same, with a cup of tea instead of the juice, and then we went upstairs. It still got dark early, which made it easier to get him into bed. We looked at a picture book for a little while, but his eyes had drooped shut before the last page. Really, I thought as I went back downstairs, for such an active child he wasn't hard to get to sleep at all. And, thank heaven, he was sleeping through the night now—or at least until just before dawn.

I did the dishes, got into my nightclothes, and as the long-threatened rain started clicking against the roof slates I ended the day as usual, with Horlicks and *Book at Bedtime*. I was still thinking intermittently about my new idea for solving the case and freeing Peter, and I could hardly wait for tomorrow to come so I could start putting it into action. It would probably be best not to tell Emily, I decided. I knew she'd think I was going to upset her former patient, and "meddling" was high on her list of my faults.

It occurred to me that the only person in the village who hadn't asked about Peter was Mr. Ivey. He probably didn't even know about the arrest. A vicar was never really one of the villagers, and Mr. Ivey would be even more isolated because he was a newcomer to Far Wychwood. He must be lonely, I thought, his wife dead and his son gone to live his own life. I really should invite him to dinner.

Before climbing the narrow staircase I went out to the potting shed with an umbrella, to check on the cat and leave a bowl of water to get him through the night. He was up on a shelf between two bags of perlite, unreachable by invaders. The look he gave me was not one of approval.

"Well, I'm sorry, all right?" I said to him. "It doesn't happen all that often, now does it? You'll be back in the house tomorrow."

I left him to sulk and went inside as the nightingale started tuning up in the woods across the road.

CHAPTER SIX

Grief, find the words; for thou hast made my brain
So dark with misty vapors which arise
From out thy heavy mold, that inbent eyes
Can scarce discern the shape of mine own pain.
                                        —Sir Philip Sidney

After Emily and Rose had embraced Archie the next morning, heard the tale of his adventures—"Dig! Twee! Baby! Cow!"—and exclaimed over his battle scars—"Bad cat!"—he and Rose went looking for the tape player while I sat down with Emily at the table in the dining corner.

"Thanks, Mom," she said. "I *am* glad you can do the nature-exposure thing, it's so educational for him."

Emily was big on educational activities, typical of her generally earnest outlook on life. She looked a little more rested this morning, and I hoped I had contributed to that. But she was still distracted and nervous, still twisting her hair and glancing around periodically as if to catch the next disaster creeping up on her.

"It was fun for both of us," I answered. "Have you had any breakfast? How about if I fix you some scrambled eggs with cheese, the way you always liked them?"

She made a disgusted face. "Mom, really I couldn't. Food just sticks in my throat. But cook yourself something if you like."

"Archie and I ate before we came. Cup of coffee, at least?"

"Please don't keep on asking."

I knew that tone of voice, so I changed the subject.

"How did the meeting with Peter and the lawyer go yesterday?"

"Well, it looks as if Mr. Billingsley is planning a defense of temporary insanity."

"Insanity! He doesn't believe his own client, then? He thinks Peter did it! That's the kind of help your father gives you, finding a lawyer who won't even *try* to prove his innocence!"

She sat silent for a minute, while from the nursery that high-pitched voice sang about Mrs. Bond and her dinner plans. Then she said quietly, "Are you finished?"

"Emily, you and I have to go and find another lawyer."

"No, Mother. Dad's spoken to several colleagues here, and they all say Mr. Billingsley is the best you can get."

"Best, my eye! If we go to London, to the Inns of Court—"

"Mother, I have faith in Mr. Billingsley and I'm going to keep him. Dad is an experienced attorney, and he agrees that unless we can get around that 999 call, no jury is going to believe us."

"What does Peter say about this?"

"He hates it, but Dad talked to him and I think he's—"

"That man is going to destroy Peter's reputation, if not his life! Even if they got him off with temporary insanity, what college or even lower school would hire a murderer? He wouldn't be able to earn a living, he'd be a marked man for the rest of his life. No, it's essential to prove he's *not guilty*, nothing less will work. Somebody has to find the real murderer."

"I don't know what else to do!" she said shakily. She closed her eyes for a few moments, as if to hide from everything. Then she opened them, and her voice was firmer. "I'm not going to alienate Dad. I'm lucky to have his advice, he knows about these matters much better than you and I. But it's true, the insanity defense could ruin our future, and if it fails they'll take Peter away from me completely. Maybe John Bennett would help us?"

"I'll ask him," I said, patting her hand. I could see my outburst had made her feel worse, so I said no more. Kind though he was, I knew from experience how over-cautious John Bennett could be. He would never investigate a case behind the backs of his superiors. I was more determined than ever now to talk to the one other person who had been in the house while the killer was there.

"Have you heard anything about Mrs. Stone?" I asked.

"Ann and Dorothy came to see Peter just as we were leaving, you remember, Cyril Aubrey's wife and Dorothy

Shipton, the tutor? Ann said she'd been to visit Perdita and found her stuffing her husband's clothes into a bin bag for Oxfam, alternately laughing and crying about the murder. She made Ann very uneasy. Perdita told her she never wanted to see me again, because my husband had killed hers—then the next minute she was giggling, saying how happy she was now." She shook her head. "Bipolarism is not a good progression in her case."

There was a knock at the door, and when Emily opened it Quin stood there, accompanied by the girlfriend with her sulky face on.

"Dad!" Emily exclaimed, with some annoyance. "I told you Mom would be here and you should wait till later."

He stepped in, pulling Miss Congeniality by the hand. "Honey, all this ducking and dodging is crazy," he said, putting his arm around Emily's shoulders. "There's no reason we can't be here when your mother is. We've got to start acting like grown-ups sometime. Hi, Kit!"

"See you," I said to Emily as I passed her, going out the door.

It was another sunny day, so I walked to the Stones' house, about forty-five minutes away. I hoped Quin wouldn't be around when I came back for my car, but I wasn't going to let him keep me from getting my exercise. What was this "grown-ups" nonsense? Did he really believe I could forgive and forget? And he'd always said I was the one who refused to face facts!

When I rang the doorbell, Geoffrey Pidgeon answered it and blinked at me in surprise.

"Hello, Mrs.—er—"

"Not Mrs. anybody," I said briskly. "Just Catherine. I'm Peter Tyler's mother-in-law, remember?"

"Of course, of course," he said heartily. "How could I forget so clumsily ruining your frock? Do please come inside." As I did, he continued, "I'm just helping Perdita to sort through her accounts, Edgar always did them and so—"

"Geoffrey!" called that deep, dramatic voice peremptorily, and he stepped quickly to the study door. It stood open as it had on the night of the murder, the broken lock still dangling. "Who is that? Tell them to go away."

She was sitting at a big oak desk, the top littered with checkbooks and papers. Although the day was mild, she was dressed in woolen slacks, a pullover, and a heavy coatlike sweater which she held wrapped tight around her as if she couldn't get warm. Her long, thick black hair had obviously not been combed for the past two days. I could see some mats that were going to have to be cut out. She looked up, narrowing her dark eyes suspiciously.

"I've seen you before," she said. "Who are you—one of Edgar's lovers?"

"Far from it," I answered. "I'm Emily Tyler's mother. You met me at Mercy College the night of—the other night."

"Oh, Emily." She went back to shuffling through the papers, dismissing me. "*She* couldn't help me to deal with him. Talk, talk, talk—that's all she could do. I knew that wasn't enough. Geoffrey, come help me with this!"

He obeyed, pulling a chair up next to hers, glancing at me apologetically. "I'm sorry, rather a difficult time, not yet ready to receive visitors, the shock, you know," he mumbled.

"Emily's concerned about you, Mrs. Stone," I said. "She's afraid you might not be taking your medications."

"Medications!" She spat the word at me, fury suddenly twisting her face. "I don't need those anymore, and you can tell her so. They make me feel—thick. They give me bad dreams. Do you know," she went on, her eyes widening with amazement, "I didn't dream of Simon last night! It was the first night since he was murdered that I haven't dreamt of him." She turned to Geoffrey and laid her hand against his chest. "Do you think his ghost was waiting for justice, like Andrea in *The Spanish Tragedy,* and now he can rest?"

Geoffrey shook his head. "No, my dear," he said gently. "The dreams were only an effect of your grief. There are no ghosts."

"How do you know?" She snatched her hand away, angry again. "You sound just like Edgar, always the *expert* on every subject!"

"I didn't mean—" he began miserably, but she rushed on, turning to me.

"Do *you* think Simon is at peace now?" she demanded.

"I don't even know who Simon was," I answered.

"He was my son," she said, turning cold and quiet. "His father murdered him. I know he'll rest now, and wait for me."

"If you can feel at last that the poor boy is at rest," said Geoffrey, "something good has come of this after all. You'll see, these things that try your mind will fall away, one by one. It only requires someone who's willing to give you kindness and understanding."

That seemed a bit overoptimistic, from what I'd seen of her.

"I'd like to ask you a couple of questions," I said quickly, since she seemed to have fallen momentarily into a quieter mood. "Didn't you see or hear anything, the night your husband was killed? You were in the house the whole time, weren't you?"

"I was asleep," she said, scowling at me. "I told the police. It was their siren that woke me, and then I ran downstairs and saw his body." Her eyes suddenly widened, and she pointed to the corner where Edgar's body had huddled. "Look, you can still see his blood all over the wall!" I didn't see any blood, but she must have thought she did, because she jumped up and cried, "I have to get out of this place! Blood everywhere—I have to go back to Tyneford, where the walls are clean—"

Geoffrey folded her in his arms, murmuring, "There, my dear, of course you'd want to move from this house. I'll look up an estate agent this very day."

Now she was weeping against his shirt. I was already exhausted by these violent mood swings and wondered how Geoffrey could even think of taking her on. But it was obvious he would do anything for the poor demented creature.

"No, not in Oxford," she went on through her sobs.

"He loved me when we lived in Tyneford, it was only after we came back here it all went wrong. You'll drive me there, won't you, Geoffrey? If I had a car I'd go by myself, but he would never buy one. Oh, God, is he really dead? How can he be dead? My poor Edgar, he shouldn't be dead! He wanted *me* dead, me and Simon, and now he—Why must I be the one to go on living? There's no point in it anymore!"

"I guess I'd better leave," I said, and Geoffrey nodded. But she heard me and pulled out of his arms.

"No, don't go," she commanded, the sobs stopping abruptly. "*You* understand, don't you? The way he betrayed me, the pain, the jealousy and the hopelessness?"

I could only stare, wondering if her mental state gave her some kind of sixth sense. Fortunately she didn't seem to require an answer.

"I don't want to look at those *bills* any longer," she told Geoffrey. "I'm sick of the sight of them, they make no sense!"

"I'll take care of them for you, my dear, don't concern yourself."

"Because I'll have plenty of money after I sell all his books." She waved her arm at the shelves that covered two walls, packed tight with books in all sorts of colors and states of preservation.

"Oh, but surely they should go to the college." Geoffrey sounded profoundly shocked. "We all assumed—I mean to say, there are some important volumes there, they must be preserved for scholars, my dear."

"They're mine now, and I'll do as I want with them!" she flared up. "A dealer can sell them for more money than Mercy College would be able to give me."

Was she as disturbed as she at first appeared, or could she be acting? I wondered suddenly. That last observation had sounded surprisingly shrewd.

"You may be disappointed in their value, my dear," Geoffrey said sadly. "Few, if any, of them are really rare. Edgar's interest in books was more scholarly than pecuniary."

"He told me some of them were *priceless*!" she insisted. "There's a first-edition Heywood in here somewhere, I've seen it many times." She started pulling books off the shelves at random, tossing them to the floor. "Well, I shall find it—and he told me there was something about this one, something important—I can't remember what it was, but a dealer will know." She was pulling out a shabby green volume with a beautiful gold sunburst pattern on the spine, the pages trying to fall out of a split binding. Geoffrey looked about ready to cry, picking up the books as she threw them down and setting them back on the shelves. I moved stealthily toward the door, longing to be gone but unwilling to provoke her by leaving openly.

"So I'll have plenty of money," she was saying, "and I'll use it to buy back our house in Tyneford. Edgar said nobody lives in it anymore, and I'll paint it and make it all lovely and then we'll be happy again."

"Please, Perdita, reconsider—"

She turned on him contemptuously. "Oh, go home, Geoffrey! Go on, leave me alone, I'm sick of your mewling."

He tried to persuade her to let him stay, but anything he said only made her angrier, and finally he and I left her sitting alone at her husband's desk, bundling up the papers.

"She really ought to have somebody with her," I said uneasily. "She might hurt herself."

"Not to worry," he said with forced cheerfulness. "I know her better than anyone, she'll quiet down now we've gone. I keep in touch with her by telephone several times a day, and a woman comes in the afternoon to take care of the housekeeping. She's been told off to ring me immediately if there's any problem."

"You're very kind to take such care of her," I said as he stood back to let me go out the gate before him.

"Not at all. I feel it a privilege. Are you going toward Mercy? I'm heading for my study to get in a bit of work, and should be glad to accompany you that way."

"Yes, I'm going to my daughter's place by Folly Bridge, where I left my car."

"Ah, then, instead of following the streets, let's go by way of Magdalen Grove. Have you seen the deer park, and the view of Magdalen Tower from Addison's Walk? No? Come along, it's one of the best sights in Oxford."

I had to walk briskly to keep up with his long legs, down a couple of residential streets and across a traffic circle, toward a large green area ahead.

"I wouldn't have the patience to deal with someone as difficult as Mrs. Stone," I said.

"Ah, but you didn't know her before." His face flushed with emotion. "Before the slings and arrows of outrageous fortune had wounded her, when she was young, when we were all young together. Her mind then was perfectly sound. One should perhaps have realized how vulnerable such a mind would be to adversity, but we only saw how dashing she was, how reckless, a free spirit—brilliant, in every sense of the word! She was a tremendous favorite in OUDS productions, played all the great parts—Cleopatra, Webster's Vittoria, Hedda Gabler. She could certainly have acted professionally, but like the rest of us she preferred academia. Her father was a well-known Shakespearean scholar, a Trinity man—even gave his children names from the plays."

"Yes, I recognized 'Perdita,' she's the heroine of—oh, dear. *The Winter's Tale*?"

"Quite right! She was herself more interested in Jonson and wrote an excellent paper on his plays in her second year, which was later published."

"So, she was into acting," I said, remembering my earlier suspicion that she might not be quite as crazy as she seemed.

"We were all mad for the stage. I was a credible Falstaff, though I say it myself. Cyril and Dorothy usually took on the secondary parts, although I remember that he did very well as Antony to Perdita's Cleopatra. It's how we became friends, and when Edgar came to Oxford, a year behind us, he made quite an impression as Iago. But soft—here we are!" he said heartily as we started down a dirt path, under a canopy of very old trees beside a slow-moving stream.

"This path," he told me, "is known as Addison's Walk. Have you read Joseph Addison?"

"Of Addison and Steele?" I ventured uncertainly.

"Yes, editors of the *Tatler* and the *Spectator* in the seventeenth century. Addison was a Magdalen man, and college tradition says he liked to walk here. I've always found him a bit didactic, although he's generally considered a great prose stylist. Terrible judge of literature, however, wrote a long ode called 'An Account of the Greatest English Poets,' including Montague, Roscommon, and Waller, but omitting all of our fellows, as well as Donne, Marlowe, and Shakespeare." We both laughed, and he went on. "If you look off to the right you'll see some fallow deer, part of a little herd they keep here."

The beautiful creatures gazed at us without fear as we passed the fence that enclosed their grazing ground. They were much smaller than American deer, and even the adults were spotted like fawns.

"How nice of the college to take care of the sweet little things!" I said.

"Well, actually, the herd was established to provide meat for the dining hall, in the eighteenth century. They've become an institution, of course, but when they're judged to be overplentiful, venison does still appear at table."

As we got closer to Magdalen College three or four tourists passed us, as well as a couple of dons who acknowledged Geoffrey with nods. A few undergraduates lounged under the trees, reading, and mallard ducks paddled slowly downstream. It was hard to believe the noise and traffic of the Oxford streets was so nearby.

We walked in silence for a while, but in the end I couldn't resist the opportunity to pump him for more information.

"How did Stone get into your little group?" I asked. "Surely you wouldn't have wanted such a nasty character as a friend!"

"His sarcastic wit seemed daring to undergraduates," he said. "We quite admired his impudence, and his acting ability did enhance our productions. He was interested in the 'other' Elizabethans too, and so we took him into our circle."

He sighed deeply and stopped for a minute, looking across the stream at the deer.

"A bit rum, repeating all this ancient history," he said with a sound of finality. I could see how uncomfortable it made him, but I was certainly not going to let British reticence get in the way of a chance like this. I hadn't been able to get anything useful out of Perdita, but if I could get Geoffrey to open up to me, now I had him started, he might inadvertently hand me the key to Peter's jail cell.

I was startled to hear him pick up that very subject, as if he had read my mind.

"Do you know, I see in Peter the same enthusiasm, the

same willingness to take chances that we all had then. His book is full of daring conjectures, exciting new interpretations, quite like the writings of the Elizabethans themselves. They were a bold lot, in and out of prison for their audacious opinions, killing one another in duels, challenging all the contemporary mores—and we, their interpreters, have lived long enough to become conservative, conventional, wary of new ideas! I quite wanted Peter to be named head, you know. Spoke to Cyril about it, but he didn't want to be the one to change the whole direction of the program, take power out of the hands of the old boys. If only the poor lad hadn't allowed himself to be goaded into precipitate action, he would have won recognition another day."

"*You* don't think he did it, surely? You were his mentor!"

He looked at me with surprise. "Is there reason to hope he's innocent, then? I'd heard the police are convinced of his guilt."

"Who cares about them?" I exclaimed impatiently. "All they want is to get the case off their books. It's his friends who have to find the evidence that will save him. You're his friend, aren't you, Geoffrey?"

"Of course, of course I am! But I don't see how—"

"Then tell me more ancient history. The real reason for the murder could lie somewhere in Edgar's past. I know it's a long shot, but we have to try everything."

"Really, I—What can I tell you that could possibly help?"

"How did Edgar come to marry Perdita? He didn't seem to love her at all."

"That couldn't be relevant to his death," he said shortly.

"Oh, come on, Geoffrey! Don't you want to help Peter? Do you want him shut up in some prison for the rest of his life?"

"Of course not, but— Well, Edgar Stone made a dead set at Perdita, and when she— They were married before the end of our last term." His face was growing redder by the sentence. It wasn't hard to guess why. Edgar must have got her pregnant and had to marry her. "We all scattered after graduation, teaching in various schools. Edgar and Perdita went to Tyneford, sixty or seventy miles from Oxford, where he taught in a preparatory school. It's since closed down, I understand."

"Didn't Perdita get a positon too, with her brilliant mind and all?"

"They had a child. He had certain needs— She gave up her career to care for him."

"Simon," I said softly.

"Yes. Look, Mrs.—er—I simply cannot discuss these things further." He stood still again, looking at the ground. "I've no right to violate the privacy of my friends, anxious though I naturally am to help Peter. Now, I wish you would look to the left, at those small purple flowers in the grass. Do you see them? Those are very rare wildflowers, fritillaria they're called, extinct in the wild. Magdalen is famous for its little colony."

I looked bleakly at the bright dots in the grass, nodding in the chilly breeze that had sprung up.

"I'm sorry," I said. "You're right, I've got no business

asking you for details about people's personal lives. I'm just scrabbling around desperately for something, anything, that might save him!"

"I quite understand," he mumbled. "I only wish I could give it you."

Eventually we came to the end of the path and went through a scrolly blue gate, along the serene cloisters of Magdalen, and out into the mayhem of High Street traffic. Geoffrey led me across the street and down a lane between college buildings, and then through another gate. Now we were on a wider path, turning at a shady bend of the river into a broad open meadow. To the right, across a playing field, rose the pale medieval buildings of Christ Church College, and to the left a little herd of black and white steers grazed the meadow grass, oblivious to tourists and students, who were much more numerous here than on Addison's Walk.

"That's Christ Church Meadow," Geoffrey said determinedly, "and this is called the Broad Walk. The little alley of trees over there was planted by Dean Liddell, whose daughter was—"

"Yes, I know, Alice in Wonderland," I finished for him. "It's very kind of you, but I'm not in the mood for sightseeing right now. I think I'll just go home and heat a can of soup. But thank you for showing me the gardens, and I apologize again for quizzing you."

I held out my hand and he took it in his big paw. "Not at all, not at all. It's really most admirable of you to take up Peter's cause like this. I say, why don't you join my colleagues and me for supper this evening? We'll be dining at High Table in the Great Hall, and people often bring guests. You might find the experience interesting, and I assure you the victuals will be better than any tinned soup."

I allowed myself to be persuaded. "High Table in the Great Hall" sounded like an experience not to be missed, and besides, it would be another chance to ask questions that might lead somewhere. Almost immediately, while he gave me directions and a time, it occurred to me that I had nothing to wear to such a grand-sounding event. I had ended up throwing the red dress away, knowing it was no use taking it to Oxfam, the British equivalent of Good Will, with that indelible stain all over it. So when we parted at the end of the Broad Walk, instead of crossing to Emily's I turned to the right and hurried up St. Aldate's toward Debenham's Department Store.

I didn't seem to have learned anything that would be helpful to Peter, I mused while pushing back dresses on the racks. I'd only got to know and like Geoffrey better, and to appreciate how disturbed Perdita Stone really was. At least, she seemed to be. Something bothered me about her behavior, maybe a bit too much Lady Macbeth? That business about the blood on the wall, for example. And how could anyone sleep while bloody murder was being committed downstairs, and not hear a thing?

I wondered, too, why she kept saying Edgar had killed the child, Simon. If he had done such a thing, why wasn't he in jail? Why was Perdita the only one who talked about it, while the others always looked embarrassed? Nasty as Edgar had been, it was a stretch to imagine any man deliberately murdering his own little boy, much less getting away with it.

Then I came upon the perfect dress, not too formal but respectful of the occasion, and trotted off to the fitting room, abandoning detection temporarily for the nervous decisions about shoes and jewelry that women have to make on such occasions.

CHAPTER SEVEN

Trust me, Plantagenet, these Oxford schools
Are richly seated near the river-side . . .
The town gorgeous with high-built colleges,
And scholars seemly in their grave attire,
Learned in searching principles of art.
—Robert Greene, *The Honorable*
History of Friar Bacon and Friar Bongay

How tragic that Peter can't be here for this lovely Dover sole! I believe it's his favorite dish. One doesn't want to think what sort of dinner he's having in that prison."

The two men, Cyril Aubrey and Geoffrey Pidgeon, murmured agreement to Dorothy Shipton's lament. I leaned back in my ornate Jacobean armchair and let my eyes roam over the Great Hall.

It was an impressive room, carrying out the Roman motif typical of eighteenth-century Adam buildings, with round stone pillars at the corners and dark paneled walls richly carved in swags of wooden fruit. Classical stone heads gazed down at us from above the big, leaded windows at either end of the room. The stone floor echoed the sounds of chairs scraping and the shoes of formally dressed servers clacking among the long trestle tables. The place was full of students producing a loud but civilized murmur of voices and clinking of tableware and glasses. Most of them were dressed, like my dinner companions, in the black gowns that I always thought of as graduation outfits, but a few wore street clothes.

"Is there a reason some students wear gowns and others don't?" I asked idly.

A sigh went round the table. Cyril Aubrey answered me sadly, "Actually, subfusc—the scholar's gown, with a dark suit under—is required for dinner in Hall, as well as on ceremonial occasions and at exams. But there is strong sentiment among the undergraduates to abolish that requirement."

"No respect for tradition," Dorothy grumbled. "Come to Hall in blue jeans, if they could!"

"Quite," Cyril agreed. "Well, the world *is* changing— if perhaps too rapidly for some of us. Subfusc has already been abolished at Cambridge, you know."

"Kind of a shame," I said. "It's such a distinctive part of the college scene."

"The ones wearing street clothes tonight are expressing solidarity with the movement for abolition, you see," Geoffrey put in. "We've decided it's not worth a fight. It would only lead to demonstrations and the like, and they're bound to have their way in the end, aren't they?"

" 'Now all the youth of England are on fire,' and why? To force even the most solemn precincts to accept their denims and underwear tops!" Dorothy declaimed.

The men chorused, "*Henry V!*" and smiled their congratulations on the aptness of her quotation.

The five of us sat at our own table on a platform slightly above and at right angles to the other tables. I'd felt at first like an actor on a stage, until I realized the kids were paying no attention at all to us. There had been sherry in the Senior Common Room before the walk across the quad, and now, with the fish, a bottle of chablis was moving around the table. I was beginning to feel kind of mellow, so I counted five minutes by the pendulum clock on the far wall before taking another sip of wine. It would be too humiliating to get silly in front of these erudite people, although *they* didn't seem to be counting. And I did want to stay alert, in case any information useful to Peter should drift my way.

"Tom and Gemma not joining us?" Cyril asked.

"Apparently not," Dorothy said gruffly. "They've become very thick again, off in corners at every chance. We shall have to speak to them, they really should put in an appearance at least once a week."

"Edgar's death has certainly changed their lives," I ventured to remark.

"Alas, poor Edgar," said Cyril Aubrey, and startled me by launching into iambic pentameter.

"Cut is the branch that might have grown full
     straight,
And burnéd is Apollo's laurel-bough
That sometime grew within that learnéd man."

Geoffrey muttered grudgingly, "I suppose one *could* describe him as 'learnéd.'"

"Come along, Pidgeon," said Aubrey, "one cannot deny he was a good scholar, and I for one still believe he would have made an excellent head of faculty."

Geoffrey burst out, "He would have been a disaster for this house!"

"There, now," Dorothy put in quickly, "what's the good wrangling over that? It's done with. Have you begun thinking which of us will be your replacement now, Aubrey?"

"Not just yet," he answered, refilling his glass. "Disrespectful of poor old Stone, you know, and I don't think the rest of us need any further disruption just now. Ann and I must just put off our plans, and stay on until a better time."

"Was that quotation from the Other Fellow too?" I asked him. "The one about 'Apollo's laurel-bough'?"

"Christopher Marlowe, actually," Aubrey replied. "*Dr. Faustus.*"

"But the O.F.'s famous line on Marlowe's murder could certainly be said to have some relevance," said Dorothy. "'A great reckoning in a little room.' And who would have thought Peter, of all people, would exact a reckoning in blood?"

"He didn't, you know," I said doggedly.

"I assure you, my dear lady," said Dorothy, "we don't want to believe it—but the evidence seems incontrovertible! I mean to say, that telephone call—"

"There's some other explanation for that," I said, "and I'm going to find out what it is. No matter how long it takes or how hard it gets, I'm going to find out what really happened."

"Certainly we hope you will!" said Aubrey heartily. "Well. Perhaps not the most suitable subject for High Table. Are you partial to Dover sole, Mrs.—er, Catherine?"

It was obvious that the recent unpleasantness was not going to be allowed to dominate the conversation. But after I had expressed my feelings about the very tasty fish, Dorothy skirted the edge of it again.

"Do you know, Aubrey, Geoffrey says Perdita is planning to sell all Edgar's books? Isn't there some way to dissuade her? Surely the college should have that collection."

"I agree, of course," Aubrey answered, "but I should be willing to wager any opposition to her plans will only harden her resolve. My wife tells me her mental state seems to be deteriorating."

"No, no, not at all," Geoffrey put in quickly. "I've spent far more time with her than Ann has since the incident, and I see definite signs of improvement. Got a bee in her bonnet at the moment about moving back to their old house at Tynesford, but that will pass."

"Come along, Pidgeon!" Dorothy said impatiently. "She'll never be well again. You must face facts. It's not only the thing about Simon, or the sick relationship she developed with Edgar—Perdita was always on the edge, even when she was young."

"She only had the artistic temperament," he said indignantly, "but she's as capable of being rational, and happy, as anyone—given time, and the kindness Edgar was never willing to expend."

"My dear fellow, you are preparing to devote your life to a hopeless cause," Dorothy persisted with some irritation. "You must give her up."

Cyril Aubrey said, almost under his breath, "Give her up, give her up, oh give her up!" We all looked at him in surprise, and saw a diffident smile spreading over his face. Then, to my bewilderment, Dorothy burst out laughing, and even Geoffrey smiled, if reluctantly.

"Sorry, old fellow," Aubrey said to him. "Couldn't resist. Come along, let's drop these unpleasant subjects and enjoy our dinner. But look, amazement on our visitor sits. That 'give her up' was rather a fateful line from an old play called *Vortigern*, you see. Amusing story, if you'd care to hear it."

"I'm determined to hear it, now!"

"One of Aubrey's techniques for defusing tensions within our little group," Dorothy told me, "coming along with a bit of a joke. Yes, *Vortigern* was thought in the eighteenth century to be by the Other Fellow, but it was actually forged by a nineteen-year-old boy."

"Extraordinary," Cyril went on, "how all the literary lights of the day leaped to believe young William Henry Ireland had *found* all these documents—Shakespeare's mortgage, an IOU, a 'love effusion' to Anne Hathaway."

"Yes," said Dorothy, "that last one contains my favorite passage of the lot:

> 'Is there on earth a man more true
> than Willy Shakespeare is to you?' "

A laugh went round the table that made some of the undergraduates glance up at us.

"People really believed Shakepeare wrote that kind of doggerel?" I asked.

"Not so surprising really," said Geoffrey. "People in those days idolized him in a completely irrational way. That's when the people of Stratford began making a nice living selling mementos of their favorite son. One wheelwright sold all sorts of things made from the wood of a crabapple tree under which he claimed Shakespeare had passed out drunk."

"No different today," Dorothy put in, "when fans tear pieces off the clothes of their musical and film idols."

"Or the enthusiasm for saints' relics in the Middle Ages," Aubrey said, "which also gave entrepreneurs a chance to profit by manufacture. There seems to be an inborn human need to touch something that has been close to the person one reveres. People wanted to believe they were actually in the presence of Shakespeare's mortgage, so they made themselves believe it. Young Ireland fooled Boswell, Edmund Burke, our own New College—"

"But when Sheridan produced *Vertigorn* at Drury Lane,

the jig was up," Geoffrey said. "The audience fell into fits of laughter at lines like the one Aubrey just quoted. Young Ireland finally confessed."

"I've always rather felt the dint of pity for William Henry Ireland," said Aubrey as the server replaced our fish with rib roast, Yorkshire pudding, brussels sprouts, and a bottle of Burgundy. "After all, the supposed experts who were fooled revealed themselves unable to tell good poetry from bad. Apart from embarrassing them, Young Ireland didn't hurt anyone."

"Any forgery hurts the cause of scholarship," Dorothy said decidedly. "But you're right, of course, in that the literati who were deceived revealed themselves to be poetically tone-deaf. Now, it would be impossible to bring off a trick like that today, but only because modern science could detect it. People like the deconstructionists in this very university deliberately denigrate the aesthetic value of literature, call it merely subjective. I've no doubt they could be taken in as easily as Edmund Burke was!"

"I hope all this history isn't boring you," Aubrey said to me with a smile.

"Not at all," I replied, putting my hand over the wineglass as he went to fill it. "What happened to young Ireland?"

"Ah well, he became old Ireland," he answered, "publishing unsuccessful novels, in and out of debtor's prison. If he'd been able to resist trying his hand at the theater, he might have lived in honor and prosperity on the proceeds of his forgeries. But it's hard for the young to resist a chance at the theatrical world. After all, none of us could! Of course, the only one who had any genuine talent was Perdita."

"Great waste, that she didn't pursue it," Dorothy said.

Geoffrey's voice deepened with emotion. "Do you remember her Hedda Gabler?"

"Of course," Aubrey answered. "No one who saw it will ever forget it. A really catlike ferocity in those last scenes. But not a patch on her Ralph in *The Knight of the Burning Pestle*!" They all murmured agreement.

"Ralph?" I said in surprise, pronouncing it in the English way as he had: "Rafe."

"Ah, yes," said Geoffrey eagerly. "That production is legendary in the annals of OUDS. Are you familiar with the play?"

"Never heard of it," I had to admit.

"Oh, a marvelous piece!" Dorothy exclaimed, pouring herself another glass of wine. Amazingly, she showed no effects from the previous ones. "Still hilarious after almost four centuries. Beaumont and Fletcher's best-known work."

"Point of fact, it's being done this season at the Globe in London," Geoffrey put in. "It's a satire of the popular romances of the time, with a grocer's apprentice named Ralph thrust into the hero's role by a series of incidents too complicated to tell now. He's rather a send-up of Don Quixote, you see, although he's just a lumbering, well-intentioned boy. Actors playing his master and his wife sit among the audience, cheering him on."

"At the curtain call, when Perdita came out and pulled off her boy's wig, her long black hair tumbling over her shoulders, and thanked them in her normal voice instead of the masculine voice she'd assumed, the audience suddenly realized that a girl had played the part," Cyril said. "At first a collective gasp went up, and then this tremendous eruption of applause. They had never guessed."

"Yes," I said slowly, "you wouldn't guess. She'd only have to lower her voice a little."

"That wasn't the only male part she played," Cyril went on. "In fact, she became well known for them. I remember how she studied recordings of a particular male actor for each part, until she could imitate him perfectly—Albert Finney, I believe, was her model for Ralph. Ah, that first time, though, that was a great experience. I played the grocer, and was onstage with her when the gasp went up. Of course, she was also impressive in women's parts. I played Antony to her Cleopatra, and Benedick to her Beatrice. Ah, well, long ago, long ago," he ended, looking at the others with a sad little smile, and they nodded solemnly.

The servers cleared away again and brought sherbet and port, which I was definitely not going to try. I felt much too relaxed as it was, my mind slower than I'd have liked at processing information, although I was sure I'd just heard something important.

"If I had been able to persuade her to go to London with me . . ." Geoffrey was saying.

"She made her own decision, old man," Cyril told him. "She always did. Stone was on the scene by then, if you remember. Now, if you'll hand me your glass, Mrs.—

er, Catherine. The college port is excellent, you really must sample it."

"Thank you, but I've had enough. I'm not used to three bottles of wine at one meal! If you'll just point the way to the bathrooms?"

They all turned puzzled faces to me as I rose.

"I'm afraid we have no bathing facilities in this building," Cyril said, genuinely apologetic. "Of course, if you'd like one of the scouts to accompany you back to the SCR, there are baths in the corridors—"

"No, no," I laughed. "I don't want to take a bath! I just mean the—well, the restroom." Their faces showed no greater comprehension.

"Do you mean a bedroom?" Cyril ventured. "You feel a need to lie down?"

"She wants the toilet," Dorothy finally decided. She stood up too. "I'll accompany you there, my dear. If we were more cosmopolitan, not so lost in the days of good Queen Bess, I'm sure we'd understand these American euphemisms."

She led the way to a stone corridor and an oak door with a sign that said, sure enough, TOILET.

"You know, it's a shock for an American, the first time you see one of those signs," I said. "That's a rude word in America. It's hard for us to bring ourselves to say it. This is the first time I've had to ask."

"Extraordinary."

She was waiting while I ran a comb through my hair, deploring my flushed cheeks. I was relieved to feel the mellow mood receding. I looked at her plain, honest face in the mirror and was suddenly moved to ask, "Dorothy, what happened to Simon?"

"Oh, Simon." She looked away uncomfortably. "Child was born with Down syndrome, you know."

"No, I didn't know. It must have been so hard for Perdita!"

"She loved him all the more. Quit her work and devoted herself to him, got involved with organizations to help other parents, push legislation and the like. Simon, and children like him, became her life. But he died at the age of five. By then they were back at Mercy. Aubrey had set up this program, and Edgar had asked to be included on the staff." She shook her head sadly. "We all tried to help her through it, but she couldn't cope with her grief. Or her bitterness toward Edgar."

"Why was she bitter? She goes around saying he *killed* Simon. Could that be true?"

She took a deep breath. "I said Perdita loved the boy. Well, Edgar hated him. Any sort of physical or mental imperfection disgusted him, and he made no attempt to disguise his feelings. He wanted her to put the child in an institution. They had blazing rows over it, as well as over his infidelities. But obviously, she never imagined he'd— One day, when Perdita was out of the house for a few hours, Simon choked on his food, and Edgar deliberately didn't call the St. John's Ambulance until it was too late to save him. Perdita was never the same again."

"He was a real monster, wasn't he?" I mused. "And yet she stayed with him! I would have been long gone, wouldn't you?"

"We all urged her to leave him, but it was as if the recrimination, the flailing at him, was all that kept her engaged with life. Do you know what I mean? I think really she stayed to punish him—since her abuse was the only punishment he was going to receive. He denied any responsibility for Simon's death, of course, and there was never any question of legal action, but we all knew he'd let the child die. She kept it before him, before everyone. To leave would have been to let him go unpunished. At any rate, that's my theory. And he, of course, got sadistic pleasure from tormenting her. So they lived for years locked in this death grip, and now it's been broken I wonder how she'll be able to stand alone."

"You couldn't live that way indefinitely," I said, talking more to myself than to her. "Sooner or later you'd have to move from words to action."

She didn't seem to have heard me. "Aubrey's quite right, dwelling on these things will only ruin our evening. Shall we rejoin them? I believe a savoury is still to come."

The savory was waiting for us when we got back to the table, triangles of white toast spread with anchovy paste and topped with sauteed mushrooms. I knew it was an old British custom to follow the sweet with something like that, though usually only observed at formal dinners nowadays. It tasted better than it sounds, but I wasn't thinking about food. With the effect of the drinks wearing off, my mind was seized with growing excitement. The three of them chatted about literary matters, occasionally addressing a polite remark to me, getting only brief, distracted answers. By the time the dinner party broke up I was ready to put my new theory before Emily, before Mr. Billingsley, before the Thames Valley Constabulary, if any of them had been available at ten o'clock at night.

I didn't at all mind being awoken before six the next morning by Muzzle's serenade. I'd had a hard time getting my brain to shut down the night before, and when the cat went off I jumped out of bed with alacrity.

Feeding Muzzle, letting him out and then back in, showering and dressing and gulping down some underdone toast and scalding coffee brought me only to six-forty, but I couldn't wait any longer. At least I could be sure Quin and Barbie wouldn't be out yet, and I had to get started saving Peter right away.

The sun was just up when I pulled into the parking lot at Emily's apartment building. The rowing crews were out on the river already, the coxswains' sharp calls punctuating the morning quiet along with the rumble of the first cars going to work. A pair of swans had built a nest beside Folly Bridge this spring, occasioning stories in the local papers, and I saw one of the famous birds sitting on it while the other sailed off down the Isis in search of food.

I used my key to get into the apartment. I knew Archie would be up, and sure enough he came charging out of the kitchen with his piece of Marmite-spread toast, leaving a brown smear on my pants leg when he hugged me. Rose was sitting sleepily at the table in her bathrobe, eating a bowl of cereal.

I answered her greeting and let Archie pull me to the picture window overlooking the river. "Sah, Nana!" he informed me, and I knew he meant the swan on the riverbank. They had a good view of the nest, and it was going to be wonderful for him to watch the birds' family life from eggs through cygnets. I let him tell me about it for a few minutes, pretending to understand, then I tiptoed to Emily's bedroom door, putting my finger to my lips as he followed.

I slipped in quietly and tried to wake her with a gentle touch on the shoulder, but Archie scrambled up on the bed yelling, "Mummy! Mummy! Sah!" She woke with a jolt and sat up, blinking her eyes rapidly.

While Archie wrapped his arms around her neck, bouncing on the bed at the same time, she muttered, "Mom? What—what's—why—"

"Sorry," I said, "I tried to be quiet, but you know how it is. I couldn't wait to come and tell you, I've learned some things that point to somebody other than Peter, somebody so obvious I can't believe nobody thought of her before."

"Her?" Archie had moved on to ransack the dresser drawers, and she was slowly lowering her feet into slippers and reaching for a terry cloth robe at the foot of the bed.

"Mrs. Stone!" I explained. "Come on, let me fix you some breakfast—all right, some coffee anyway, and I'll tell you what I found out about her."

A few minutes later, her eyes brighter, her blonde hair hanging disheveled around her shoulders, she sat down at the table in the alcove between living room and kitchen. She said, in her patient-expert voice, "Mrs. Stone has a depressive personality disorder, which appears to be developing into bipolarism. That particular axis is unlikely to result in homicidal behavior, Mother."

I had asked Rose to supervise Archie's investigations in the bedroom and restore the place when he'd finished, so I could explain without distraction. I poured boiling water over instant coffee, handed her the mug, and sat down opposite her, trying to repress my excitement.

"You gave me that diagnosis before, but I seem to remember you also saying she was 'explosive.'"

She thought about it for a few minutes. "That's true. She does exhibit intermittent explosive disorder, although that's rare in combination with DPD." She looked up at me with a little more interest. "What's this new information you've got, then?"

"Okay, I had dinner last night with Peter's colleagues at Mercy College. They started talking about the old days when they were all in the Oxford Drama Society, and what a really good actress Perdita was. Well, I'd been to her house the day before, and I'd kind of wondered if there wasn't a bit of acting going on, all that now-I'm-happy now-I'm-mad business."

She was frowning. "That's classic bipolar behavior, Mother. I *do* know something about the subject, and that woman is not acting. She's very sick."

I didn't argue, although I wasn't convinced. "All right, anyway, they talked about her performances in plays where she did men's roles, did them so well the audience hadn't a clue until she took off her wig and *spoke in her normal voice* at the end. You see? If she could imitate a male voice that convincingly, why couldn't she have practiced imitating her husband's voice until she could do it well enough to fool 999 and the people who worked with him? After all, it was *her* identification of the voice on the tape the police mostly went by."

"Well, we all heard it, and it did sound just like him. No, Mother, you're jumping—"

"Okay, listen to how it adds up: she was alone in the house with her husband that evening, she's a terrific actress and can do different voices, and she'd hated him for years."

"She did. She blamed him for the death of their child." I could see she was beginning, reluntantly, to consider the possibility that I was on to something.

Then there was a knock at the door. As we stared at each other apprehensively, I got that sinking feeling in my stomach and whispered, "No. It couldn't be."

But it was. At least, it was Quin, uncharacteristically dressed in sweatpants and a T-shirt, smiling tentatively at her, as if unsure of his welcome. When he stepped inside and saw me, the smile became an embarrassed grimace.

He said, "Fancy meeting you here," at the same moment I said, "Oh, for God's sake!" and jumped up to take refuge in the kitchen.

"Sorry, baby," I heard him saying as I snatched milk and eggs from the fridge, cursing under my breath. "I never thought your mom would be here so early. I hurried over so I could bounce an idea off you before we see Billingsley again." He raised his voice. "Come on, Kit, you don't have to hide in there. See what you think about this."

"I am making Emily breakfast!" I shouted back indignantly. "If you think I'd hide from you, you're even—even more—Oh, forget it!"

I slammed a measuring bowl down on the counter and made as much noise as I could, beating the eggs and milk, to prove I was cooking.

"Mom, I'm really not hungry," she said in a resigned sort of way.

"I'm not going to let you get sick from malnutrition," I called back. "That won't help Peter, now will it?"

"No use arguing with her," I heard him say. "You know how she is when she gets her mind set on something. Remember the dancing lessons?"

He laughed, and she tried to. Right, bring up something stupid I'd done, he was always good at that! So I'd thought a girl needed to know ballroom dancing, and dragged her to Arthur Murray's once a week despite her protests, when she was twelve. How was I supposed to know teenagers didn't dance that way anymore?

"You must have been the only kid in eighth grade who knew how to polka," he went on.

"It's all right, Dad," she said. "I'll eat a few bites of whatever she's making. I just don't want you and her— you know."

"Sure, sweetheart, don't worry. Sit down and I'll tell you what I started thinking about last night. We ought to get Billingsley, or the police, to look more closely at Mrs. Stone."

I dropped the skillet with a loud clang.

"Mom, are you all right?" Emily called, and I stepped into the doorway, staring at him. He looked back at me, now wearing his familiar cocky grin.

"See what you think of this, Kit. Perdita Stone never made a secret of hating her husband, in fact she went around telling the world what a bastard he was, how he killed their kid. That had to be a delusion, but she did hate his guts. There's your motive. The murder weapon was right there in plain view on Stone's desk all the time, he used it for a letter opener. There's your means. And she was alone in the house with him that evening until Peter barged in. There's your opportunity. On top of all that, she's a real nut case." I saw Emily flinch. "And that story of hers about sleeping through all the ruckus downstairs, that's pretty suspicious in itself. Of course, none of that explains the 999 call, which is our biggest problem, but I think we should try to talk the police into getting some better answers out of her than she's given so far." He put his head on one side curiously. "What's the matter? Drop the pan on your foot?"

"*No*, I didn't drop the— Where exactly did you get this idea? Were you listening at the door or something?"

"Mom, he couldn't have heard through that door," Emily said. "You've just both happened to come up with the same suspect. Weird."

"No kidding?" he said. "Well—I guess it shows our minds still work the same way."

"All it shows," I retorted, keeping my eyes on Emily, "is what a plausible suspect she is. Somebody else realized how many suspicious facts there were, without even knowing all the things *I* know about her."

"What things?" he asked, but I turned back to the stove and poured the eggs into the skillet, ignoring him.

"Mom's learned that Perdita Stone has a talent for imitating men's voices. She used to do it onstage. And she did have reason to accuse her husband of killing their child—"

"Danda!" I heard Archie yell, and Quin answered, "Hi there, sport!" I was laying pieces of cheddar cheese on top of the scrambled eggs and didn't look until I heard Emily say tensely, "Dad, I wish you wouldn't do that! He really doesn't need to fall on his head again."

I turned around and saw Archie just missing the ceiling while Quin waited for him to land in his arms. Rose and Emily both watched wide-eyed with alarm, but Archie was screaming in delight. Quin caught him and turned him upside down, increasing his hilarity.

"Dad! I said I wish you wouldn't!" Emily repeated as I dished up the eggs and brought them in to her.

"Oh, come on, baby. A boy needs some roughhousing. You don't want him to be a little sissy, do you?"

"You and Mom both have this idea that you know what he needs better than I do—it's enough to drive anybody to distraction!"

I could tell she was pretty near the end of her rope. "You're right, love," I said, going over to put an arm around her shoulders. "We should never argue with your way of raising Archie. You're doing a great job."

Quin set Archie down and came over to us.

"Yeah, we don't mean to be critical," he said. "It's just hard for two old meddlers like us to mind our own business."

Our eyes met. I could see he understood how distraught Emily was. She looked up at him, then at me, and a little smile came to her lips. For just a moment we were a unit again, instead of two warring camps.

A dangerous moment. I never should have let "we" and "us" sneak into the conversation. I cut it short by sneering, "Where's Barbie, then?"

"Who?" he asked.

Emily sat down with a sigh. "Oh, what difference does it make now? It's what Mom and I have always called Janet. We expected her to be younger and more—well, remember my Barbie dolls?"

"Your mother always hated them," Quin said slowly.

"Yes, she never wanted me to have them," Emily agreed. "She only gave in when I convinced her I was becoming a social outcast because I couldn't do Barbies with my friends. Remember, Mom?" she almost begged me.

I knew she wanted to bring back that moment of rapport, but I just couldn't do it for her. I turned away abruptly and picked up the phone.

"I'm going to call John Bennett and see if I can talk to him this morning," I said and started dialling.

But he wasn't at the station, nor expected back that day. I asked for the detectives in charge of the case and got the same answer.

"Damn!" I banged down the phone.

"Now, calm down," Quin said in that too-familiar patronizing tone. "We're going to see the solicitor tomorrow and file a motion for bail—"

"Oh yes, the great Billingsley!" I snapped. "If you ask me, he's a dud. If we—if everybody waits for him to do something, Peter will spend days and days in jail unnecessarily. Well," I went on, grabbing up my purse from a chair, "I'm not going to hang around. I'm going to talk to Perdita myself."

"Mother!" Emily protested, rising from her chair. "That woman is in a very precarious psychological condition. You just can't go over there and start harassing her, there's no telling what could result."

"I'm sorry, dear, but *somebody* has to do something about this, and not next month, or next week, or tomorrow. She's just crazy—I mean, disturbed enough to break down and confess if she's presented with—"

"Mother, you can't do that! You have no idea how to approach someone in her condition. Will you for once listen to me?"

"Why don't you go too?" Quin said. "You're the only one who knows how to deal with her, after all you were her therapist."

"She doesn't want to see me." But I could see she was thinking about it, so I chimed in.

"It would be a good use of your expertise. You might get her to open up, and if there's even the smallest chance of saving Peter, don't you think you should try?"

Quin saluted my cunning with a thumbs-up, behind her. I pretended not to see it.

"You're right," she finally said, "I can't let you go to her on your own, and I know you will. Just wait while I get dressed."

I was hoping Quin would leave, but he only raised my blood pressure higher by sitting down and starting to eat my rejected scrambled eggs. I wanted to put the plate in his face, but instead I went into the nursery, where I listened while Archie played his nursery rhymes for a quarter of an hour. When Emily came to get me, dressed in one of her dark power suits, with her long hair bundled up behind her head, I knew she was serious about the coming interview. She had put on her professional-therapist persona.

Unfortunately, we were not going to do it alone. Quin fell into step on the other side of her, and the three of us climbed St. Aldate's looking, to any passing pedestrian, like a nice American family. There was nothing I could do about it except to keep my eyes straight ahead and my mind on the goal of clearing Peter. I could put up with anything, even Quin, for that.

CHAPTER EIGHT

Wish me good speed;
For I am going into a wilderness
Where I shall find nor path nor friendly clue
To be my guide.

— John Webster, *Duchess of Malfi*

Cows, by God. Only in England would you see cows grazing on a college campus," Quin said as I led him and Emily down the Broad Walk beside Christ Church Meadow.

"I'm impressed," he went on. "You really know your Oxford. How did you find out about this shortcut?"

When I pretended not to hear, Emily said with some irritation, "Mother, will you please just be polite and answer him?"

"Look, Emily," I began, and then gave up. It wasn't worth quarreling over. I wouldn't turn my eyes toward him, but I answered shortly, "Geoffrey Pidgeon showed it to me."

"Huh. I didn't know you were so friendly with that guy," he said.

"There's a lot you don't know."

After that we continued in silence until Addison's Walk, when he exclaimed, "Cows at one end and deer at the other! And it's not exactly an agriculture college, is it?" That actually got a small giggle from Emily, and I was glad to hear it. He'd always been able to make her laugh.

The blinds were drawn on the downstairs windows at Perdita Stone's house. There was no light coming through, and a full milk bottle stood uncollected on the doorstep. After knocking for almost ten minutes, we had to conclude she was either asleep or not at home.

"There's no car in the driveway," I remarked.

"They never had a car," Emily reminded me. "Why didn't we call first? Or at least bring *my* car. That walk was exhausting, and all for nothing."

"You need to get more exercise," I told her and immediately regretted it as I heard her taking a deep breath preparatory to defending her lifestyle.

"There must be a back door," Quin cut in quickly. "Let's go knock on it. Maybe she's in the back of the house."

We went around into a neglected yard and knocked again, with no more success. I noticed an open window, low enough to look through, and I leaned toward it from the doorstep and called, "Mrs. Stone, are you in there? It's Catherine Penny. I'm—I have something really interesting to show you."

"What?" Emily asked, and I shrugged, holding out my empty hands. It had seemed like a good lure to get her to open the door. But there was no sound inside.

I gave the window a push and it went up farther. "I'm going inside," I informed them, getting ready to launch myself from the step.

Sounds of consternation arose behind me. "Mother, don't even think of sneaking into that house!" Emily ordered, and Quin barked, "That's breaking and entering, you know."

"Don't be silly," I retorted as I got one leg over the windowsill.

I grabbed the sides of the window and pulled myself up with some difficulty until I was sitting with my legs inside while he continued to fume: "It's not going to help anybody to have you in jail too!" and she threatened, "Mother, I'm leaving. Do you hear me? I'm not going to be a party to criminal behavior!"

I slid down slowly until my feet were on the kitchen floor, then went and flipped the latch on the door and opened it.

"You can come in or not," I said to her, "but I'm not going to neglect a chance like this to find evidence."

"Get out of there, Kit," Quin said urgently. "Stop and think for once. If you're right and that woman's a crazy killer, do you really want to surprise her in there?"

That gave me pause for a few seconds, long enough for Emily to add, "And if she's not there, she might come back at any time and find you searching her house!"

"Then why don't you wait out there, and shout if you

see her coming?" I turned away to begin my investigations before she could give me an argument.

I left the kitchen and went through the hall to the murder scene, the library. The house was so still it felt eerie, and when I heard a footstep behind me I spun around with a pounding heart. It was Quin, shaking his head and frowning at me.

"You'll never learn to think things over before jumping in, will you?" he said in a stage-whisper.

"Why don't you go have sex with your girlfriend?" I hissed back. "I don't need your help!"

"You will if Mrs. Stone shows up with a knife," he said grimly.

I turned my back on him and started opening the drawers of the desk, rummaging through the things you'd expect to find there—pens and pencils, old receipts, paper clips. I opened the rosewood writing box that sat on the desk and found only bundles of old, yellowed letters tied with red ribbon.

They didn't look like evidence, so I moved on to the bookshelves on the wall behind, pulling out books at random to look behind them. Some of them were so old and badly preserved, pages fell out and had to be pushed back in. I gave up on them and went to peer up the chimney.

Quin stood in the doorway and watched me, his arms folded. Finally he said, "Kit, don't you think the police have done all that?"

"Oh, shut up!" I answered imaginatively. I went back to the hall and started up the stairs. With one of his exasperated sighs, he followed me.

She wasn't in either of the bedrooms, but some sweaters and a long green dress lay on one of the beds. When I went into the room I found the wardrobe door open and nothing but empty hangers inside.

"Looks like she's skipped town," Quin said. I opened the drawers of the handsome oak dresser. There were some socks scattered around in the top drawer, but no nightgowns or underwear.

So Perdita had slipped away before she could be questioned. Could she have found out I suspected her? But how could that be, unless someone at High Table last night had guessed it by something I'd done or said, and told her? Geoffrey, of course. And that must mean he knew she'd killed Edgar—why else would she have to escape?

"Had enough?" Quin said. "You know the police picked up any evidence there was, and the lady's not here to be questioned, so let's just put our idea in the hands of Billingsley, or your friend Bennett. I'll bet they'll want to find her and question her."

"Oh, so there couldn't be evidence of her guilt left *after* the murder, after the police got through searching and focused all their attention on Peter? That's how much you know."

I took a look in the other bedroom, which appeared to have been Edgar's, austerely masculine and seemingly untouched since the murder. I poked around, feeling a bit of a shudder as I went through the pockets of the dead man's jackets in the closet. Eventually I gave it up and went back downstairs, Quin shadowing me all the way.

I really hated to leave empty-handed and let him be right. I gave the study one more chance, and at last, on the telephone table in the corner, I found a notepad with just one notation, scrawled in pencil: 257 lv 11:04 ar 11:28

"Come on, Kit," I heard Quin saying, "you're not going to find any—"

"I *have* found something! It's a train schedule, I think. See that?" I thrust the notepad at him triumphantly, and he looked at it with the first sign of interest he'd shown.

"She could have copied it after calling the National Rail," he said. "Don't take that, I'll write the numbers down and we can show them to the police."

But I was already going through the telephone book that lay beside the notepad. When I had the number for train information at Oxford station, I dialed it and muttered some choice words under my breath when a recorded voice asked me to wait for the next available assistant.

"Got you on hold, eh?" Quin said with a grin.

They'd got me well and truly on hold. After ten minutes of canned music assaulting my ear, I slammed the receiver down and tore the sheet of paper off the pad.

"Okay, so far we've got breaking and entering *and* tampering with evidence," Quin said to my back as I strode out where Emily stood, biting her lip. On my way I had folded the paper and slipped it into my pocket.

"She's packed up and gone away," I told her. "Guess there's nothing we can do until she turns up again. I'll go and tell the police about it. I'm sure they can locate her."

She was immediately relieved. "Yes, that's the best

plan. You don't know how glad I am she wasn't in there! I'm going to take the bus back, get my car, and go to the hospital for my ten o'clock group, so you go ahead and ask the police what they think about this. Did you relock the door, Dad?" I heard him saying that he had while I made my way ahead of them to the front gate. "Mom, don't tell the police you went into her house!" she called after me. "Just say she's not answering the phone and you're concerned, so they can—"

"Don't worry, best beloved!" I called over my shoulder. "I'll be very discreet."

I cut through the deer park again, but then turned right and got myself on Broad Street, alternately jogging and race-walking past Wren's golden Sheldonian Theatre, the incomparable Blackwell's bookstore, the ornate blue gates of Trinity College, and Debenham's glass entrance doors, until I emerged into Hythe Bridge Street and the ugly modern buildings around the railroad station. It wasn't an easy walk, because Oxford's sidewalks are always crowded with pedestrians, all following different traffic laws. I had finally learned that the English walk, as well as drive, on the left, but Americans and other foreigners keep to the right, so there is a lot of last-minute swerving to avoid collisions. You might even be forced to step off the curb, sometimes right into the path of a speeding bicycle. I was quite proud to have covered that distance so quickly without being upended by some bewildered tourist. It was always heartening to see evidence that I wasn't yet ready to start pricing rocking chairs.

I entered the train station feeling strong and fit, quite

capable of carrying out the risky plan I'd evolved on the way. Then as I headed toward the information booth, from the corner of my eye I saw Quin standing by a rank of telephones, watching me while he spoke into a receiver. I started toward the booth again, but before I reached it he was beside me.

"I already asked them," he said. "The two-fifty-seven is the train to Manchester, and the next one leaves in ten minutes from track twelve."

"What are you *doing* here?" I demanded. "I don't *want* you here."

"I knew you'd go looking for Perdita Stone on your own, so I flagged a cab. You didn't fool me with that stuff about putting it in the hands of the police. Emily doesn't understand how your mind works, but I do. I'm not going to let you go into danger alone."

"What makes you think you have anything to say about it?"

He held up a couple of slips of paper. "Two tickets to Manchester. Come on."

"But why would she want to go there? I never heard that she—does that train make any stops on the way there?"

"Don't know. You think she was heading for someplace between here and there?"

I didn't answer him but went over to the information booth, where I had to wait five minutes or so behind a turbaned Sikh having trouble understanding the train schedule. When I finally put my question to the attendant, he started rattling off a list of town names. I thanked him hurriedly and bought my own ticket for the third name on the list—Tyneford.

Quin was right at my shoulder as I trotted toward track twelve. "You think she's gone to this Tyneford?" he said. "What's there? Why are we—"

"*We* aren't doing anything!" I snapped, turning on him as we reached the train. "For the last and final time, leave me alone!"

But he was right behind me going up the steps into the train, and there was nothing I could do to prevent it, except maybe turn around and kick him.

"Look, I want to clear Peter as much as you do," he said. "I called Janet and told her I'm following a lead and won't be back for a few hours. She'll just have to live with it. I'm not going to let you go after some nut alone. And *you'll* have to live with that."

"Don't tell me what I have to do," I said automatically, but I'd given up.

The train was surprisingly crowded. Maybe people commuted to Manchester at this time in the morning, at any rate all the seats were filled and people were standing with their hands wrapped around straps hanging from the ceiling. I got hold of one of these, but an older man, complete with bowler hat and furled umbrella, rose from a nearby front-facing seat and gestured for me to take it. Strong and capable though I like to think myself, I was touched by the old-fashioned gesture and sat down thankfully. I hadn't been looking forward to standing for half an hour or so on a swaying train after tramping all those miles through Oxford.

Quin took a strap and stood over me. His very presence made me feel like running somewhere, anywhere, just escaping. For thirty years that presence had been the most comforting thing in my life, never really thought about, just a necessity that would always be there, like dinner or a roof over my head. Now it made me edgy, angry, almost afraid. I caught a faint whiff of the scent of pipe tobacco that always hung around him, evocative of thousands of moments I wouldn't let myself remember.

He said nothing but kept his eyes on me. At the first stop, just outside Oxford, the fellow in the side-facing seat in front of mine got up and left the train. Quin took the seat, of course. Now we were pretty much face-to-face. I stared out the window determinedly, watching stone walls, power lines, and tracks slide by faster and faster. I thought I knew how a rabbit must feel with its leg caught in a trap.

"Do you remember the Thalia?" I heard him say.

That was a question I couldn't have predicted. Befuddled, I had to look at him.

"All the classic movies we saw there," he went on, "when we were young and poor, and that was the only entertainment we could afford? I feel like we're in the middle of one of them now, one of those early Hitchcocks about murder and train travel—*The Lady Vanishes*, *The Thirty-Nine Steps*."

He laughed. I didn't.

"Remember," he persisted, "the night we sneaked in some cheap champagne and drank it while we watched

Notorious, to celebrate how I got that kid off, that cop killer?"

"I thought you proved he didn't—" I began, then caught myself and turned my gaze back to the window where now fields and houses rushed by. "No, I don't remember that. I don't remember anything!"

He said softly, "Being young together—I know you remember that."

Anger boiled up in my chest at the lowdown nerve of him, but I held it back and laid a steady gaze on his face. For the first time I noticed a faint, healed scar on his cheek that hadn't been there last year. I started to wonder how he'd got it but then remembered that I didn't care.

"I like being old alone," I said deliberately.

He frowned and leaned forward earnestly. "But I don't want you to be old alone, Kit. I want to stay in your life and help you out. I know, I know," he said quickly as I started to protest, "you don't need help. But when that changes, and it will, I want us to be on speaking terms. It scares the hell out of me to think of you needing money, or advice, or just friendship, five or ten years down the road, and not asking me for it."

Suddenly I saw something clearly for the first time. "Yes, you *are* scared, aren't you? But not for me—for yourself. You're afraid of being old. Having a gray-haired woman around reminded you of it, but Barbie makes you feel twenty years younger, doesn't she? Twenty years further from the end."

He sat back again, looking uncomfortable. "You're saying *you* aren't scared?"

Times I'd forgotten my keys, or left my purse behind, or searched my brain for the word that wouldn't come, rose up before me. Of course I was scared. Everyone over fifty nowadays lives with the fear of Alzheimer's, that empty-skulled specter that beckons us down the path to our future. But I wouldn't let him checkmate me.

"Don't you equate my feelings with yours!" I retorted. "I could never be so scared of anything that I'd abandon people who trusted me."

"I don't know, what you said—it mght have been somewhere in the back of my mind," he said brusquely, "but it wasn't the big reason. You and I weren't the same people we'd been when we started out together, and after Emily was gone it didn't seem like there was much between us anymore. You must have felt it too."

"No, I never felt that!" What was he talking about? I'd felt only what the vicar had described—"the comfort of a long-lasting partnership"—and never had a hint that he was feeling anything else.

"Come on—I'd finally made it into a top firm, my work was the biggest part of my life, and you weren't interested. I'd try to tell you about a case, maybe a strategy I was working on, and you'd either look bored and change the subject, or tell me I shouldn't have taken it! You were more interested in those damn charity groups of yours than in what I was accomplishing."

"Don't you dare try to put the blame on me!" I exploded. Passengers looked at us nervously, and I forced my voice lower. "You poor baby, didn't I gaze at you adoringly and tell you how great you were ten times a day? *She* did, didn't she? She knew how to get herself a successful lawyer with plenty of money, instead of the low-profit husband she had—just flatter that old male ego. Well, I'd never put myself on that level with you or anybody else."

"You're wrong about her," he said, with the first trace of irritation he'd shown.

"Oh, I didn't mean that was the *only* trick in her bag."

"You know, it's kind of nice for a man to hear that his work's interesting, that he's good at it. It's kind of nice to know a woman thinks you're worth some time and attention."

"Anne Stinson told me that woman used to sit and gaze at you as if you were the second coming, and run to the ladies' to do her makeup over if you called her in for dictation!"

His lips curved into a little smile. "Yeah, the whole office used to pull my leg about it. But down inside I liked it, and when they sent her to a different branch, I missed it. Missed her. Then I ran into her on the street one day—"

"Did I say I wanted to hear your sordid reminiscences? No, I did not."

He stopped talking as the train pulled into another station and people got off and on. As it started again with a jerk, I couldn't stop myself from saying, "You never wanted to know about my 'damn charities,' either, and they did the world a lot more good than your 'strategies' for getting rich people off the hook!"

He looked at me silently for a few moments and then

said, "I wonder, if we'd had this fight a couple of years ago, would things have turned out differently?"

"You always left the room when I tried to talk about feelings or problems or—anything deeper than what's-for-dinner. We never had a fight, don't you *remember*?"

"Yeah, I guess I've never felt comfortable talking about—all that stuff women want to talk about. You're not the only one who complains about that. But it's just how I am. My dad was the same way."

"He was worse," I said. "He'd duck if I tried to kiss him good-bye. And even when he was dying, if you asked him how things were he'd tell you everything was great, fine, couldn't be better. There was no way to get near him."

"He always liked you, though. He told me once, 'She's a feisty broad. You're lucky.' "

I started to laugh at his imitation of his father's gravelly voice but caught myself with a start and turned my eyes to the window again, furious with myself for that slip. The houses outside were going by more slowly, the brakes started hissing, and in the next minute we were pulling to a stop beside a platform with a sign that said TYNEFORD.

Once we stood on that platform, I realized my plan had run out. I was sure Perdita had come here, but this was no village of thirty cottages, like Far Wychwood. The station building was large, snack kiosks and newspaper stands lined one side, baggage carts and scores of passengers pushed past us. I heard traffic sounds beyond the exit doors. I had no plan for finding a fugitive in a large town.

"Have you got an address or something?" Quin was saying. I shook my head. "So why did we come here? Is this where her people live?"

"No. She lived here with her husband when they were first married," I answered grudgingly. "But—I don't know where their house is."

"Wait here." He walked over to the information booth and spoke to the young man behind the counter. I saw a lot of head shaking going on. Quin turned away, then turned back quickly and spoke to the fellow again, and this time he started pointing, ahead, to the left, to the right. Quin came back with a big grin on his face.

"He's never heard of the Stones, but he gave me directions to the town hall. That's where the records will be. Let's go."

So I had to follow him, out of the station, straight down to the next corner, left onto a busy boulevard dominated by a Sainsbury's supermarket, and right after two blocks onto High Street. Halfway down we walked into a little Beaux-Arts beauty with TOWN HALL carved into the stone above its door.

We stepped up to a counter where a bespectacled middle-aged woman sat behind a computer. She leaned forward, her arms crossed on the desk, with a questioning smile.

I spoke up quickly, determined not to let him take over the investigation, as he was so obviously trying to do.

"We're looking for the former address of a couple named Stone, Edgar and Perdita, who moved to Oxford at least a decade ago. You do have house listings by name, don't you?"

"Of course. All on the computer now. S-t-o-n-e? If you'd like to have a seat over there, it will take just a few minutes."

But the few minutes passed, and she hadn't come up with an address. In fact, she hadn't found a single "Stone" in the property database.

"You're sure you got the town right?" Quin asked me. "Okay, okay, calm down! Is there maybe another Tyneford around here?" he asked the woman.

She shook her head. "I don't believe there is another town of the name in England. I *am* sorry, I wish I could help you. Perhaps the name is a bit off?"

"No, it's not," I said in mounting frustration. "I know they lived here, I heard her say so! All right, I'm going to walk around and ask any old people I see if they knew the Stones. Eventually I'm bound to meet one who did. Law of averages."

Quin was starting to give me his opinion of that plan when the clerk burst out, "Oh yes, old people! Wait just a moment," and nipped behind a wall, to return a few minutes later with an incredibly thin, bald, but very upright old man in tweeds, who looked at us suspiciously through cataract clouds.

"This is Mr. Folke," said the woman loudly. "He's near ninety and still working, isn't that wonderful? His memory for the long ago is amazingly sharp, although"—she lowered her voice drastically—"not so good for the short term, you understand."

"What's that?" Mr. Folke bellowed.

"I'm just telling them how well you remember things. These people are looking for some people who left Tyneford a decade or more ago, and I thought you might have known them. Stone, their name was. They had a house here, the lady says, but I can't find any record of it."

Mr. Folke pulled a cigar from his jacket pocket and lit it, drawing the smoke into his lungs avidly while he shifted mental gears.

"Stone? Stone?" he finally shouted. "I knowed a Stone, yes—taught my boy Francis at Branton School."

"Yes, he was a teacher!" I exclaimed. "Edgar Stone, right?"

He peered at me with some hostility. "Yank?" he demanded. " I remember them doughboys well. Randy lot they were. Well, they do say it takes all kinds to make a world."

"But where was the Stones' house?" I asked impatiently.

"Stone never owned a house here."

"But Mrs. Stone said—"

"*Rented* a house!" he cackled triumphantly. "Old McCreary's place, outside of the town. Then when they moved away, people named Howard lived in it, and after they left, and McCreary died, his daughter left the place without a tenant."

"Oh, I know the place you mean, Mr. Folke," the woman said, with great relief. "I was so afraid I shouldn't be able to help you," she went on to us, "but it's quite all right now. Mr. Folke never fails when it's a matter of

Tyneford's past. I can give you directions to the old Mc-
Creary place. Although, mind you, it's been untenanted
for years, and the owner never comes near it, so it's in no
sort of condition."

"That's all right," I assured her. "How far is it?"

"Oh, at least a mile and a half. You can use my phone
to ring up the taxi."

"I don't mind a little walk—" I began, but Quin cut in.

"We've walked eight or ten miles already, Kit. I'm calling the taxi."

"If you're too big a wuss to walk a mile, go back to Oxford! I'm looking to take her by surprise. If she sees a taxi
coming to the house she'll lock herself in, or run for it."

"Run for it?" said the woman behind the counter, her
eyes widening. "You mean there's somebody hiding in the
old McCreary place? Oh, dear—what are you planning
to *do?*"

"We only want to help a poor homeless woman," I assured her, and she seemed to believe me.

"Oh, my yes, the homeless problem! Do you know,
they sit begging right in our town square! How kind of
you."

"All right," Quin said grimly. "We'll walk."

The woman told us to follow the High until we saw
the sign for Upper Barrow Farm, follow that road to the
bottom of the hill, and then look back among the trees
for the old McCreary place. She said it was called The
Lindens, but there was no sign, nor lindens either anymore, only a tangle of briars and ancient oaks around it.

Mr. Folke came out onto the front steps to see us off

and startled us by singing the first verse of "Over There" at the top of his cracked old voice, waving his cigar in the air until his kindly coworker came and led him back inside.

"Thirty years," said Quin. He grinned when I looked over at him, wondering what he was on about now. "You and I've got about that long until we turn into Mr. Folke. Well, it's a pretty good stretch."

"Yes, a nice thirty-year downward spiral," I answered gloomily, more to myself than him. "And people would say that man's lucky—he's still doing a job, at least."

"Do you think he does a job? I'll bet they only keep him on because the welfare state's outlawed age discrimination. He probably just wanders around boring everybody stiff with his long-term memory."

"If you get plenty of exercise and eat right and keep challenging your mind, you don't end up like that," I said, stepping out briskly, ignoring my aching calves and toes.

He gave a snort of laughter. "If Mr. Folke's any criterion, you'd be better off taking up cigars. Enjoy it while you've got it, that's my philosophy. Carpe diem all the way."

"Right, that *would* be your philosophy—the same one my cat lives by."

"You've got a cat? Hey, we were always dog people! I seem to recall you saying cats only put up with people for what they can get out of them."

"That pretty well describes my cat's attitude toward me."

Tyneford had petered out to just the occasional house

now, and a two-lane motorway had taken the place of the High Street. The sun was warm, sheep were grazing, wildflowers splashed color across the hedgerows. It was an altogether perfect spring day in one of the most beautiful countrysides on earth.

"This is the first time I've seen the famous English countryside up close," Quin said. "Pretty, isn't it? A really *green* green, with sort of—soft edges." He laughed self-consciously, and I frowned. It made me nervous to have us thinking of the same thing at the same moment, the way we'd done when we were together.

"Is it like this where you live?" he went on.

"The whole country's like this," I answered shortly.

"You're telling me all of England is green fields and sheep and little hills?"

"Oh, they have mountains too, and seacoasts, and things," I said vaguely. "I haven't seen the whole country yet, but I'm going to. I'm going to walk all over it."

"That doesn't sound too safe," he said as a car swished past us, powdering our clothes with the dust of the shoulder. "You're liable to end up roadkill."

"No, no, there are these footpaths all over the country, following the fields and rivers and hills, leading from one village to another—you don't have to see a car all day. But you can stay at inns and pubs, you don't have to sleep in a tent like on the Appalachian Trail. Remember how Ellie Markham and I used to say we were going to walk the trail from Bear Mountain to—"

I broke off, feeling as if I were hopping out of the way of one of those speeding cars. I glanced quickly at him and then away. He was smiling down at me, and his blue eyes were softer, not arrogant or mocking now.

"Yeah, I remember that. And Frank and I used to make fun of you. He drew that picture of a bear chasing you two up a tree, and Ellie got it framed and hung it in the hall?"

I couldn't help smiling. "Frank was a good cartoonist, for an accountant."

"You know, their second boy got married last month—Mark, remember him? They asked me to come, but—Really big wedding, I heard. Out in Connecticut."

He didn't have to tell me why he hadn't gone. I wondered how many of our old friends' events he had missed because Janet wasn't welcome. Serves him right, I told myself staunchly.

"There it is," he said, and I looked where he pointed, to a small dirt road leading up a hill on our left. There was a sign at the junction with a crude hand-painted picture of a cow and the words TOP BARROW FARM.

"What do you think—could Frank do a better cow than that?" he asked as we started up the little road. This time I let myself laugh out loud.

At the top of the hill stood the old stone farmhouse and a cluster of outbuildings. A boy was pouring grain into a trough in the barnyard, black and white cows pushing around him to get at it. He smiled as we passed, unconcerned about the big beasts almost trampling him.

"You the artist?" Quin called.

The boy looked uncertain, and I gestured back down the hill and said, "The cow picture."

"Oh. Nah, me brother done that. Awful, i'n it?"

Quin and I laughed and started down the other side of the hill, with forest on our right and a fallow field on the left. There had been a lovely breeze at the top, but it diminished as we came down into a deserted little valley, and I felt sweat running down the back of my neck. The farm ended abruptly with a wire fence, and the fields gave way to weedy, uncultivated open land and patchy woods. There was no sign of human habitation, no animals grazing down there. The silence was so profound that I strained my ears to pick up some sound, the call of a bird, the rustle of leaves. But there was nothing.

"Hell of a change from the other side, isn't it?" Quin said.

I hated to admit it, but I was glad I wasn't alone in that desolate landscape. Tramping through strange ground toward the bolt-hole of a mad woman, I couldn't really tell myself I'd rather be alone.

"Think that's it?" he said a few minutes later, and again I followed his pointing finger. Through a tangle of branches and vines, a few hundred yards off the road, you could just make out the shape of a fairly large brick house. I was reminded of the picture of Sleeping Beauty's castle in Emily's old fairy-tale book, entwined with wild roses and briars, holding the royal family and its retinue in charmed slumber.

"Looks like that Sleeping Beauty picture, doesn't it?" Quin almost whispered. It seemed appropriate to whisper as we approached the house, pushing our way through the overgrown vegetation, especially when we saw that the front door was standing open. Up close, I could tell it had been a nice, substantial house before McCreary's daughter had abandoned it. But now the woodwork was almost bare of paint, bricks were missing from the walls, windowpanes were broken, roof slates lay shattered on the ground.

"What a shame," I said.

"The woman's got to be terminally nutty if she's moved into this place," Quin remarked.

"Believe me, she is. But I'm not giving up now, not after coming all this way." I started through the door, and he followed me.

The inside was worse than the outside. Rain and snow had come through the broken windows and roof, stained and warped the floorboards, soaked the furniture the tenants had left behind. The whole place smelled sickeningly of rot and mold.

"Kit, there's no way she could be here," Quin whispered. "Even a crazy woman would have taken one look and run for the Oxford train. Let's get out of this hole."

I called, "Mrs. Stone! Perdita? It's Catherine Penny. Are you here?"

Nobody answered. There was a doorway on each side of the hall, and I forced myself to go through the one on my left. The room was dark, the windows completely covered by overgrown bushes. A small, dark shape ran from one corner to another. I backed out quickly into the hall. It stretched back at least ten feet and ended behind a staircase with missing risers. Since there were no windows, it got darker and darker as it went, finally too dark to make out anything, or anyone, who might be lurking there.

"Come on, Kit," Quin said aloud. "There's nobody here!"

"I have to know for sure," I whispered, shaking him off. With a hammering heart, I stepped into the room on the right, and then I knew for sure.

Perdita sat in a dark red velvet chair, staring at me. Her arms, in a long-sleeved white blouse rolled up to the elbows, stretched along the arms of the chair. I was briefly reminded of a queen receiving homage from her throne. I whispered her name and stepped closer, and suddenly I realized that her black eyes were not focused on my face. They were blank, like a doll's eyes. They didn't blink. Then I saw that the arms of the chair were crusted with dried blood. It had run down to form twin pools on the floor at either side, still wet. I saw the deep, red open gashes in her wrists and the razor blade still clutched in her left hand.

I stopped abruptly, and I must have made some sort of noise, because Quin's voice said in my ear, "It's all right, baby, she can't hurt anybody now." He stepped over to the corpse while I backed away from it, and picked up a scrap of paper from its lap. He shook his head as he read it. Then he showed it to me.

I killed him. Some crimes are beyond forgiveness.

Perdita Stone

My legs were suddenly too weak to hold me. I staggered and immediately felt his arms around me, turning me to face him, drawing me against him while his gruff voice murmured words I couldn't understand. I grabbed hold of his shirt and hung on as if survival depended on it, enveloped in the old, familiar smell of his tobacco, letting myself weep for Perdita Stone.

CHAPTER NINE

Tonight, grave sir, both my poor house and I
Do equally desire your company;
Not that we think us worthy such a guest,
But that your worth will dignify our feast.
                                        —Ben Jonson

L ighten our darkness, we beseech thee, O Lord, and
by thy great mercy defend us from all perils and dan-
gers of this night, for the love of Jesus Christ."

Mr. Ivey sat down in the celebrant's chair, and the village choir stood up. Their earnest, slightly discordant
rendition of the Twenty-third Psalm floated over us from
the rear pews like a soft breeze: "The Lord is my Shep-
herd, I shall not want, He maketh me to lie down in
green pastures, He restoreth my soul . . ."

It had been four days since we'd found Perdita Stone,
and I was still shaky. I had come to Evensong to get my
soul restored, to try to rid myself of images of mutilated
arms and dead eyes, and it was helping. Sitting between
Alice White and Fiona Bennett, surrounded by solid

Norman stone and listening to the beautiful Jacobean English Mr. Ivey had restored to our services, I did feel calmer. Maybe I wouldn't have a bad dream tonight.

Of course, it wasn't just the horror of finding the body that had me upset. However much I'd have liked to, I couldn't very well tell myself the other thing hadn't happened. I had to face the appalling fact that I had fallen into Quin's arms and stayed there for a while.

It hadn't been very long, I was sure of that. He had drawn me out of the house and we had climbed the hill again to the dairy farm in shocked silence, his hand tight around mine. The farmer's astonished wife had showed him to the phone and he'd called the Tyneford police. They had arrived in a very few minutes, sirens screaming, and Quin had taken them back to the abandoned house while I turned down offers of tea and biscuits and heard at length about how awful I must be feeling. The boy from the barnyard came and stood in the doorway, staring at me with avid curiosity. I didn't want to be rude, but I just couldn't bring myself to speak.

We were driven to the Tyneford police station where Quin had recounted our story, and I'd just nodded or shaken my head whenever a question was addressed to me. They'd called the Thames Valley Constabulary, and eventually we'd been taken back to Oxford, to be questioned again. Then I'd driven home and had been there ever since. I talked to the Tylers after Peter came home again. But Quin and I hadn't seen or spoken to each other.

I'd heard through Fiona that Perdita's only living relative, a sister, had come from Kent and identified the handwriting in the suicide note from letters she'd received years ago. They hadn't been in touch since Perdita had somehow insulted her, back when her mind had started going. She'd seen to the cremation specified in the will and, as sole heir, was now moving out the contents of the Oxford house preparatory to selling it.

"I will dwell in the house of the Lord forever," the choir finished and rustled back into its seats. Mr. Ivey stepped to the altar and invoked "The grace of our Lord Jesus Christ, and the love of God, and the fellowship of the Holy Ghost" on us, and Evensong was over. As we got into our jackets and picked up our handbags, I wondered if Perdita dwelt in the house of the Lord now. I wasn't sure about any of it, but if there was a God who welcomed the good to his house and condemned the wicked to some dark, eternal homelessness, he'd surely have found a corner for a poor sick woman like Perdita. On the other hand, maybe she'd simply been snuffed out, like a guttering candle that couldn't give a steady light, and hadn't gone anywhere at all. As I approached the south porch where Mr. Ivey stood shaking hands, I wondered why he had chosen to devote his life to something nobody could prove positively, why his face shone with such serenity, as if he possessed some secret knowledge closed to people like me.

"Ah, Catherine," he exclaimed when I gave him my hand. "How good it was to hear of Peter's release! You must be tremendously relieved to know he is cleared of suspicion, and largely through your agency."

"Oh, I am, vicar," I assured him. "I'm very happy."

"If I may say so without offense, your aspect suggests disquiet more than happiness," he said, peering into my face with concern. "Is something still amiss?"

"No, I assure you all is well." It was devilishly easy to pick up his speech patterns. "I suppose I feel some regret because the killer didn't turn out to be a really evil person who deserved a bad end."

"Yes, poor lady," said Alice White, beside me. "Hearing of such things makes one feel fortunate to be a spinster. Marriage so often leads to violent death, doesn't it?"

"Not nearly so often as it leads to perfect love and peace," Fiona said briskly.

"Ah, yes, the words of the marriage ceremony," said Mr. Ivey with delight. "And based on my own experience I should certainly agree with you, Fiona."

The subject was making me uncomfortable.

"I suppose I'll be seeing your son tomorrow evening, vicar," I put in, to change it. "I've been invited to dinner at Cyril Aubrey's with the faculty—sort of a joint celebration of Peter's freedom and commemoration of Perdita and, I suppose, Edgar Stone too."

"Have you indeed? I didn't know about that. I haven't heard from Tom for several days," he said rather wistfully. "It was a mistake, I think, to express any misgiving at his relationship with that young woman. Do greet him in my name, won't you, if he is there?"

Fiona, Alice, and I left him soon after and hurried down the churchyard path. It had rained most of the day, and the enormous oaks dripped on the gravestones, the blossoms of ragged robin that dotted the grass, and us. The ancient stone cross beside the church was so soaked it looked darker than it really was, its delicately carved scenes from the life of Christ almost indistinguishable. The grass had grown back over the ground beside it, and no sign remained of the hole that was opened there on my first day in Far Wychwood. I shuddered a little at the memory, but I remembered how the two women walking with me had come into my life the same day, and that warmed me.

"Why don't both of you come back to Rowan Cottage for dinner?" I asked them.

"I'd love to," Fiona said without hesitation. "John's on a case and will be out until all hours, and you know I'm not fond of eating alone."

"Oh dear," Alice began timidly. "I should like to come, Catherine, only—well, I don't like to miss tonight's episode of *Doctors*, the young Indian pediatrician is treating a little boy for a most mysterious condition, and his sweetheart, I mean of course the pediatrician's sweetheart, appears to be developing an attachment to the new houseman, not at all a nice young man—"

"I understand," I said quickly. "Another time, then."

She scurried off, exuding apologies, when we reached my gate. Fiona and I crossed the road to take a look at the slab of cement that would form the foundation of the new house. I had watched the pouring process from my front window two days before. It covered a lot more of the property than George Crocker's hovel had.

"I predict three or four people, at least, will be living in that house," Fiona said.

"Well, not even a single person would want to live in the amount of space George did."

"And yet his parents raised four children there, and his grandparents even more! I wonder what kind of people the new owners will be—perhaps a nice little family with kiddies for Archie to play with when he comes over."

"That would be wonderful," I said. "But as long as they aren't weekend people or long-distance commuters, I'll be satisfied."

Muzzle was sitting on the doorstep, and as we got closer I saw a dead field mouse lying at his feet. Fiona and I both stopped and made disgusted sounds, and the cat stood up and greeted us with a trilling kind of meow, looking smug.

"That's a token of esteem, I believe," Fiona said. "I'm sure I've heard somewhere that a gift of vermin is considered a very high honor among cats."

I kicked the little victim off the step, into the high grass. "I'm afraid I'd rather be treated with his usual disdain than honored like that," I said. "I guess I'll have to get out the shovel and bury the poor thing later." Muzzle sat down again and withdrew his gaze from me reproachfully.

But he slipped into the cottage when I opened the door and accompanied us to the kitchen, meowing loudly. I put his food down before starting on our meal.

"You know, the vicar was right," Fiona said as I rummaged in the cabinets. "You don't look as happy as you might, what with Peter being free and all. And I don't think it's all sorrow for that woman's suicide. You're worrying over something more personal."

I put the opener to a can of tomatoes, and sighed. "Oh, Fiona, I'll feel like such a fool telling you!"

"Rubbish, my dear. Didn't I tell you about that silly argument I had with my sister last fortnight? It certainly showed me up for a mug, and yet you were as supportive as one could wish. Let me return the favor."

I turned to look at her, still holding the can opener. "I don't know how it happened. I was *over* him. I was okay with how things had turned out. I can't understand it!"

"Oh, my dear, you haven't got involved with your ex-husband again?"

"No, not *involved*! What happened was, when we went to look for Perdita Stone, somehow he got me talking to him after I'd sworn I'd never do it, and by the time we found her, well, I was shocked, of course, and—I actually let him take me in his arms."

"Good heavens. And?"

"There's no 'and'! He just held me for a few minutes. But it felt good, Fiona! It felt *right*, you know? And I've been wondering if it felt that way to him too. And whether it meant he still—But of course I don't want him to! I dread going to the Aubreys' tomorrow night, but at the same time I've got to see how he acts when we meet again. Isn't this the dumbest thing you've ever heard?"

I slammed the can of tomatoes down on the counter, and the juice splashed against the wall.

"My poor girl, come and sit down. Do you know, I always thought you protested too much. If you'd really got over him, you wouldn't have been so furious with him all the time, unable even to hear him mentioned without going all mental. No, let me finish—you *can* get over him, but it will take more time than you've given it. And perhaps—now, don't get shirty with me—perhaps he's finally realized what he's lost. It's not impossible."

"Listen to what I'm saying, will you? I do not *want* him realizing what he's lost. Whatever this is, it's happening completely against my will." I dumped the tomatoes into an enamel pot and set it on the surface of my Aga stove. "I must have walked the equivalent of the distance to London in the past four days, and it hasn't helped a bit."

She came over and moved the furiously boiling tomatoes to a cooler spot. I was not yet an expert at Aga cooking, which involves a good bit of instinct. The cast-iron monsters cook by storing heat and radiating it over a broad surface, not by lighting a gas flame or electric element. It takes a while to get used to finding the spot with the right temperature, instead of turning a dial.

"What are you making?" Fiona asked.

"Vegetable soup, if that's all right with you."

"Yes, lovely. I'll get started slicing the onions."

We talked about my dilemma while we chopped vegetables and simmered them, and while we ate our soup with "biscuits," which to me were still crackers. We never came to a conclusion, because of course there was none. If exercise and evensong hadn't rid me of this revolting weakness, I didn't know what else to try. But it was good to get it off my chest.

After she'd gone, when I settled in the wing chair by the fireplace to listen to the penultimate chapter of *Cranford*, I felt a pang of regret that I wouldn't be in my place for its ending tomorrow night. Good, Catherine, I encouraged myself silently. In your own cottage, with your radio and your cat and your books, that's where you're happiest, and safest. Don't let anybody interfere with what you've created here. Well, of course I won't! I answered myself fiercely.

But another voice whispered that I sounded just a bit like Alice White, experiencing life and love through characters in a television show because people so often get hurt when they take chances on real life.

That's ridiculous, I grumbled inwardly, sipping my Horlicks. I don't even own a TV.

They started framing the new house the next day. When I left for the dinner party in the early evening, the wooden skeleton was starting to take shape, laid out on the concrete slab. The hammering and drilling didn't even annoy me, although it drove Muzzle to parts unknown. It was exciting to think I'd soon see my neighbors moving in.

I happened to glance at the dashboard as I drove through the village and was surprised to see my gas tank was close to empty. Forgetful as I was, one thing I'd never done was run out of gas. I'd always imagined that to be one of life's ultimate humiliations. But it tended to slip my mind more since I'd moved to England, probably because gas cost about five times what it did in the States, making filling up a painful experience one would rather not think about.

Fortunately the village petrol station was still ahead of me, at the junction with the big road to Oxford. As I pulled in and Harry Ames ran out to pump my gas, I saw Audrey, his wife, holding her baby daughter in the doorway. She waved Diana's tiny hand at me, and I waved back. After Harry was inside again and I was starting away, I caught a glimpse of them together, their arms around each other's waists, working up to a kiss.

Take away the leather and the nose ring and the orange hair, and Audrey reminded me of myself thirty years ago, in love and full of hope. It was pretty hard to envision, but someday she'd probably be a grandmother too. I wondered if Harry would still be at her side. Of course not, I thought bitterly, she'd be alone like me, and he'd be off with a girl from Nether Stowey or someplace. The wonderful *completed* feeling marriage brought would be part of the vanished past, and she wouldn't even let him stir the memory of it again, if he—I sighed and beat my hand on the steering wheel to chase away that stream of thought, knowing it wasn't really about Audrey at all.

In Oxford, I drove over Magdalen Bridge to the south side of the River Cherwell, which bisects Oxford pretty cleanly into town and gown. The colleges are all to the north of the river, their Oxford of narrow medieval streets fading off into atmospheric Victorian suburbs like Jericho and Park Town. Across the river, Oxford is a city of working-class Britons and immigrants, students needing cheap lodgings, and here and there, gentrifiers.

The little street where Ann and Cyril lived had fallen into the hands of the latter. It was lined with small row houses, run-down toward the top where a broad traffic artery crossed it, freshly painted and adorned with flower boxes toward the bottom where the houses had been discovered by north-bank people in search of a good buy. Their own house was different from these, however, older, larger, and built of mellowed, rosy bricks. It stood next to a waist-high brick wall that made a very definite end to the street. I thought there must be a stream beyond, because you could see a thick line of trees on the other side, and I heard a chorus of quacking over there as I got out of the car and crossed a patch of lawn to the Aubreys' door.

"No, it's the Cherwell," Ann told me as she took my coat in the entrance foyer. "The same river that runs through Addison's Walk, though it's much smaller there. This part of Oxford is such a lovely backwater, Cyril and I fell in love with it and with this old house, a couple of decades ago. The house was in very bad shape when we bought it, and the street was rather rough. But we knew things would improve. We've spent no end of money restoring the place, and I think it's come out rather nice."

That was, of course, typical British understatment. Walls must have been knocked out to create the spacious, white-walled dining room into which Ann led me first, and they had put in a window wall that paralleled the long, highly polished oak table with its pink-upholstered armchairs. It looked over the little river and the thick copse of trees and bushes on its other side, already in full leaf.

"There," she said when we stood looking out, "that's what sold the house to us. It backs right on the river, and you can just see Angel Meadow behind the trees on the other side, a beautiful place for dogs and little boys to run about. There's a rustic bridge, farther down the footpath, that takes you over there. It's actually a flood meadow, so it can never be built upon. In winter it becomes part of the river, and one sees swans floating about on it. Then, just behind the trees at the other side of the meadow, is the deer park—Geoffrey Pidgeon told us he showed it you the other day."

"What a wonderful find!" I exclaimed. "And this house was actually derelict, in this great location?"

"Yes, well, even now this isn't a fashionable part of Oxford. This house stood alone in the nineteenth century, the row houses weren't built until 1902. It had its own access to the water when we bought it. We think it was a waterman's house. You can see the steps leading to the water, where a boat would have been moored—down there."

I looked where she pointed and saw a rusty iron gate in the wall that separated their small back garden from the riverbank. Four or five crumbling stone steps led straight down from it, into the water.

I was fascinated by this insight into an Oxford a tourist would never see. She led me through a set of folding doors into the drawing room, obviously created from two or three smaller rooms and decorated in eclectic style, with some beautiful antique side pieces set off by big, puffy modern sofas and chairs that invited lounging. One of the Aubreys obviously had an eye for art; the walls were like a gallery of abstract and avant-garde paintings.

"Yes, it's rather a passion of mine," said Ann when I remarked on them. "I must show you my latest discovery, although as usual Cyril grumbles about the cost. But spending on art, especially by lesser-known artists, is an investment, isn't it? This young man"—she led me to a canvas just inside the drawing room door—"is going to take the art world by storm one day, I'm quite certain. Of course to many people, like my stuffy old husband, his work is quite outrageous, but I find it exciting."

I gazed at six random orange and purple slashes of paint and tried to think of something intelligent to say about them. Luckily, a young woman in a maid's uniform came up and murmured urgently to Ann so that she hurried off with a quick apology to deal with some culinary emergency.

"Looks like somebody's brother done it," I heard Quin say, right behind me.

I couldn't help bursting into laughter, and when I turned I saw him grinning at me. Janet, beside him, gave a painfully forced laugh while the big brown eyes darted nervously between us.

"You're so *funny*, Tibby!" she exclaimed.

A brief flash of annoyance crossed his face. "Not in public, remember?" he said to her.

The phony smile immediately fell into a hurt scowl, and she retorted, "You never said that back home!" The big brown eyes turned to me, absolutely glittering with hatred. "It's just because *she's* here—"

"Stop it right now," he said quietly, "or I'll take you back to the inn."

"All right, let's *go* back to the inn!" She stood on tiptoe and tried to whisper in his ear, but he shook his head.

"No. I'll take you there, then I'll come back to the party."

She looked away, biting her lip as if she was trying not to cry. I was about as uncomfortable as I wanted to be, so I hurried to join Emily and Peter at the other side of the room. They were with Tom and Gemma, who looked much happier than she had in the Eagle and Child. The engagement ring sparkled on her left hand.

"I must say," he told me, after I'd kissed my daughter and son-in-law, "we're all very grateful to you for following and finding Mrs. Stone. Of course, somebody would have found her eventually, but Peter might have been on trial by then, or even convicted."

"Oh, I think not," Peter said. "Geoffrey would have missed her before the day was out, and found that notation about the train. Hard as it is on the poor fellow, I'd rather he had found her than you, Catherine. I very much regret that you and Quin had to go through such an unpleasant experience."

"Poor Geoffrey," said Dorothy Shipton, sitting a little apart from the young people. "He's in a sad way. I rang him up this afternoon, tried all I could to get him to join us but he wouldn't consider it. Quite distracted with grief. One who loved not wisely but too well."

She was the only one dressed in black, and I wondered if her severe dress was meant to represent old-fashioned mourning weeds.

"Are *you* all right, Mom?" Emily asked. "You sounded so unnerved that evening, I wanted to come out to you, but you insisted on staying there alone."

"I'm over it now," I said. "And I wasn't alone, I've had my friends in the village for company. I wanted to take some long walks and sort out my thoughts. And I wanted you and Peter to have some time to yourselves."

Cyril Aubrey shambled into the room with a tray of sherry glasses. "How do you do, Mrs.— Catherine!" he exclaimed, handing me one of them. "What a very odd situation, isn't it? We are all overjoyed to see Peter at large again, yet at the same time we've lost two old friends in the most horrific fashion. Ann and I thought it might be helpful to all to get together and discuss these events, although it's hard to say which emotion most animates us. You don't think it tasteless, do you?" I smiled and shook my head. " Mr.— Sorry, Quin, do you?"

"I know what's animating me," he answered, accepting two sherries and handing one to Janet. " I didn't know the Stones, so I can't share your feelings on that score. I'm just happy for Peter and Emily, that's all, and I want to propose a toast to their future." He held his glass out toward them, and the rest of us followed his lead. "Nothing but roses from here on, kids."

"Thank you, Daddy," Emily said. "And Cyril and Ann, thank you for having us over. *I* think it was a very good idea. Since Mrs. Stone's sister had her cremated without a ceremony, her friends need a chance to express their feelings. You can imagine how I feel about Peter being cleared, but even though it was Mrs. Stone's fault, I feel sad for her, and a little guilty. I should have been able to help her. No, it's all right," she went on, as a general objection went up, "that's how therapists always feel when a patient self-destructs. I know I did everything I could, but still—"

"My dear, no one could have saved Perdita," Dorothy said firmly. "Geoffrey deludes himself with the idea that he could have made her happy, but I'm quite sure she was determined to die. The *Times* reports that there was no house key found on her. It was left behind on a table, where they always kept it. So she wasn't planning on coming back—she went to Tyneford to take her own life."

We stood silent for a few minutes, then Gemma said artlessly, "But they kept a second key under the soil of a plant pot in the yard, Edgar showed it me." She blushed as everyone looked at her, coming to the obvious conclusion. "So she could have changed her mind and come back, you see," she went on with irritation.

"Well, she didn't," Dorothy said, scowling at her. "Shouldn't have thought Edgar would be so foolish." As Gemma started to retort, she went on, "To leave a key where someone could find it, I mean!"

"It *is* foolish, I suppose," Ann put in, with a little grimace, "but it does save a lot of inconvenience when you forget to take the proper key. I must confess," she whispered conspiratorially, "we keep one hidden by the door too."

"Not a high-crime area, this little street," Cyril said, coming to her defense. "It's most unlikely anyone would seek about for the spare key and come in with robbery in mind."

"There *was* that attempted burglary at the Bodleian last year but one," Peter said.

Cyril laughed. "I do possess a few valuable books, but this is hardly the Bodleian!"

"Well," Emily returned to the subject, "I just meant to say that it's a very good idea to express our feelings—the worst thing for our own mental health would be to keep them to ourselves, like Geoffrey."

"Quite right," said Cyril. " 'The silent griefs which cut the heart-strings,' eh?"

"John Ford," Dorothy responded approvingly.

Quin said, "John Ford? *Stagecoach*? *Fort Apache*?"

The scholars stared at him blankly, except for Peter, who explained, "There was an American film director of that name."

"Indeed?" said Cyril in amazement. "No, no, in this case, John Ford, *'Tis Pity She's a Whore*."

"Oh, one of your playwrights!" Quin said, glancing at me with a conspiratorial smile. I had to admit the movie director had been my first thought too. "That's quite a title."

"Not at all relevant to the content of the play," Dorothy sniffed. "I've always thought it a piece of sensationalism intended only to sell tickets."

"The play's actually a dark, perverted tragedy, and that title makes it sound like a comedy, doesn't it?" Tom put in.

"It's rather amusing how Ford tries to justify it by sticking it in as the very last line, spoken while the bodies of all the main characters are being dragged off the stage!"

"It's totally inaccurate, as well." Dorothy was well wound up now. "Annabella is no whore, but a victim of the lusts of the male characters!"

"Yes, but don't you think—" Aubrey began.

"*I* think Eileen is waiting for us to come to dinner," Ann put in firmly, "before our visitors are bored to tears by all this literary esoterica." As she led us toward the dining room, she added, "Emily's quite right. Let each of us say a few sentences in commemoration of the old friends we've lost, before the dinner is served. Then the rest of the evening can be Peter's."

We sat down around the table, spread now with white linen and lighted by two silver candelabra. Dark had fallen, so rose-colored drapes had been pulled across the long window. The scholars seemed self-conscious, frowning as they tried to compose eulogies in their heads. Quin sat across from me, intercepting a glance I couldn't control. The candlelight deepened the age lines beside his mouth and the little hollow at the base of his neck. Beside him, Janet shot beams of malevolence at me through the floral arrangement.

"I'll begin, then," said Dorothy, still a bit agitated. "I shan't speak of Edgar, terrible that he had to go like that, but he made his wife's existence hell and was without doubt responsible for Simon's—"

"Please, Dorothy," said Ann quietly. "*De mortuis nil nisi bonum,* don't you think?"

"Very well," she answered unwillingly, "No ill of the dead. I'll say only that Perdita was a wonderfully gifted girl who threw her life away on a bully and a hopeless child, and that's as great a tragedy as anything John Webster ever wrote."

Roughly, she wiped away tears that had begun to seep from under her glasses and then took a long drink of water.

"I shall always remember those performances in our OUDS days," Ann said quietly, "and however life changed her later on, I shall miss her." She looked around the table. "Anyone else?"

"I don't think there's much point in the three of us speaking," Peter said. "We didn't know her well, and our relationships with Edgar were—complicated. Probably best if we keep quiet." He threw a meaningful look at Tom, who nodded, and at Gemma who seemed to be preparing to burst forth with an encomium for Edgar.

She gave in and looked down at her plate, only murmuring, "None of you understood him!" Tom gave her shoulder a comforting pat.

"Do you know," said Aubrey suddenly, "when my wife spoke of Perdita's stage appearances long ago, it occurred to me that there is a way to give our younger colleagues, as well as our American guests, an idea what we mean when we speak of her talent—a sort of memorial evening, as well as a way of bringing to life our chosen field, which may indeed seem overly esoteric. The Globe in London—you've heard, of course, of the reproduction of Shakespeare's theater, built near the spot where it stood?—is performing *The Knight of the Burning Pestle* for several more weeks. As it was Perdita's most famous role, and a highly entertaining piece as well, why mightn't we organize a theater party some evening?"

The English people responded enthusiastically. And when I heard Janet whining softly to Quin, "Oh, do we have to?" and saw that look of annoyance cross his face again, I leaned over the table and called to Cyril, "What a wonderful idea! I've always wanted to see that theater."

It was quite true, although a chance of ruining another evening for her definitely increased my relish.

"I shall go over and speak to Geoffrey tomorrow," Cyril Aubrey went on, beaming at the success of his inspiration. "If it's presented to him as a commemoration of Perdita, he may be persuaded to come along. He can't be allowed to stop at home brooding any longer."

"That's so true," Emily said decidedly. "Bereavement issues can be very dangerous."

"I'll go with you," Peter put in. "Between us, we should be able to persuade him."

Ann had rung a little bell to summon her Eileen, a hefty Irish girl, and now over a creamy chicken soup—which she told me was called Queen Victoria's Soup—followed by a crown roast of pork with brussels sprouts and chestnuts, a green salad and gooseberry fool, we discussed less depressing subjects, all but one of us cheered by the prospect of our outing. Ann and Cyril talked with great pride about their two grown sons, and I was interested to learn about the organization they had created and ran together, which set up and ran schools in developing countries. They were presently working in Biafra, and their parents were looking forward to their annual visit next week to attend "May Morning," the Oxford spring ceremony. We finalized plans for the theater party, and Quin, to my surprise, said he and Janet would be coming along.

Aubrey brushed off the complaints of Peter and Tom about the college losing Edgar's rare-book collection, as Perdita's sister was determined to sell it to outside collectors. He was right, of course; they had no grounds for challenging the will, although I too thought it was a shame.

Of course there were a few apposite quotations from the Elizabethans and exchanges about their works— there was no way to exclude those boys from the gathering entirely, although Ann made sure their appearances were brief. Altogether, by the time the long, relaxing dinner was over, we all felt much closer and were looking forward to meeting again at the weekend. Except, of course, for Janet.

When we were getting our things together preparatory to leaving, I noticed that she had drawn Quin off to the side again and was whispering in his ear, her hand twined around his like wisteria choking a tree. Outwardly I was bidding Ann good-bye, but in my head I was imagining what that woman was saying to him—probably more of her trademark transparent flattery, or nagging to leave early and go back to New York, where she had the home-turf advantage.

And then, as I started down the five steps from the

door to the pavement, I heard his voice right behind me again.

"Are you over Tyneford, Kit?"

I jumped and turned around. "I'm fine!" I exclaimed breathlessly.

The gray strands in his hair shone in the light from the door, and the lines at the corners of his eyes were deeper as they always were when he smiled. His gaze traveled over my face—maybe looking for signs of lingering distress—from my eyes to my mouth, and back again. The voices of the other guests called good night all around us and laughed at farewell witticisms. I smelled the Old Spice he had always put on for occasions like this, and my mind flashed on family gatherings, suppers with friends, birthday parties. I took a couple of steps back, away from him.

"I knew you were pretty bummed out," he went on in a low voice. "I called you a couple of times to see how you were doing, and there was no answer." He waited, but I said nothing, letting him know I didn't have to account to him for my movements. "Okay—so you're all over it, then?"

"I said I'm *fine*."

"Great. So—a couple of days, I'll see you again at this play." He was dragging it out, as if he didn't want to separate. "The plane tickets are for May second, you know—that's only five more days." He took a deep breath. "Look, why don't I call you tonight, or tomorrow? We ought to talk before it's too late—"

"No," I cut in. "No. It's already too late."

"What's going on?" Emily's voice said brightly. She and Peter had joined us, and there was the hint of a hopeful smile on her face as she looked from one of us to the other.

Over his shoulder, I caught a glimpse of Janet standing in the doorway. Tom and Gemma were stepping around her with apologies. She was watching us so intently she didn't even notice them.

"Nothing's going on, Emily," I said, bringing my eyes back to Quin's face. I suddenly felt very sad. "Just saying good-bye."

I thought I heard him start to speak as I turned away and walked toward my car, but if he did, I couldn't hear what he said.

CHAPTER TEN

Speak, gentlemen, what shall we do today?
Drink some brave health upon the Dutch carouse?
Or shall we go to the Globe and see a play?
—Samuel Rowlands, *The Letting of Humours*

It was the evening of the theater party, and I was doddering around, trying on my few pieces of jewelry in hopes of making something of the green dress. I was sick of staring at my wiry, flat-chested image in the long mirror, wondering why I'd ever bought a dress with a top low enough to show my wrinkled neck, in that "princess" shape that only looks good on somebody with hips and a bosom. I could hear Muzzle outside batting at the back doorknob, the teakettle had started shrieking on the Aga, I'd just decided to wash off the powder and rouge I'd bought from Enid that morning and admit defeat, when the phone started up.

I hadn't answered it for the past two days, in case it was Quin. Now that I knew he'd been trying to reach me before, while I'd been out on those marathon walks, I was afraid to pick it up. I couldn't stand to find myself trapped again in an anecdote about some moment we'd shared twenty-seven years ago. I figured if I made sure to see him only in a group, like tonight, he couldn't get personal, and I told myself I was only agonizing over my appearance to avoid embarrassing Emily.

I went to open the kitchen door and let Muzzle in, took the kettle off the hottest part of the stove surface, and got out a mug and a bag of Earl Grey. The phone continued jangling while I poured on the water. Suddenly I couldn't stand it anymore. I went into the parlor and picked it up, ready to cut him off with a pithy retort.

"My dear, I've been worrying over your dilemma," said Fiona, starting out without a greeting as she always did, "and here's what you must do. Although I know she's simply glued to his side, you must make arrangements to meet him for a really good talk. It's the only way, get things out in the open, find out for once in a way how *both* of you feel, before he's gone."

While I listened to her, I noticed Muzzle sitting in the doorway. Another dead mouse dangled by its tail from his mouth.

"Oh, damn it!" I cried. "Damn it, damn it, damn it!"

"There you are, any mention of the man and you go crackers! Doesn't that tell you something? If he can still move you so much—"

"Fiona, I can't talk right now! I'll ring you tomorrow. And for heaven's sake, stop worrying!"

I hurried out to the garden shed and came back with a shovel. Muzzle looked on quizzically while I scooped up my gift from the floor where he had dropped it. He followed me to the back garden and watched me dig the tiny grave. I buried today's mouse next to the other one, in a spot at the side of the garden where I was pretty sure I wouldn't acccidentally disinter them if I ever got a chance to dig in the perennial border again.

"This has got to stop!" I snapped as I passed him, stomping inside with stains from the wet grass on my suede shoes and a smudge of dirt on the hem of my dress. Putting water on that material would probably only make a more noticeable stain, so I convinced myself it was in an inconspicuous spot. I washed my hands thoroughly but refused to look in the mirror another time. He—or rather, Emily—would just have to put up with me as I was.

It hadn't rained since early morning, but it was a typical overcast English afternoon with a chilly breeze. When I got to the Aubreys' house by the river, Cyril showed me where to park. It seemed the theater party was to be divided among his car, Peter's, and Tom's.

"I hope you'll ride with Ann and me," he said confidentially, "as poor Geoffrey's to do so, and he does like you. Dorothy always tends to put her foot in it, and of course your—er, Quin, and his—er—well, pretty much strangers to him in comparison, aren't they? But I feel sure you'll think of the right thing to say."

I didn't feel so sure. Geoffrey was already in the black Daimler, bent forward, his hands hanging between his knees, staring at the back of the front seat. He was an intimidating prospect for any comforter. His big, square face was drained of color, his eyes were red-rimmed, there was at least a day's worth of stubble on his cheeks and chin. I certainly wasn't going to tell him that things weren't really so bad, or that he would feel better if he gave it some time. I'd always hated it when people had repeated such trite consolations to me.

But Aubrey, settling himself in the driver's seat, did a donnish variation on them. "Remember, old fellow," he said, " 'Things being at the worst begin to mend.' "

"Webster, *Duchess*," Geoffrey murmured automatically.

"Quite right!" Aubrey exclaimed heartily.

I had managed to avoid Quin. Tom's car pulled out first, Gemma beside him in the front seat and Dorothy in the rear. I watched Peter's car leave the curb a little ahead of us, and I recognized Quin's head through the back window, beside that woman's. It was over an hour's drive to London, so I could breathe a sigh of relief for the present and relax against the velvety seat covers.

"Do you want to talk about it, Geoffrey?" I asked hesitantly.

He shook his head, but a few minutes later he asked, as if it were being pulled out of him with pliers, "How did her face look? I mean to say, were there signs—signs of suffering?"

I could answer truthfully, "No, she had no expression at all on her face. I imagine she'd lost consciousness pretty early in the process."

"I hope to God she had!" He put his hands over his face, and his shoulders shook. I saw Cyril Aubrey's face in the rearview mirror watching him anxiously.

I didn't know what to say after that. Tell him she was at peace, in a better place? I wanted it to be true, but I couldn't claim any inside information. He'd never accept the only thing I *was* sure about, that he was better off without her. I tried to remember how I'd felt when my mother had died, but I'd been only a kid. A grown man who'd lost the woman he loved had to be in a whole different world of grief. So we just sat in gloomy silence while the car sped along the motorway in heavy traffic.

Eventually Ann and Cyril started telling me about the play and the new Globe Theatre, and soon we were in the London suburbs and then the city itself.

When we got out in a car park right behind the Tylers' car, Emily stared at me. She pulled a tissue from her handbag and gave it to me, whispering, "Mother, you have a great brown *smudge* on your left cheek!"

I wiped at it until she gave a discreet nod, then shoved the tissue in my pocket. I felt, rather than saw, Quin and Janet on the other side of the car with Peter and Dorothy. The four of them walked toward the theater just ahead of Emily, the Aubreys and me, and Tom and Gemma joined them. I stole a glance at Janet's latest fashion statement— a loose ankle-length black dress with a matching crocheted jacket long enough to cover those hips, accessorized by a long rope of what looked like small semiprecious stones.

"Mother," Emily murmured, "whatever have you been doing? Your dress is all dirty, and your shoes are a mess. Don't tell me you've been working in the garden in your good clothes!"

I resigned myself to feeling like a chimney sweep all evening.

Peter was telling them about the theater, gesturing right and left, and Quin was listening with interest while Janet kept her eyes fixed on him, looking worried.

"It was in point of fact a countryman of yours, an American actor named Sam Wanamaker, who provided the momentum to rebuild the Globe in the 1980s," Cyril told me.

"It's surprising nobody had tried to build a model of Shakespeare's theater before that," I remarked.

He frowned. "Well, you know, it wasn't actually *Shakespeare's* theater! He was only one shareholder in the acting company that owned the Globe, and the works of some of our fellows were produced there as well—"

"But he *was* the principal playwright of the Lord Chamberlain's Company," Ann put in, sharing with me a little smile at her husband's competitiveness on behalf of his "fellows." "And the Globe was their theater. At any rate, Beaumont and Fletcher wrote the play we're going to see for the Globe."

"Quite," Cyril agreed. "Now, you must conceive of this part of London, Southwark"—he pronounced it "Suthuk," to my amusement—"as a bustling, disorderly place in Elizabethan and Jacobean times, full of taverns and brothels, soap yards and breweries and prisons, but the home as well of an amazing community of artists. It was outside the city then, and in attending the theaters along the riverbank Londoners thought they were engaging in daring, even disreputable, behavior. Ironic, considering that the plays written for these theaters are now considered high culture!"

It was certainly not a disreputable area now. A neat brick walkway had been laid overlooking the Thames, St. Paul's dome on the other side, and the church spires and attempts at skyscrapers that poked up here and there around it. Farther north along the walkway I could just catch a glimpse of London's newest art museum, The Tate Modern, converted from a power plant, and the minimalist silver arch of the Millennium Bridge on which you can walk across the Thames.

Emily had joined Quin's party, since I was safe under the Aubreys' wing. She looked back and threw me an encouraging smile as they entered the small building adjoining the theater that houses the souvenir shop, restrooms, and other modern amenities.

"Of course, the theater is not *precisely* the same as the original," Aubrey went on. "The average Elizabethan, for example, was ten percent smaller than a modern adult. It was suggested during the planning period that if the new theater were built to the same scale, it would accomodate only the shortest of actors playing to parties of school-children! So it has been scaled up for the bulk of a modern audience."

"And a very good thing too," said Ann. "Come along, now, darling—the rest of the party have left us behind."

We followed the crowd through the modern building and out the other side onto a brick-paved entrance court-yard to the theater, where Cyril rented cushions for all of us, assuring me it was not an extravagance when you would be sitting on oak benches for several hours. Then we climbed three long sets of stairs to the very top row of the theater. He'd explained that since he had reserved the tickets at the last minute, nothing lower was available. We were sitting right under the theater's roof, which my close-up view revealed to be covered with thatch.

"How did they ever get away with that?" I asked. "Isn't it dangerous? I've heard the original Globe burned down because of a thatch fire!"

"Oh, it involved quite a battle," Cyril assured me with relish, "between the designers and the fire commissioners. The latter almost prevailed and forced them to install a tile roof. They didn't care that in the 1613 fire there had been three thousand spectators in the place and every one of them had escaped unharmed. But while they were arguing, a new fire-retardant spray for thatched roofs came out, the first one insurance companies would accept. The fire brigade were finally convinced it would be quite safe if that were applied, the thatch laid over fire boards, and a sprinkler system incorporated into the roof."

"So you needn't worry about that, at any rate!" Ann said, laughing.

Dorothy, dressed in her usual black suit and sensible shoes, greeted us warmly, and Geoffrey muttered something as we sat down beside them. There were only three rows of benches on this level. Gemma and Tom were whispering together on the next row down, and Emily and Peter sat next to Quin at the front of the gallery, Janet still attached to his arm.

It was impossible not to watch them, even after the

play started. In fact, I discovered that watching a play in the open and in daylight was completely different from watching one in the usual darkened indoor theater. There were so many distractions, like the pigeons that strutted around on the wooden roof of the stage, right in front of us, and the planes making their approach to Heathrow, drowning out whole lines of dialogue. The audience too was visible all the time, especially the "groundlings," the crowd of cheap-ticket holders who had to stand on the ground in front of the stage, exposed to the elements and necessarily strong of limb—no umbrellas or folding seats being allowed. They were actually the most serious and attentive of the spectators, and I was glad for them that it didn't rain that afternoon.

The play itself was hilarious, with action back and forth between the stage and the galleries, the actors playing the grocer and his wife emerging from among the spectators to take over an attempted production by the Globe players and insert their apprentice, the hapless Ralph, as leading actor. It was fascinating to imagine Perdita Stone in that part, and I could see how she could have brought it off. The audience was in gales of laughter most of the time.

But I couldn't help looking down at Quin pretty often, watching how Janet insisted on whispering to him, laying her head on his shoulder, almost forcing him to look her way even though I could tell it annoyed him. That self-assured air I had noticed when I'd first met her was steadily slipping away. I realized that underneath she was insecure, afraid he might be starting to have second thoughts.

And was she right? Had she been only a midlife aberration, a year's refuge from the relentless approach of old age? If I had been the one sitting beside him we would have been laughing together. She didn't seem to understand that flattery and sex weren't going to be enough for the long haul, that after a while a man as sharp as Quin was going to need a woman he could match wits with, a woman who presented a bit of a challenge.

As the play neared its end I began to be nervous too. Ann had told me we were going to have dinner at The Anchor, a nearby inn that was there in Shakespeare's day. I didn't want to sit across a table from him as I had the other night. I understood how the old cliché about butterflies in the stomach had come about, it really felt as if something was fluttering back and forth in mine. I could feel his eyes on me as we made our slow way down the stairs in the crowd and walked along the river promenade in the twilight. Everybody was talking about the play, but I said little. I was conscious of him walking just behind me as we crossed The Anchor's riverside terrace, its wooden picnic tables all empty on that chilly evening.

Inside, the inn was large, well worn, and comfortable. A table was reserved for us in the main room, where horse brasses gleamed in the light of a steady fire. I made sure to sit farther down the table and on the other side from Quin and Janet. I hadn't met his eyes yet. Every now and then the butterflies fluttered up from my stomach into my chest and made me gasp for breath.

Everybody was laughing and joking, except for Geoffrey—who was still sunken within himself, looking

around with irritation at the general party atmosphere—
and, of course, Janet. A waiter took our drinks orders, and
when Dorothy said apple cider, I figured that should be
safe.

"Strongbow or scrumpy?" the waiter persisted.

I didn't know the difference, but "scrumpy" sounded
cute, so I ordered that.

It turned out to be nothing like the cider we used to
buy at roadside stands when we'd drive out to Connecticut to see the fall leaves. "Scrumpy" was hard cider with a
real kick—but it was certainly tasty, and after a half pint
the butterflies all migrated out of my stomach. I felt so
much better that when we ordered our meals, I asked for
another one.

The waiter brought green salads and bread along with
the dinner drinks.

"Now this is beautiful lettuce!" Ann exclaimed. "Nothing like the tired stuff one gets in some establishments."

" 'It is said that the effect of eating too much lettuce is
soporific,' " I announced, a little woozily.

Everyone stared. I looked at Emily expectantly, and
after a moment she burst out laughing. I heard a snort of
laughter from Quin too and looked around with satisfaction at the flustered scholars.

"Beatrix Potter, *Tale of the Flopsy Bunnies*, page one,
line one," I intoned solemnly.

"Of course, I remember!" Ann Aubrey exclaimed,
smiling at the three of us. "I read all those dear little
books to my boys, long long ago."

Everyone except the two party poopers had summoned up a sheepish smile at my coup. Cyril laughed and said, "Touché," and Dorothy said grudgingly, "One sees the joke. Perhaps we do indulge too much in quotation."

"No, no, no," I said. "I love it! That line just popped into my head when I heard 'lettuce.' "

"There's nobody wittier than Potter," Quin said. "Kit and I had more fun than Emily when we read those books to her, because we were old enough to appreciate the subtleties." This time, when he looked at me, I returned a steady gaze, my heart swelling with new, scrumpy courage. "You never forget discovering things like that together."

I knew I was answering his smile, and I took another sip.

Janet was alarmed by the smile. "You just wouldn't *believe* how witty Quin can be," she said quickly, assuming the worshipful gaze, trying to get his attention back.

"That's one author I can quote from anytime," I went on boldly, "like some people I could name ought to 'fill their little sacks with nuts and sail away home'—*Squirrel Nutkin*."

Quin leaned his forearms on the table, and his grin widened, his blue eyes glittering with enjoyment.

"Wait a minute, wait a minute," he said, "okay—with that mud on your dress and shoes, you remind me of that bunch of kittens that got all dressed up and then 'trod upon their pinafores and fell on their noses.' "

"Oh, right," Emily exclaimed, "and they took off their clothes and the ducks got them! 'Mr. Drake Puddleduck advanced in a slow sideways manner' and stole Tom Kitten's little blue suit." She was flushed with happiness at what was going on. I had to put a stop to it.

"Or there's the line I used to remember a lot, about a year and a half ago," I said, staring him down. " 'What do you mean by tumbling into my bed all covered with *smuts*?' " I leaned back and waited for him to top that one. "*Tale of Samuel Whiskers*."

"Yeah," he said ruefully, "he was a rat, wasn't he?"

The English people were staring at us, completely nonplussed. Fortunately the entrées arrived just then, and the usual comments broke out, of delight at their appearance and confusion about who got which.

Emily leaned over and murmured, "Maybe you'd better not have any more of that strong cider, Mother. You know you're not used to alcohol."

"Don't worry," I answered, "I'm not going to disgrace you! I may be dirty, but I am not inconsiderate."

And then the conversation stopped as Geoffrey suddenly rose and hurried toward the exit, knocking over an empty chair at another party's table. After only a brief pause the English people resumed talking about the food, as if nothing had happened. Their code of good taste obviously forbade recognizing an emotional crisis in public, but I kept looking after the poor man as he blundered out of the inn, going God knew where. He shouldn't be wandering around London alone in his state, of that I was sure.

"I'm going after him," I told Emily. I made my way to the door less clumsily than Geoffrey, although the floor did seem to be shifting alarmingly. Probably needed bracing, old building like that, I thought. Behind me, I heard Quin asking indignantly, "Why's she chasing after that guy?" and Emily hushing him while the others went on talking, perhaps a little louder.

I found Geoffrey on the terrace that overlooked the Thames and the city. He stood beside the low brick wall, looking out at the river, the full moon reflected in the ripples left behind the sightseeing boats. St. Paul's dome seemed to float above Ludgate Hill in floodlit serenity. As I came up to him I saw that tears were streaming down his cheeks.

"How can they laugh and talk as if things were still the same?" he demanded, without looking at me. "I don't think I shall ever laugh again."

I didn't know how to answer him.

After a few minutes he burst out again. "She knew I loved her, and she didn't *care*. When I told her, she didn't even listen. All the plans I had made for our future—they meant nothing to her. I couldn't—I couldn't—"

He broke off abruptly and glanced down at me, as if he had suddenly remembered my presence. Then he pressed his lips firmly together and looked away again. If he could have stopped crying, I knew he would have. Such a painfully inhibited Englishman, I thought, had to be humiliated that a mere acquaintance saw him grieve so openly.

My eyes filled with the easy tears of the slightly inebriated. Geoffrey stood impassively while I wiped the tears from his cheeks with the tissue Emily had given me. Then he reached inside his jacket and brought out a grubby piece of paper. He unfolded it and handed it to me.

"I carry it with me always," he explained in a choked voice.

It was a brief note, in the handwriting I recognized from Perdita's suicide note:

> Dear, dear Geoffrey.
>   You are the most patient man on earth to put up with my silly tantrums. You really shouldn't marry me, it will be the ruin of your quiet life. But if you don't, it will be the ruin of me, because I do love you terribly!
>
>   Your ridiculous
>   Perdita

"In less than a fortnight Edgar, damned Edgar, came into the theater group," he said, "and I lost her for the first time. But you see, she did love me once!"

I'd seen something else too, and it startled me.

"Geoffrey," I said slowly, "could you lend me this note until tomorrow?"

"Lend you— Why?" He stared at me in bewilderment.

"I want to show it to the police."

"The *police*?" His whole expression changed. His body straightened from its hopeless, stooped posture, and his eyes widened with what almost looked like alarm. Then he said, rather breathlessly, "No—no, it's all I have left of her!" He took the note back quickly and stuffed it into his jacket again.

"Well, all right," I said, rather jolted by the vehemence of his response. "It's only that I saw something in it that makes me wonder if she really—"

For some reason I didn't want to finish the sentence.

Now he was looking at something behind me, and I turned to see what it was. Quin stood in the doorway of the inn, his arms crossed over his chest, his face rumpled in a scowl, watching us. He had his nerve, I thought with a sudden charge of anger, following me around, acting as if he had a right to monitor my behavior.

Defiantly, I reached up and kissed Geoffrey soundly on the cheek. He jumped back, as if I had tried to stab him.

"Oh, I say," he mumbled, turning bright red. "No need for—I should not have made such a—entirely my fault if you—certainly didn't mean—"

I was heartened to hear the old, repressed Geoffrey breaking through.

"It's all right," I said. "It was only a friendly kiss, and I like people to show some honest emotion. My daughter says the stiff-upper-lip thing causes a lot of neuroses among Englishmen."

"Best if I return to the group," he said nervously.

He left me hurriedly, and I stood looking at the boats on the river and the cars moving along Victoria Embankment on the other side. My slightly muzzy mind was working on the new idea I'd got from Geoffrey's memento, in fact it was working so busily I didn't hear the quick footsteps crunching the gravel behind me or realize Quin was there until he took hold of my shoulders and turned me to face him. The anger in his face was something I never remembered seeing before, not in the years we'd spent together, not in the bewildering encounters of the past fortnight. We gazed at each other for a few seconds, and then he pulled me against him. A feeling like an electrical shock hit the pit of my stomach. He pressed his lips against mine in a long, hard kiss that left me breathless.

When it ended I wrenched myself loose and fled back into the inn. We didn't speak again in the half hour or so the party lingered in The Anchor. I was back to avoiding even eye contact. My heart kept pounding wildly as I got back into the Aubreys' car beside Geoffrey, as they carried me through the night back to Oxford, as I hurried to my own car outside their house. I didn't say good night to anybody, in fact I seemed unable to speak or even to think coherently and only realized I was driving on the right when a pair of headlights coming straight at me forced me to swerve to the left just in time. I pulled onto the shoulder and sat there until the maelstrom in my head subsided to, at least, white-water rapids. I couldn't blame my condition on the hard cider anymore, it had worn off long before. It was Quin who had put me in this state. I should have been able to work up some indignation toward him, but I couldn't, any more than I could stop myself from reliving over and over that kiss, which had felt like homecoming after a long, hard journey.

CHAPTER ELEVEN

*The month of May was come, when every
lusty heart beginneth to blossom, and to bring
forth fruit; for like as herbs and trees bring forth
fruit and flourish in May, in likewise every
lusty heart that is in any manner a lover,
springeth and flourisheth in lusty deeds. For
it giveth unto all lovers courage, that lusty month
of May.*

    —Sir Thomas Malory, *Le Morte d'Arthur*

It was completely different from the one in the suicide note," I told John Bennett, sitting opposite him in his comfortably messy, antique-filled sitting room. "There, it was a printed *I*—you know, 'I *killed him*'—and in the note Geoffrey showed me it was a script *I*,—'*I do love you terribly*'—although all the other letters were written exactly the same in both."

He sipped his coffee, eyeing me skeptically.

"But Geoffrey Pidgeon's note was very old, you said. People sometimes change their styles of writing."

"Why would Perdita only change the way she wrote one letter? If you're going to change, you just make all your letters lean a different way or something, and anyway, how many middle-aged people fool around with their handwriting? That's a kid sort of thing to do, isn't it?"

He smiled indulgently. "A slender reed on which to rest a murder theory, Catherine."

"If she didn't write the suicide note, she was murdered too," I said flatly.

"It *is* possible, isn't it, John?" Fiona put in. She stood in the doorway between sitting room and kitchen, wiping one of the breakfast dishes. John set his empty cup on a Hepplewhite pie table and stood up.

"I suppose anything is possible. But there was a post-mortem, you know, and no evidence was found of drugs, or of bruising, as there would be if she'd been tied or held down. Are you suggesting Mrs. Stone sat there quietly and allowed someone to cut her wrists?"

"Well," I said weakly, "maybe she was tricked some-how. If the real murderer was somebody she trusted, couldn't she have—sort of cooperated, until it was too late to fight back?"

"Most unlikely. I'm not prepared to abandon a sce-nario that makes perfect sense," John said, getting into his coat, "for one that creates more problems than it solves. And all on the basis of a single vowel."

"What if I could bring the note to the police station?" I asked. "If I told Geoffrey how it proves Perdita didn't kill herself, I bet he'd let me borrow it."

"I would really prefer not to raise false hopes in a man as grief-stricken as you've described," John said with a frown. The telephone started ringing.

As Fiona picked up the receiver he gave her a quick kiss and bade me good-bye. I just sat there, sunk in disappointment. I had hurried over that morning with such excitement to catch him before he left for work. And I still felt sure the difference in those two *I*s was significant. Thinking about it last night, I'd pictured the "suicide note" in my mind, only two lines at the top of a piece of paper: "*Ikilled him. Some crimes are beyond forgiveness.*" I'd dwelt on that *I*, the way it was squeezed up against the next word, and I'd felt more and more sure it was the end of a longer composition, innocently written by Perdita to the killer and brought to the scene because it could so easily be misinterpreted. The word at the bottom of the preceding page, the one that really came before "killed him," was no doubt "Edgar," and the killing referred to the death of little Simon. I'd hardly slept for working out all these details, and John had just dismissed my whole theory out of hand.

"For you, Catherine," Fiona said.

"Goodness, who'd be calling me here?"

"It's Emily," she said, with her hand covering the speaker, and a warning expression on her face. I took the phone, and my daughter started right in.

"Mother, where have you been?" she demanded. "I called you three times yesterday, and every time I got a busy signal! When I couldn't get you in the evening I was going to drive out there and make sure you were all right, but Peter convinced me to wait and call again this morning, and when it was still busy *then*, he suggested trying Fiona's. Now I know you weren't on the phone all that time! Why did you leave it off the hook?"

"Darling, I—I was afraid it would be Dad."

"Oh. He's been calling you?" Her voice softened. "What's happening between you two, Mom?"

"I have no idea." A scared feeling hit me, and I sat down. "I guess something *is* happening. I'm trying not to think about it."

"Are you— Do you—" She stopped, then murmured, "I'm afraid to ask."

"Oh yes, I hope you won't! It's all getting very, very strange. I don't think he expected things to be like this, any more than I did. Look, he'll be going home in a couple of days, so I figure if I don't see him or talk to him again, everything will—"

"But you can't miss May Morning tomorrow!" she exclaimed. "I want you to see how lovely it is, and afterward we're all going to the Aubreys' for breakfast. And you know, Mom, you *have* to see him again, you have to talk to him—otherwise you'll always wonder what might have happened." I started to protest, but she went on, urgently, "Do it for me. Give yourselves a chance, and maybe—Mistakes can be corrected, Mom, people *can* get back what they've lost. I've seen it happen."

I could have wept, hearing her beg like that. Maybe, as Quin said, I'd been partly to blame for hurting her. She had a right to ask me to give these untimely emotions a last chance, and deep down inside I knew my misgivings were not strong enough anymore to protect me.

"All right, love," I said. "I'll come."

Emily's happy sigh floated down the phone line. We said good-bye, and I quickly got out of there before Fiona could throw any questions my way, as she was obviously longing to do.

I hadn't mentioned that kiss to her or to anyone else. I knew it meant something bigger than taking refuge in his arms after finding Perdita dead, something too big to talk about yet, even with my best friend.

I walked home slowly, thinking about last night, and tomorrow, and the rest of my life. Could it really turn around again and take me back to the world I used to live in, the love I had been sure was gone forever? Did I want it to?

The workmen were hammering at the frame of the new house across the road, fastening the timbers together on the concrete slab, ready to be raised. I wondered if I'd be there when the new people came to live in it, or if the village would be only a memory by then, a dream I'd had before Quin and I came back to our senses.

May Morning in Oxford starts officially at 6 A.M., although a lot of the celebrants have been partying all night when the little choirboys of Magdalen College School sing their Latin invocation to summer from the college tower. High Street and Magdalen Bridge are closed to traffic and packed with people, and this year I was among them, at the entrance to Magdalen's cloisters, where Geoffrey and I had emerged from Addison's Walk. I generally hate crowds, but this was such a jubilant group, the students greeting the beginning of their last term before the long summer break, the townspeople and tourists enjoying the spectacle, I didn't mind being backed up against the college walls by the press of bodies. It was a spectacular morning, the bright sun rising into a blue sky as if cued up by the hymn floating from among the tower's bristly spires and glistening gold weather vanes.

When the choristers' sweet falsetto voices had faded away, a cheer went up, and Morris dancers took over the middle of the street, the bells around their legs jingling merrily as they went into their bizarre heel-slapping, stick-batting dance. Mimes and street musicians moved through the crowd, students made boisterous attempts to maneuver past the police stationed at the bridge to keep them from diving off. Peter said diving had been a tradition on May Morning until a student broke his neck a few years before and it was finally banned.

"This is really the only event university people and townspeople celebrate together," Emily was saying. "The rest of the year the colleges have their boat races and balls, and the regular people have street fairs and city-sponsored fetes in the parks—but everybody comes to May Morning, and the town-and-gown resentments are put aside for a little while. Isn't that nice?"

I was making my way through the crowd between her and Peter, who carried Archie on his shoulders. I could see the Aubreys ahead of us, accompanied by their two visiting sons, Ann turning now and then to be sure everybody was coming along as we crossed jam-packed Magdalen Bridge. The rest of the faculty were scattered through the mob, all heading for the Aubreys' little street, just a few blocks along on the other side of the Cherwell. Breakfast at their house on May Morning was a Mercy tradition.

And somewhere behind us, I knew, Quin walked with Janet. I had glimpsed them before the choir started singing, her hands wrapped around his arm as if to keep him from escaping. His eyes had been searching the crowd, and I knew he was looking for me. I'd turned my eyes away quickly. Cowardly, I knew, but there were such contradictory emotions churning inside me, I couldn't help myself.

"Dad was over last night," Emily said, as if reading my mind. "He wanted to make sure you were coming this morning. This is his last day in England, you know. His flight leaves tomorrow at—"

"Yes, darling, I know! I absolutely know."

"I'm sorry," she said quickly, and turned away to tie Archie's shoe. He was having a wonderful time, seeing the whole show from his perch on Peter's shoulders and giving a running commentary in his own private language.

We all trailed down the street, through the gate, and into the Aubreys' house, where Cyril and his sons brought us little glasses of orange juice as we stood around in the drawing room, and Ann hurried off to the kitchen. The two sons, introduced as Eric and Graham, were tall, blond, and strikingly handsome, as well as quite modest about all the good they were doing overseas.

They could make a lot of money from their looks, I thought, go into modeling or films or even sales, and instead they devoted themselves to helping children in the poorest countries on earth. Cyril and Ann were lucky to have raised such great kids, and they obviously knew it.

This was where things would get dicey, I knew. I was miserably conscious of Quin's presence, although I stayed on the other side of the room, making conversation with Dorothy. I knew every time he looked my way, although I wouldn't look at him. When we went into the dining room and took seats at the long table in front of the window wall, I cast a quick glance at Janet. Her flowered cotton dress looked too loose on her, and her face seemed thinner too, so that the brown eyes looked even larger. Her former sulky look had been replaced by an edgy, almost hunted expression. She and Quin didn't seem to have much to say to each other. He looked tense as well, but when I sat down beside Emily and finally met his eyes, he smiled, and I felt the uncertain beginning of a smile touch my lips.

"What a beautiful day!" Cyril Aubrey said expansively, beaming around the table like a father with his brood. "One always wishes to have this weather for May Morning, but seldom is such a wish granted in this climate. I believe this is the last full day you and your lady are to spend with us, Quin, and so you will remember sunshine and flowers as your last impressions of our island. Most gratifying."

"One only wishes poor Geoffrey had joined us," Ann added, taking her seat at one end.

Eileen bustled in with platters of scrambled eggs, fat sausages, broiled tomatoes, and bacon, and Ann helped herself and started it around the table while the maid returned to the kitchen. A few minutes later she carried in a plate piled high with buttered triangles of white and brown toast, and on her third appearance, a big silver coffeepot. As we ate she came back several times with marmalade, honey, cream, sugar, and the steak sauce the English inexplicably like to pour on eggs.

Archie as usual had no interest in sitting at the table but tottered around the room, exploring. With no breakables in reach, he soon started showing signs of boredom. Emily handed him a piece of toast, and he plopped down in a corner to tear it up.

Ann started telling us about the boating party the whole family was going to at midday, and the sons joined in with wisecracks about another May Day when they'd gone punting and Cyril had inadvertently landed them in the river. They got us all laughing, while he tried to defend his ability with the pole in a half-serious way. And so conversation went on, full of literary allusion as usual, intelligent and amusing. But I couldn't concentrate on anything except the two across the table. Janet took a spoonful of eggs and a triangle of white toast, but she didn't eat them. She only sipped at her coffee, looking from Quin to me to her plate. Ann drew him into conversation, but his eyes kept darting to me while he talked to her. Emily watched us discreetly, her cheeks flushed.

Peter was absorbed in a friendly dispute as to whether Beaumont and Fletcher had been influenced by Cervantes in writing the play we'd seen in London, when Emily suddenly half-rose, exclaiming, "Where's Archie?" I looked around and saw scraps of toast scattered around in the corner, but no sign of the baby.

"You stay here, love, I'll go and find him," I said quickly. I'd been feeling desperate to escape from the tension anyway. I jumped up and hurried into the hallway.

There were four doors on the right side of the hall. The first was closed. I turned the knob and opened it just a crack, peeking in and calling his name softly. It looked like a pantry, and there was no sign of Archie there, nor in the next room.

As I got farther from the dining room I lost the sounds of talk and laughter. It was very quiet at the far end of the hall. And then when I came out of the third room, a small one with no furniture except a piano and some bookshelves, I heard a voice. The last door stood open, and I headed for it.

Before I got there I stopped in my tracks, and a chill went down my backbone. It wasn't Archie talking in that room. It was Edgar Stone.

"A man named Peter Tyler is outside the door threatening me with a knife— He'll kill me if he gets—"

The harsh, almost whispering voice broke off, then repeated, a little lower, "He'll kill me if he gets through—if he gets through the door." It went slightly higher. "He'll kill me if he gets through the door."

I stepped slowly toward the room. Then Cyril Aubrey spoke from within it. "No, damn it," he said, as if to himself. "Needs more force." And then Edgar again, with increased intensity: "He'll *kill* me if he gets through the door!"

I stepped into the room. It was an oak-paneled study, with an elaborately carved desk, an empty leather swivel chair and side chair, and a wall of floor-to-ceiling bookshelves. A wheeled wooden ladder was fixed to a track on the ceiling, slanted toward the books. On the topmost rung I saw my grandson standing precariously, gazing at a small black radio-tape player a lot like the one Quin had given him, right in front of his nose on the highest bookshelf. He was waiting for it to do its magic trick again, but the tape must have run out.

My legs began to shake. I knew in that instant what had happened. Our affable host, my son-in-law's greatest booster, had practiced the murder victim's voice until he got it perfect. Then he had killed him, called Peter from the murder scene to lure him there, and made the 999 call that had laid the blame on Peter. Which meant he must have killed Perdita as well—God alone knew why! I had been right about that letter after all.

"Archie," I said as quietly as possible, "stay there till I bring you and the tape player down."

He jumped, startled, and tried to turn around. I could see him starting to lose his balance.

"Wait, wait," I cried, running toward the ladder, "don't move till I get you!"

Before I could reach the ladder he fell, with a little yip of surprise. I tried instinctively to catch him, so of course he landed right on top of me. I was thrown to the floor on my back, all the breath knocked out of my body.

Archie, his fall conveniently cushioned, was immediately up and jumping around me, saying something I couldn't hear through the ringing in my ears. I lay there like a beached whale, gasping for air, wondering what I had broken and how long it would be before Cyril Aubrey walked in.

After a while my hearing started to come back. Archie was yelling, "No, no, bad Nana!" and pulling on my arm with a worried face. All right, that arm wasn't broken, because he wasn't hurting me. Gingerly, I felt the other one, then my neck and my shoulders. Everything I could reach without sitting up felt okay, but I was still pulling in air as loudly as the Creature from the Black Lagoon, and every breath hurt my chest horribly.

I gathered all my courage and started to push myself up, when I heard footsteps in the hall. Oh, God, I thought, he would know what had happened. I could see the tape player sitting askew on the shelf, not straight as it had been. I was scrabbling madly at the carpet to get to a sitting position when a man's voice said, "Hello-ello! Having a problem?"

I looked around and saw the Aubreys' two tall blond sons standing in the doorway, wearing bemused smiles. Relief flooded through me.

"Taypay," Archie explained to them. " Fa-down."

"What's that, young fellow-me-lad?" said the younger of them. "Fall down? I should say she did."

He came over and offered me his hand. I rose slowly, still gasping and speechless, but free of major pain. He got me into a nearby chair and offered to fetch a glass of water. I could only shake my head. All I wanted was to get myself and the baby out of that room before Cyril Aubrey found us. I pointed toward the door and looked up at his son pleadingly.

He had such a nice face, concerned and sensitive. What suffering was I going to lay on him when I told the police what I now knew about his father? I wondered sadly.

I stood up, rather wobbly, and leaning on the young man's arm—Eric, I suddenly remembered—I limped toward the door.

The one who remained nameless to me herded Archie along, laughing, while we made our slow way toward the dining room. By the time I could hear the talk and laughter, I had started to breathe more normally and was able to whisper, "Thank you."

"Not at all," he answered cheerfully. I wanted to ask him not to tell anyone where he'd found us but knew I couldn't get out that many words.

The party looked up in amazement as we came in, and Emily cried, "Mother, what have you done to yourself this time?" as Archie climbed into her lap.

"Taypay!" he kept trying to explain.

"Playing with the baby," I wheezed.

"We found them on the floor in Dad's study," Eric added helpfully. "It looked as if she'd taken a fall, not surprising when you watch this young tearaway in operation."

I kept my eyes away from Cyril but I could feel his on me, as the others exclaimed and offered me advice. Emily insisted on my sitting down, and Quin took Janet's untouched glass of water and, leaning across the table, set it in front of me while she watched in dumb misery.

What was I to do? I couldn't very well stand up, point down the table at Cyril, and shout, *J'accuse!* There he sat, quoting yet another obscure playwright, his wife smiling fondly at him, his sons teasing him affectionately, Dorothy nodding approvingly at a point he'd made, none of them imagining he was a murderer.

Bookish, rumpled, kindly Cyril Aubrey—how could he be capable of such things? And *why* would he kill two people who had been his friends for decades?

I was starting to feel a persistent ache in my back now, and I was slightly sick besides, more from the knowledge I was holding inside than from the fall. I pulled myself up with the help of the chair back and said, "I'm sorry, I think I really must go home and rest."

There was a general murmur of concern, while Peter and Emily insisted I come to their place until I felt better. I refused, but evidently I had started a trend, because everyone started getting up and gathering belongings together. Cyril and Ann of course protested politely, but we all moved gradually toward the front door, Emily and Peter still trying to convince me I wasn't fit to drive.

I kissed them good-bye at the gate. Archie was still worried about me. He kept repeating, "Fa-down!" and "Ow!" as we went out into the street. I looked back to see the Aubreys standing in the doorway, waving to their departing guests, holding hands. I wished I could go back and unlearn what I had learned.

I was just opening my car door when I heard Quin's voice at my shoulder. "I've got to talk to you," he murmured huskily.

I turned and looked up at him.

"Yes," I said. "I've got to talk to you too. I've got something really important to tell you."

"Have you?" His eyes lighted. "That's good. Not right now, though. Meet me in an hour or so, after I explain— Should I come to your house?"

I balked at the idea of letting him into my little sanctuary. Somehow I knew Rowan Cottage would never be the same once he'd stepped over the threshold.

"No," I said. "Someplace else. There's a pub, the Eagle and Child, on St. Giles, just a little north of your hotel. I'll meet you there."

"Right. I'll see you in an hour."

He turned and went to his car. I saw Janet sitting huddled in the front seat, hugging herself. I certainly felt no pity for her, but I did feel a frisson of fear, realizing what I had just agreed to. I had to tell him about my discovery in the study, I had to get his help, but I knew this meeting was going to decide things between us as well. I was going to have to choose between Far Wychwood and New York, between solitude and companionship, and I was going to have to do it in only one hour.

CHAPTER TWELVE

. . . what's past is prologue, what to come
In yours and my discharge.

Shakespeare, *The Tempest*

Parking in Oxford is a royal pain. The closest space I could find to the Bird and Baby was on Keble Road, several hundred yards away. I had to feed the meter, a big black box on a post that took the money for four or five parked cars. I put in enough coins for an hour—surely we'd be on our way to Aubrey's house by then—pressed a button, and put the resulting ticket on the dashboard so it showed through my windshield.

Sore all over by now, and tense as a strummed string, I walked toward the pub through the grounds of Keble College, a redbrick intruder in the golden stone of Oxford. I'd always liked the scallops and stripes and checkerboards of white and yellow brick that enliven its facades, and the happy superfluity of Victorian Gothic turrets and gables.

It was still more than half an hour until I had to meet

Quin. I didn't want to sit conspicuously alone in the pub that long, but my body insisted on sitting somewhere, so I crossed the sunken quad to the college chapel. I'd always got a kick out of its overdecorated interior, especially the mosaics of biblical events going around the walls like a pre-Raphaelite comic strip. There was nobody else in the vast stone interior. I sank wearily into a pew, my stomach churning with apprehension. Maybe I could just sit here for a while until Quin gave up on me and went away. If I did, and if I took the phone off the hook tonight, the whole crisis would be over because he would be gone tomorrow, back to America with Janet. She'd be cheerful again in her own environment, and he'd sink back into his world of affluence and adoration and forget this temporary madness.

How had I let it happen? Was I really so weak that a few caring words, a shared adventure, a single kiss could win me back? I hadn't been lonely before he came, I hadn't been afraid of the future or hungry for affection. I'd shed the skin that had loved his touch and grown a new, harder one. At least, I'd thought I had.

A mosaic God the Father glared down at me from above the altar, a bearded old man with a stern, impassive face, a sword sort of floating on his shoulder and one hand held up, with a star in the palm. I half wished I were one of those people who believed you could get your problems solved by talking to someone you couldn't see. When I was a child in Cincinnati, my mother took me and my brothers to church every Sunday, and I obediently repeated the magic formulas she'd taught me, picturing the man with the beard listening sympathetically, even though I never got the pony. But when she died despite my frantic repetition of every Episcopal mantra I knew, my faith began to slip away. My father wasn't a churchgoer, so the boys and I gradually dropped it, and I'd been a skeptic ever since.

I stared back at the mosaic face scowling down in disapproval, as if I'd somehow let God the Father down. But *he* was the one who'd decreed my mother should have a fatal stroke at thirty-three.

Still, I liked churches, the quiet, the smell of candle wax and flowers, the way nobody bothers you. A church is a great place to get your thoughts together. I decided to rest there for a while, and then just go home. I didn't *have* to talk to Quin, after all. I didn't have to put myself through all this misery. It would serve him right to be stood up.

As soon as I'd made the decision, I relaxed. No longer obsessed by the prospect of meeting him, my thoughts shot back to my other problem, Cyril Aubrey. When I gave John Bennett that tape player he would have no doubt who the killer was. But I had to get hold of it first. Could I risk breaking into that house alone? I thought I'd seen Aubrey throw me a startled look when his son said I'd been in his study. Had he remembered the tape was still there, even though he had put it on such a high shelf, where no one would be expected to climb? Or had he just left it there and forgotten it? It was kind of amazing that he'd held on to something so incriminating. Anyway, I had to get back there and grab it while he was out boating. I had to do it now, as soon as possible, and, I admitted reluctantly, I was going to need help. Quin hadn't been willing to let me go into danger alone before. He was the only person I was sure would go with me. Suddenly I was irritated with myself, hiding there like a coward, when I needed to take control of this situation.

All right, I'd go to the Eagle and Child, not to discuss this thing that had happened between us, but to tell him what I'd found and demand his help. I would be very firm in squelching any talk about our future.

I stood up, not without a groan, and hurried out of the chapel before I could change my mind yet again.

"Kit—over here."

I heard his voice as I passed the two rooms just inside the front door of the Eagle and Child, and when I looked to the right, behind me, I saw him sitting on the bench that ran along the front wall of that room. He was leaning on a low, round table, holding his pipe. When I went in, he half-rose, then sat down again as I took the other bench, at one side of the table. He hit the pipe bowl a few times against an ash tray to empty it. The sound flashed me back to New York, to nights reading in bed, knowing the next sound after that would be the click of the living room light going off, then his footsteps coming down the hall to join me.

The room was small and intimate, and we had it to ourselves. There was one casement window, behind Quin on the front wall, the only other light two old-fashioned wall lamps, high up, casting yellow circles on the embossed ceiling. The walls were dark green above almost black wainscoting, interrupted on the opposite side by a little fireplace.

"Quin, something really important has happened," I began quickly.

"I know," he answered. "Something neither of us expected."

"You see, this morning I was—"

"No," he said. "Let me tell you first. Then you can tell me."

I really had meant to be very firm, but sitting there, looking at his face and hearing his voice, was totally different from sitting in Keble Chapel making theoretical plans. Now I didn't want to stop him.

"I came to England to offer you any help you needed, to try to get us acting like adults again. That's the real reason I came, Kit, not just for a visit with Emily. It was a hell of a job to get Janet to let me come, and it turns out she was right about everything. Emily didn't want her around, she knew that would happen, and when I saw you again—"

"Take your order, then?" a chipper young man in an apron demanded, leaning in the door.

Quin scowled at him and said shortly, "Lager."

"Pint, sir?" the waiter asked, and Quin nodded, blowing out an angry sigh. "And the lady?"

"What do you have that's not alcoholic?" I asked him. "I need my wits about me."

"What about a nice squash?"

"Squash?" I pictured a glass of liquefied zucchini, and

it must have shown in my expression, because the waiter laughed.

"Quite tasty, actually, lot like a lemonade."

"For God's sake, bring her a squash!" Quin exploded. Obviously he was at least as tightly wound as I was.

When the waiter had gone I said tartly, "I didn't come to hear about *her*!"

"You're wrong about her, you know. It's not an act, she really loves me."

I swallowed the question I wanted to ask, the one about his feelings for her, and took refuge in sarcasm.

" 'Whatever love means,' " I quoted. "Prince Charles, announcement of engagement."

"I don't want to get into one of these go-arounds with you about what things 'mean'! We've already agreed I'm no good at that stuff." He leaned toward me, his blue eyes full of intensity. "Listen, I lied just now. It's not true I only wanted to get on a more adult footing with you. I told myself that was it, but—I missed you, Kit. I worried about you."

He leaned back, releasing his tension in another of his noisy sighs as the waiter set our drinks down. I took a sip of my lemony soda, he took a long swallow of his beer, and we sat in silence for a few moments. Outside, a sidewalk grate clanked periodically as passersby stepped on it. Emily had told me a few days before he'd said he missed me. It had made me angry then, but it didn't now.

Finally he said, with a touch of impatience, "So didn't you miss me at all?"

"Back in New York I thought I'd go crazy from missing you. And after I got here—yes, I thought about you, and our past, a whole lot more than I'd expected to. I'd thought once I was far away it would be easy to forget, but it wasn't. It took me weeks to cure myself of thinking about you, and now— Oh, it's not fair! What do you *want*, Quin? Are you planning to move all your women into a big house together, like Brigham Young?"

"No," he said, smiling for the first time. "One at a time's enough to deal with."

He reached across the table and took my hand, and I felt the same shock in the pit of my stomach as when he'd held and kissed me.

"Now," he said softly, "you tell me."

I took a deep breath.

"I want you to help me break into Cyril Aubrey's house."

He drew back and dropped my hand, looking stunned. "To do *what*?"

"Okay, I'll explain," I hurried on. "This morning, when I went to look for Archie, I found this tape recorder in the study, and the tape was of Aubrey practicing Edgar's voice saying what he said on the 999 tape. You know, that Peter was about to kill him? So Cyril Aubrey made that call! Which means he killed Edgar, and he must have killed Perdita too, because I know she didn't commit suicide from the way the *I* in her note was written, so we've got to get that tape and take it to the police." I stopped to get my breath.

He just stared at me for another minute.

Then his face flushed and he burst out, "What is this?

I came here to talk about *us*, you and me, whether we can start over—not about another cockamamie murder theory you've cooked up!"

I started to respond angrily too, then forced myself to quiet down, to be conciliatory.

"Just help me, Quin, the way you did before, and *then* we'll talk about us. I know we need to, but this has to be done right away, before he—"

"You're going off half-cocked again, the way you've done as long as I've known you! Look." He leaned across the table again, gazing at me earnestly. "Peter's free, Emily's got him back, so she's happy again, and that's all I ever cared about. It's over. Perdita Stone killed her husband and herself, nice neat package, all wrapped up and bought by everybody. Forget about it."

"No, you don't understand—it's unjust to Perdita to leave it like this. If Cyril Aubrey really killed them he has to bear the responsibility!"

"I don't give a damn about that. It's better for everybody if a dead woman gets the blame. *If* Aubrey did it he had a rational motive, he's not some serial killer. It'd be painful for a lot of people if he went down, and a big black eye for the police, which I can tell you they wouldn't appreciate. *You* don't understand, baby—nobody cares who really killed the Stones."

I drew back, as if to avoid touching a live wire laid across the table between us.

"*I* care," I almost whispered.

He leaned back with an exasperated sigh. "God, I'd forgotten that absolutism, that right-and-wrong garbage you were always full of. Like you never got over what they told you in Sunday school. Used to drive me crazy."

I let silence fall between us for a few minutes. Clank.

"Yes, I remember," I said slowly.

"There's no absolute right and wrong, Kit. Never was, never will be, and people who believe there is don't make it to the top—not in the real world."

"What about justice?" I demanded.

He shrugged. "Justice is an effect of the wallet. If you can afford Quin Freeman, you'll probably walk, even if you're the guiltiest guy alive. If you have to settle for the public defender you'll probably go down, though you're innocent as a newborn baby."

"That used to bother you."

"I used to be a kid. I grew up."

I saw in my mind's eye the shaggy young fellow I'd first met in front of the Capitol Building, his eyes shining with conviction. I remembered him shouting "Sellouts!" at some of the most powerful figures in the government, and I heard him telling me in a Greenwich Village coffeeshop about the poor and ignorant people trapped in the legal system who someday would not need to be afraid, because of him.

"You know," I said, "that day on the train, you said when Emily left there wasn't much between us anymore. I didn't see it then, but now I do. It was because over the years you'd 'grown up,' if that's what you want to call it, and I hadn't." A strange new feeling was taking over inside me, a sort of lightness, as if, minute by minute, something heavy was being lifted off my shoulders. "I'm sixty years old, and I haven't grown up yet."

A puzzled anger kindled in his eyes. "Yeah, don't I know it! And if I hadn't been there to take care of you, to rein you in when you'd go haring off on one of your impulses, how much trouble would you have gotten yourself into?"

"Probably about as much as I've been getting into since you left." Now there was a bubble of laughter bouncing around in my chest, just waiting to burst.

"Exactly. And I don't want to think about you getting in trouble. You've always needed me to protect you, because you've never understood what the world's really like."

The laughter burst out, startling both of us. "You know, you had me convinced of that for most of my life! Dumb old me, needing all that protection from somebody who'd long ago sold his soul for money and prestige."

"Look, I'm not ashamed of my work! I'm damn proud of the career I've built *and* the money I've made. And I did it all without my wife giving me so much as an occasional pat on the back!"

"You're right, you're absolutely right. When you'd talk about how cleverly you got some rich client off it made me uncomfortable, but I wouldn't let myself think about it. I never was that supportive little woman you wanted. And now that I've had a taste of life on my own terms, I'm even worse!"

That burden I'd been carrying for so long was quite

gone now. I'd never felt such relief and delight except on the delivery table, forty pounds lighter and about to turn the page on an exciting new chapter in my story.

I could see in his eyes he realized something had changed.

"Kit, calm down!" came the familiar order. "This is a perfect example of what I just said, you're jumping to another crazy conclusion. I know we've got problems, but we can work them out. I want you back in spite of all that."

"No, you don't want me, Quin," I said. "You want what we had in the old days—before you grew up."

"Damn it, I know what I want! Okay, you're so hung up on the truth, let's hear *you* tell it. This is about that Geoffrey guy, isn't it? All that high-minded talk isn't worth a damn, you just don't want to admit you're involved with another man!"

I couldn't contain another burst of laughter.

"Oh, Quin, it's not Geoffrey! I don't *want* to do the whole thing over with a different man. I've lived that life, and now I want something else. I want my freedom."

"It's the first time you've ever talked like that," he said scornfully.

"Because I've been learning since I came to the village, although I didn't know it. I've been learning to be myself, with no apologies. And I like it."

As I stood up and edged out from behind the table he said furiously, "All right, I'll go to Aubrey's with you, if that's what started you on this tantrum! But this time I'm not going to let you do anything illegal—"

I had already started for the door.

"No, I don't want you to come with me, Quin. I can do it alone. Let's make this good-bye. Go tell Janet she doesn't have to worry anymore."

"Kit, come back here!" he bellowed.

I stopped at the door and shook my head. "No," I said, "I'm not coming back," and I left him sitting there.

CHAPTER THIRTEEN

There are a many ways that conduct to
seeming honour, and some of them
very dirty ones.

—John Webster, *Duchess of Malfi*

I hurried back to Keble Road to get my car, feeling the
way an ex-con must feel when the prison gate slams
shut behind him. I was unreasonably happy, unduly relieved, and irrationally confident. I could get into Aubrey's
and make away with that evidence without anybody's help.

It had been a narrow escape, but if Quin hadn't come
and pushed me to the brink, I knew I'd have gone on in my
new life always regretting the old one and wasting my en-
ergy on bitterness. I could really begin to live on my own
terms now. If I hadn't gone to the Bird and Baby today, if
I'd hidden and let him leave without that confrontation, I
would never have understood the lessons Far Wychwood
had been teaching me.

Magdalen Bridge being closed to traffic this morning
while revelers still packed the streets, I had to get out my

Oxford A to Z map book and work out an alternate route to the Aubreys' street. I could hardly concentrate, so many different ideas were pulsing in my brain, but finally had to admit there was no way except the long way, north on the Banbury Road and then a big loop around to the south again.

Driving past the unaesthetic modern university buildings concentrated north of the historic area, my thoughts traveled from what had just happened, to what was waiting for me. I was sure there was still enough time to grab the tape player before the Aubreys came home. I could have it in John Bennett's hands before Cyril missed it. Without that evidence, there was no way anybody would believe he had murdered two people. I could hardly believe it myself.

Why would a man like Cyril Aubrey kill two of his oldest friends? A romantic triangle? Impossible to believe he'd betray Ann, he just wasn't the kind. But of course, that's what I'd believed about Quin, wasn't it? I shook my head, making the right turn onto Marston Ferry Road. No, there was no doubt about the Aubreys' devotion to each other, and no one had ever linked Cyril with Perdita. Maybe he'd just felt sorry for her and wanted to free her from Edgar's mistreatment—but in that case, why would he kill her too?

All right, there were other common motives—how about blackmail? Edgar might have known something that could harm Cyril or his precious family. That would explain the conferral of the headship on the one man least suited to the position. Cyril had to have known what Edgar Stone was, if the rest of the faculty did. The more I thought about it, the more false his attempts to justify his choice had sounded. And Stone had loved exercising power over people—no doubt he would have resented a man who held power over him. I could even imagine how he might have burned with jealousy watching Aubrey's two handsome, intelligent sons, roughly the same age as his Simon, grow up and make their mark in the world. To force Cyril to bow before him, to wrench from him control over the whole faculty, that would have been Edgar Stone's idea of real merrymaking.

Maybe Perdita found out about all that, somehow put two and two together and realized Cyril had killed her husband? Then he'd have to eliminate her as well. I couldn't see him as a cold-blooded executioner, but whatever desperate act Edgar might have driven him to, it was still hard to comprehend how he could murder Perdita or frame Peter.

The Aubreys' little street was very quiet—everybody would be at the festivities, of course. There were no lights in the house by the river, although the beautiful morning had turned cloudy. A swan was floating past, making an upside-down image in the dark water as I drew up to the curb. The garage door was open and the car gone. Obviously there was nobody home, but I almost tiptoed, approaching the front door. I remembered what I'd heard Ann say at the dinner party, and sure enough, after a quick search, found the key hidden in a niche between the mailbox and the wall of the house.

I unlocked the front door and stepped into the foyer,

further exhilarated by my newly discovered talent for housebreaking.

I hurried down the hallway to the study. There was the tape player, right where Archie had left it, askew on the topmost shelf. My heart pounded with excitement as I pushed the ladder over and started climbing, not even feeling my usual queasiness about high places—not today!

I had the tape player in my hand and was repositioning my feet to start backing down, when I saw something familiar on the next shelf below. It was the spine of an old book, split down the middle, its green coloring scraped away in places so the brown leather beneath showed through. A distinctive pattern of gold sunbursts ran down the middle.

That book belonged in another library. I knew I had seen it somewhere else, but I couldn't remember where. I pried it loose with my free hand. The pages tried to fall out, but I held them down with my thumb. Awkwardly, I turned the cover back and saw the title page.

Marching across the sheet of brittle vellum on a slight downward slant, those roughly printed letters told me the whole reason for the murders, although it took me a few minutes to realize it:

The most excellent and tragicall historie
of Hamlet, Prince of Denmarke.
By Mr. William Shakespeare
of the Right honourable the Queen's
Company.

Printed by Valentine Sims
to be fold in Paules church-yard at the figne
of the Greene Dragon.
1588.

Gradually, a memory seeped into my mind—the Senior Common Room, the murmur of literate conversation, Peter telling me about the *Ur-Hamlet* mentioned by theatergoers before Shakespeare's earliest known play was performed, and believed never to have been published. What had he said—the *Hamlet* we know wasn't written until 1600 or so? I was pretty sure of that, and I knew Peter's first words on introducing me had been about Cyril Aubrey's great coup, the finding of a letter that proved Thomas Kyd had written the *Ur-Hamlet*. The best seller in which he'd revealed his find had brought him acclaim in the academic world, and the headship with all its money and perks.

I turned back the title page. Beneath "Act I, scene I" was not the familiar opening I expected, the guards on the parapet discussing the ghost, but one set in the queen's chamber, the prince arguing with his mother about her hasty marriage. This was a whole different *Hamlet*, I realized with a little chill down the backbone. I was holding in my hands proof that Cyril Aubrey's whole career was a sham.

He must have forged the Kyd letter—as a scholar he would know all about Elizabethan documents, the composition of ink, the style of penmanship. Paper of the time wouldn't be hard to find, for an expert in the field. Had he done it for the sake of reputation, I wondered, or money?

And now I remembered where I had seen the green book before. Perdita had grabbed it from her shelves, that day she told Geoffrey and me she was going to sell Edgar's books. She'd been planning to call in rare-book dealers, and they would definitely have recognized the significance of this one. Cyril would have been exposed and discredited.

Edgar Stone must somehow have found the *Ur-Hamlet* and used it to blackmail his way into the headship. Any normal person would have revealed such a find right away for the fame and fortune it would bring, but Edgar was far from normal—judging by what I knew of him, he would prefer to enjoy his petty tyrannies first. There would be time enough to reveal his discovery to the world once he got bored with watching his colleagues suffer.

Cyril must have known that. So he had silenced Edgar permanently, then done away with Perdita to keep her from selling the precious volume that would reveal his lie to the world. Why couldn't he just have stolen it from her, I wondered miserably, why did he have to kill her as well? And framing Peter, now that was absolutely—

"Fie on it, ah, fie!" said a voice behind me. "How all occasions do conspire against me! If only we hadn't encountered Graham's old schoolmaster, I should have been here an hour since and had that tape erased. Oh, dear—I see you've found the incriminating manuscript, as well!

We are caught in a conundrum indeed, Mrs.—er, Catherine. Are we not?"

I twisted around to look over my shoulder at Cyril Aubrey. He stood there in the doorway shaking his shaggy head, his face furrowed with genuine distress. Then he stepped inside the room and closed the door behind him. As I turned back to the shelves before I lost my balance, my glance swept over the tape recorder hanging from one hand, and an idea came to me. I slipped my finger furtively across the top of it and rewound the tape just a little, not enough to erase his Edgar imitation, then pressed the Record button. Faintly, I heard the little wheels start turning inside.

"When Eric said you and the child had been in this room," he went on, speaking quickly, in a sort of controlled panic, "I thought it unlikely that you had found anything. But then I saw the tape player had been moved on the shelf. I should, of course, have erased that tape long ago, but I'm afraid my vanity won out. I did some acting in my youth, you know, and was rather proud of my performance as Edgar, especially the 999 call, although my summons to Peter was fairly credible as well. A useful lesson in the sin of pride—"

"That's not much of a sin compared to two murders!" I exclaimed.

"Please, let me explain all that!" he burst out in anguish. "You mustn't think I killed Edgar and Perdita just for myself— But come down, won't you? I don't want to hurt you! If you'll permit me to tell you *why* I killed them, perhaps we can agree to let it go no further."

"I don't think so!" I said indignantly. "Not when you tried to put my son-in-law in prison for your crime."

"I quite hated doing that, but he *was* the obvious suspect. Everyone knew his dislike for Stone, and so that evening, with all the faculty watching, I had only to reveal Edgar's behavior toward Emily and offer him an excuse to threaten Peter's job, to suggest quite a superfluity of motives. But afterward—I did repent me when I saw the effect on you, on Emily, on all our friends. Quite a different thing, developing a foolproof plan in theory, from watching it play out in reality. Alas, I did not employ the principles of my philosophy when I chose a man with many friends. Do come down, won't you? I can explain so much better face-to-face."

The tape had run out. I was sure it contained enough of that explanation to convict him, along with the Edgar imitation and the *Ur-Hamlet*. I knew I had to get past him and out of there with all the pieces of the puzzle. So I began loosening a large leather-bound book, obscured by the lower part of my body, as I tried to divert his attention.

"How could you be sure Edgar's manuscript was genuine? Did you get it tested?" I asked innocently.

"Oh, no—I couldn't let anyone examine it, or the game would have been up! But I do have some expertise in these matters—my Kyd letter, after all, fooled everyone—and it appears genuine to me. At any rate, how could I take the chance that it was? He was a sadistic man, you know. He actually quoted from the *Ur-Hamlet* that night in front of everyone—'Roscius, when once he spoke a speech in Rome'—a threat to expose me, because I protested his conduct toward Perdita. Yes, he deserved killing. Perhaps you are nervous about descending the ladder, Catherine. Come, give me your hand and I'll help you to—"

As he came near, I pulled the big book out and, looking over my shoulder, threw it at him as hard as I could. Of course it missed by inches and fell splayed open on the carpet.

Cyril cried out and knelt beside it, smoothing the pages tenderly. He clutched it to his chest and looked up at me with bewildered indignation.

"This is a first-edition Marlowe!" He struggled to his feet and laid it carefully on the desk. "I must insist that you come away from my books, if you are inclined to fling them about like that!"

I gave up and climbed down the ladder, but when he reached for the *Ur-Hamlet* I quickly swung it, and the tape recorder, behind my back.

"Cyril, you simply can't commit murder without paying for it," I explained patiently.

"You can tell the police all these reasons you had, but you've got to take the responsibility."

"No, no," he implored, the panic in his voice now unbridled. "You don't understand, I can't do that to Ann and the boys! I can't let them know those things—their respect is everything to me. Look, you think I forged the Kyd letter for my own aggrandizement, don't you? Not so, far otherwise. The admiration of my peers was gratifying, certainly—but what I really meant to do was to give Graham and Eric the money they needed to set up their philanthropic venture. They are born teachers and longed to bring learning to children in the poorest countries. But they weren't able to raise enough, and actually spoke of giving up their dream. So I forged the letter, and money started flowing in, for the book, for speaking engagements, for the headship. It was the happiest time of my life when I could give them the funds they needed and see the project become reality. Their gratitude was so precious to me—and only look at all the good they've done!"

"Cyril, whatever your intentions, forgery is a crime, and murder is—"

"Are you familiar with the philosophy of Jeremy Bentham?"

"Who?" The sudden change of subject threw me off balance. "Well—no."

"John Stuart Mill?" He cocked his head to one side, an eager professorial smile taking the place of his former anguished expression.

"No, but what I mean—"

"I thought as much. Utilitarianism, my dear lady! A system of ethics which I embrace wholeheartedly. The rightness of an act, you see, depends entirely upon its consequences, and one may decide that by measuring its contribution to 'the greatest good of the greatest number.' It was all formulated in Bentham's *Principles of Morals and Legislation*, in 1789. And you see, the world *is* a better place as a result of my little forgery. Uncounted numbers of children who would be trapped in poverty and ignorance will improve their lot, and quite possibly that of their people, because of what I did."

"You lied, Cyril. You led the scholarly world to believe something that wasn't true."

"I say again, fie on it," he replied, raising his chin defiantly. "Is not human welfare vastly more important than an esoteric point of scholarship?"

It was hard to argue with that. I actually felt myself moving, unwillingly, toward his point of view. Then I remembered that this had gone further than scholarly deception.

"Maybe so. But we're also talking about murder."

He collapsed, as if that last word had been a spike, puncturing the balloon of philosophical justification he'd puffed up. His hand shook, pushing his hair back from his sweaty forehead, and his candid brown eyes again pleaded with me for understanding.

"Murder—yes, the knife going in, and in, and the smell of his blood—it was more horrible than I can say! But it had to be done, don't you see? Edgar Stone would have played cat-and-mouse with me for a while, forcing me into retirement, destroying what I've built at Mercy, but he would eventually have exposed me to the world, to my family, as a forger."

"I can see that," I said, clinging with determination to the main point, although I couldn't repress a twinge of sympathy. "But you didn't have to kill poor Perdita. And you can't tell me you didn't plan her killing—you must have doctored that page from one of her letters, and that's premeditation."

"Let me tell you about a modern development of Bentham's school of thought," he said desperately. "Utilitarian bioethics—it takes the original philosophy to its logical end, you see. If the greatest happiness of the greatest number is the criterion of good, then euthanising the hopelessly unhappy is a net positive value, isn't it? Perdita's death not only kept my secret safe, it also reduced the sum total of misery in the world! I had created a situation, in Peter's arrest, that had brought unhappiness to an unforeseen number of good people. This was completely at odds with my philosophy! And there was Perdita, with no hope of happiness, and for whom no one but Geoffrey would grieve very much."

"We don't have the right to make those decisions for other people!"

"Do we not? Any utilitarian would disagree, my dear Catherine. She didn't fight for her life, you know, nor even plead for it. When I came to her house that evening, carrying the 'suicide' note and the razor in my pocket, she was outside, waiting for a cab to take her to the railway station. She was determined to go to Tyneford, wouldn't let me into the house where I could have taken the *Ur-Hamlet* once the deed was done. Not knowing about that key hidden in the flowerpot, I realized I should have to come back with her own house key, to search for the incriminating volume. I knew that Edgar had concealed it in a different cover, so I had no idea of its appearance, nor where he kept it. I looked for it after killing him, until Tyler's car pulled up and I had to make a hasty exit through the rear door. So I persuaded Perdita to let me drive her to Tyneford. Of course she was shattered when we reached the old house. Her last refuge lay in ruins around her. She wept and would not be comforted, declaring that there was nothing left, nowhere to go, nothing to hope for. I knew then that my decision had been correct. I promised that if she would trust me, I would give her peace. She looked into my eyes while I released her blood, and I saw no fear in her eyes, only a sort of numb relief. It was, in the end, a last favor for an old friend— Ah, Catherine, if you had known her twenty years ago!"

I was amazed to see that his eyes were brimming with tears.

"You didn't have the right," I said stubbornly.

He heaved a deep sigh. "I *abhor* the thought of ever killing again—it is a monstrous maze with no way out! Blood leads on to blood, I've learnt the truth of that. Just tell me you will keep my secret, Catherine. Let the dead be blamed, let it all be forgotten."

Quin had given me an argument very like that, I mused, only based in cynical self-interest rather than cloudy philosophical rationalizations. Without realizing it, I shook my head.

"Oh, God," he moaned. He stepped behind his desk and opened a drawer, and in the next moment I was looking down the barrel of a revolver.

"You must understand, I've not come so far only to be ruined now," he said wretchedly. "I cannot let you take those things away from here. I am in blood stepped in so far that should I wade no more, Returning were as tedious as go o'er.' I understand perfectly what Macbeth meant, although *tedious* is not the most apposite word—*agonizing* would be more true, in my experience. And of course, some scholars believe *steeped* is the correct reading, rather than *stepped,* although personally I have always felt—"

"Cyril, this isn't some academic panel discussion!" I burst out. "This is my *life* you're playing with! Put that thing down before it goes off."

"I do know how to use it," he said, "more or less—although it's never been out of the drawer before, as I mentioned no burglar has yet threatened my book collection. But I don't *want* to employ it, Catherine, and I will not, if I can only believe you will keep my secrets!"

"Okay," I lied, "I will, Cyril. I'll take all the evidence and hide it, and say nothing."

He scrutinized me for a few minutes, and then an expression of great sadness came into his eyes. "You have no talent for deception, Catherine. Your face betrays your real intent. I'd thought you could understand, once I explained, but I see that I was mistaken. 'False hearts speak fair to those they intend most mischief.' " He waited expectantly, as if I were one of his colleagues, always ready for their game of one-upmanship.

"What? I don't know! Shakespeare?"

"Certainly not," he said with a disappointed sigh. *"Duchess of Malfi."* He started fooling with the hammer of the gun, apparently unsure which way to pull it.

"You won't shoot me, Cyril," I said. "How would you explain a dead lady in the library when your family comes home?"

"I could—conceal your remains in the scullery, and remove them by night?" he suggested uncertainly.

"But the blood would still be here—and it would get all over your precious books, wouldn't it?"

That stopped him. "I shall—I shall just have to take you elsewhere, then! Come along, we must hurry—the back garden will be unobserved."

Then the door behind him swung open. Both of us gasped in shock, and Cyril spun around to see what was happening. Quin stood there, looking quite dumbfounded.

I jumped toward the desk, picked up the first-edition Marlowe, and slammed it with all my strength into the back of Cyril's head. He staggered and fell forward, dropping the gun. Quin snatched it up and trained it on him. Cyril lay staring at him in a befuddled way.

"Stay still," Quin warned him. "I know my way around a gun."

"Oh, absolutely," Cyril said groggily, obediently stiffening his whole body. "I didn't mean to—I tried not to—I mean to say, your lady was in no—" He gave up, realizing finally that his excuses were not going to influence either of us.

Quin looked over at me. His eyes held a sort of grim resignation and no longer the hope I had seen when I'd sat down opposite him in the Eagle and Child.

"You followed me," I said.

He nodded. "After I stewed for a while. I finally decided I couldn't let you come alone, just in case you were right. And I guess you were."

As I started to pick up the telephone on the desk, sounds floated from outside the house—car doors slamming, footsteps and laughter. A feeling of impending doom came over me.

"Oh God," I said, "it's his family."

Cyril sat up, throwing me a glance of acute supplication. Then he drew his knees up, laid his face against them, and started to cry in great shuddering sobs that shook his whole body.

"You'll have to call 999," I told Quin, pushing the phone toward him. "I'll give the police the evidence when they get here—this book, and a tape in this machine." I set them on the desk, far from Cyril, and then took a deep, unsteady breath. "I've got to go out and tell Ann and the boys, before they walk in on this."

When I'd almost reached the door he said, quietly, "Kit." I turned impatiently. He stood holding the phone in one hand, gazing at me intently, and he said in a low voice, "Just— I'm sorry."

"You know, that's the first time you've ever said it," I answered. "But it doesn't matter now. You just saved my life, and that's enough to make us quits."

I turned and hurried out to face Cyril Aubrey's family.

EPILOGUE

Farewell, love, and all thy laws forever,
Thy baited hooks shall tangle me no more.
                                    —Thomas Wyatt

"So that's that."

I put the letter back into its envelope, folded it in quarters, and dropped it on the grass.

"What's what?" Fiona asked.

I leaned back in my lawn chair and looked at the cloudless blue sky through the leaves of my apple tree. I could just make out the robin's nest in the crotch of a branch, and the mother bird sitting still as a decoy on her eggs. I would be here to see the babies, to watch them learn to fly and to keep the cat away until they could look out for themselves. Contentment filled me to the brim.

"It's a letter from an old friend in New York—Ellie. I don't know if I've ever mentioned her to you? Anyway, she says Quin and Janet got married." I smiled to show her everything was okay, but she still looked at me with concern. "They've gone to Mexico on their honeymoon.

She's definitely going to have a better time there than she had here!"

"Not—problematic?" Fiona asked.

I reached over and patted her hand reassuringly. "Not a bit," I said. "You should have stopped worrying about that weeks ago."

I glanced quickly through the rest of my mail. Walter, the postman, was just disappearing down the road on his red bicycle, jingling his bell at Mick Jenkins's old dog as it slowly crossed in front of him.

There was an envelope with the return address of Dan Vincent, an American widower I'd met at the time of our village murder. It was the second letter I'd had from him since he'd gone back to New Jersey. I'd had a hard time thinking of anything to tell him about when I answered the first one, but that certainly wouldn't be a problem this time! Such a nice man, and obviously lonely, I mused as I dropped it on the grass with the bills, to be opened later. I hoped he would find a nice, compatible Jersey girl pretty soon, and start a new life.

It was late June, and Cyril Aubrey was locked up, awaiting trial and certain conviction, having been unable to convert the police to Utilitarianism. Ann was sticking by him, and her many friends, as well as her sons, were sticking by her. I'd always feel bad for them, but I didn't see how I could have acted any differently.

Peter had been unanimously chosen to replace Cyril as head and had already hired two young tutors with provocative new approaches to Elizabethan drama. Geoffrey, still inconsolable, had taken a long sabbatical, traveling on the Continent with an old friend. Everybody hoped that when he came back he would finally be resigned to a world without Perdita.

The hardest part of the aftermath for me had been Emily's disappointed face when I told her why Quin and Janet had left on schedule for the States. But by now she had, as she put it, "reconciled her abandonment issues"—in plain English, faced the fact that her parents were divorced for good.

"Well," said Alice, "I really wonder if Enid could have been wrong about the new neighbors? The afternoon is getting on, with no sign of them."

The welcoming committee had settled in my front garden a couple of hours before, Alice and Fiona on the rustic bench I had bought last week at Debenham's, John and I on the two lawn chairs that had been left in the shed by the previous owners, Audrey and Jilly on the stone wall, and little Diana napping in her carry-cot on the ground. Enid Cobb had told me yesterday, in her unshakably positive style, that today was the day the new people would be moving into the house across the road. It had turned out quite attractive, fitting into the village as well as a modern house could, with its whitewashed stucco walls, casement windows, and steeply pitched slate roof. Fiona and I had stood on tiptoe to peek into the first-floor windows, quite covetous of the big eat-in kitchen with a countertop stove and wall oven instead of an Aga, and a ceramic tile floor with patterns of plants baked into each tile. We had concluded the new neighbors were a lot better fixed financially than either of us were.

"Has Enid ever been known to be wrong?" John asked drily.

"If she has," Fiona answered, "nobody would dare to remember. Jilly—oh, do take those things out of your ears!" she added irritably, raising her voice. Jilly removed the earphones that attached her to her Walkman, and Audrey did the same.

"Extraordinary, the way young people today seem to require a musical background to every activity," said Alice.

"If you care to call that music," Fiona snorted.

"Lumme, Fiona, it's Radiohead!" Audrey exclaimed, as if the evocation of Oxford's homegrown rock stars should end all argument.

Fiona rolled her eyes. "I was going to ask you, Jilly, if that carpenter of yours had told you anything about the new people coming today."

"Who, Bert?" She blushed, and Audrey grinned and nudged her with her elbow. Jilly had taken up with one of the young workmen while the house was being built across the road. "No, we never talked about that." The two girls looked at each other and giggled, putting the earphones back into their ears.

"Nor about anything else much, I'd wager," Fiona said shrewdly. "I hope that girl's got a mite more sense than Audrey had. But there's not much sign of it, is there?"

Audrey's pregnancy was not concealed by maternity clothes and was pretty obvious now. I had to admit, I didn't appreciate the current fashion for letting the abdomen swell under nothing but a skintight T-shirt. At least she didn't wear just a halter top, as I'd seen pregnant celebrities doing in magazines.

A black Cortina pulled over to the shoulder of the road, next to my wall, and Reverend Ivey's pale, ascetic face smiled out of the open window.

"Good afternoon," he called. "Most sensible of all of you, to take advantage of such a beautiful day! My radio tells me a storm is expected tomorrow. Oh dear, how awkward I am, bringing bad news into your little party, I do apologize—"

"Not at all, vicar," I responded. "Come and join us."

"I only stopped to tell you that the headstone is to be delivered tomorrow," he said diffidently. The village had finally got up a collection for a nice granite headstone, with inscription, for George Crocker's grave. "I thought you might want to come and see it erected. And I have another announcement, as well. May I indeed join you?"

"Do, please," I called to him.

"We're awaiting the arrival of the new inhabitants," Alice said, waving her arm toward the house.

"Ah, they arrive today? I should be here to meet them, shouldn't I?" he asked, as if seeking our advice. "Yes, yes, if you're sure I won't be imposing, it would certainly be appropriate for me to welcome them to the village."

Poor man, nobody had thought to tell him they were coming. He got out of his car, soliciting our opinions on whether it was safely parked, and once reassured he dithered over to join us. I had to stifle a smile at the way he abruptly averted his eyes when they strayed to Audrey's belly, and how pink his face became. John went into the house and brought out a kitchen chair for him.

"Extraordinarily kind of you!" said the vicar. "It *is* good to see you, Sergeant Bennett, a very rare treat indeed."

John looked slightly uncomfortable, and the rest of us smiled at one another, because he almost never went to church. Apparently Mr. Ivey noticed, and he started apologizing again.

"Oh, I am most awfully sorry, I was not referring to—I mean to say, it is purely a matter of conscience whether one attends services or not, that is, free will is a most important—"

"It's all right, vicar," John said with a smile.

"What I referred to, of course, was your very demanding vocation, which allows you so little time at home. In point of fact, I'm particularly glad to have a chance to talk with you, because I've been anxious to learn one result of your latest coup—I mean the Aubrey case."

"Not exactly a coup," John said ruefully. "Actually, we fixed on the wrong suspect *twice.*"

"Ah, but you did bring the right one to justice at last," the vicar went on regardless.

"But how about your other announcement?" I reminded him. "First tell us that."

"Ah, yes. That one is most gratifying. My son, Tom, and his beloved, Gemma, have asked me to conduct their wedding, at the end of this month. Of course you are all invited!"

Congratulations and best wishes rose all around. Jilly and Audrey took out their earphones belatedly and the news had to be repeated for them.

Then John said, "Very well, vicar, what's this question you have about the Aubrey case? Don't know if I can answer it, mind, but I'll do my best for you."

"Well, I've been wondering whether there are any plans to place the *Ur-Hamlet* on public view? Quite understandable that the police should want to use it as evidence at the trial, but it would be a rare treat actually to see such an important piece of our literary history before it is consigned to a museum."

"Well, vicar," said John, settling back and taking his pipe from his pocket, "I'm afraid I've some bad news for you there."

"Good heavens, it has not been lost again!"

"No, we've still got it. The problem is, when we turned it over to a well-known expert in disputed manuscripts, it took her less than a day to pronounce it a fake."

"A fake?" I sat up and stared, appalled. "You mean two people died, Peter almost lost his freedom, and I could have been shot—over a forged manuscript?"

"Afraid so." He had finished packing the pipe bowl with tobacco and paused to light it. When he took it from his lips he couldn't repress a wry grin. "Mind you, very skillfully done. Only detectable by the most sophisticated technology. Must have taken Edgar Stone years."

"Then the author of the real work is still unknown," said the vicar, shaking his head sadly. "Perhaps it may always be so."

"Well, I'll be darned." I sank back again, smiling too at the irony of it.

"Any more questions?" John asked, after another draw at his pipe.

"You know," I said, "I was always suspicious of Perdita's story about sleeping through the murder. Did you ever learn what she was really doing?"

"Oh, she was asleep, all right. Cecil Aubrey slipped a sleeping draught into her sherry at the party. He didn't want her interfering with his carefully worked-out—"

"It's them!" Jilly exclaimed, pointing toward the new house. John broke off his explanation, and we all gazed avidly at a dark green car, the kind the British call an "estate car," longer than the usual sedan. It was just pulling up in front of the place, and we all rose and hurried down to my gate, led by the vicar.

There was a woman in the driver's seat, a man beside her, and what looked like a couple of teenagers in the back. A moving van was coming down the road, pulling up behind the car. The woman got out and saw us, and her face broke into an irresistible smile.

She was plump and big-bosomed, in a bright blue dress with a pattern of large red flowers. Obviously she wasn't worried about hiding her amplitude. Her hair was a brassy shade of blonde, in those big fat curls you have to set every night on rollers. Her blue eyes sparkled with delight.

"Hello, then!" she called in a north-country accent. "You lot the welcome committee?"

She started out to meet us halfway across the road, limping heavily on her right leg. But the man from the passenger seat now emerged, with some difficulty. The young man and woman each held one of his arms and almost lifted him out. He was dark-haired and white-faced, quite emaciated, and the look in his black eyes as they darted to the blonde woman gave me the shivers.

He yelled at her, quite savagely, "Get yer arse back here! Yer meant to be finding me med'cines, not lollygaggin' in the road with some strangers!"

"Dear me!" said the vicar.

The woman's smile shrank and her happy expression turned fearful. We stopped on the shoulder of the road, and three of the newcomers looked over with embarrassment. The teenaged girl threw us a little pinched smile. She was very pretty, slight and graceful with long dark hair hanging nearly to her waist.

Jilly called over to her, "Need any help, then?" and the girl shook her head silently.

The young man resembled her, the same brown eyes and full lips, but otherwise they were a contrast. He looked none too clean, there was a growth of stubble on his jaw, his hair was dragged back in a tail tied with a string. But he called to us, "Thanks for the thought, but Dad's not been very well the past week or two and we—"

"Sorry," the woman broke in abruptly. "Me husband's fallen ill, as Michael says. After we're settled in—"

She stopped and shrugged helplessly at us, then limped back to open the trunk of the car. After a few minutes of rummaging she emerged with a handful of pill bottles. The young people had supported the man up the brick path and into the house by then. The blonde woman threw us a last smile and a wave and followed them inside while the movers started unloading sofas and chairs.

"Well, that was interesting!" said Fiona as we moved back to my garden. "Do you think we'll ever get as far as introducing ourselves?"

"The poor man *is* ill," Alice said charitably.

"How unfortunate for them," the vicar said, "to have built in a village without a doctor! Of course, they weren't to know a family member would fall ill. The gentleman did look very weak, didn't he?"

"I don't know that I'd call him a gentleman," Fiona responded, "with the mouth he's got on him!"

"Girl looked a bit of a prat," said Audrey. She picked up her daughter, who had started to fuss, and stuck a pacifier in the baby's mouth.

"Pre-Dead," Jilly responded enigmatically. "But did you have a dekko at the brother? Wicked!" From the look on her face, I figured that was not a criticism.

"He's all right," said Audrey coolly. "Not a patch on *my* man, though."

"Well, I'm going to give them a chance," I said staunchly. "I need some nice neighbors, and at least they're not weekenders! I'll go over tomorrow, I'm sure they'll be more approachable then."

Everyone dispersed soon after and I turned back to the cottage, looking forward to starting the fourth act of *The Duchess of Malfi*, which Peter said would curl my hair. I'd picked it up at the public library in Oxford and was reading it slowly, one act a day, savoring the gorgeous poetry but always emerging with relief from half an hour in Webster's merciless world.

Starting up the path, I caught a flash of black in front of me and focused on it long enough to see Muzzle going through the door with, I was pretty sure, a little gray corpse clenched in his teeth.

"Oh, hell," I muttered. He hadn't brought a mouse home for a couple of weeks, and I'd thought he finally understood I didn't appreciate his generosity. But it didn't bother me the way it had a month before. There was all the time in the world to get through to him, I wasn't going anywhere. I stood on the path for a few minutes just looking around, thinking how close I had come to losing it all—Rowan Cottage, the perennial border I was definitely starting tomorrow, the robins in the apple tree, Far Wychwood and its people.

I heaved a sigh of relief and turned toward the potting shed to get the shovel.

Solve a murder or two before bedtime with these intriguing mysteries from Pocket Books.

Verse of the Vampyre
A Poetic Death Mystery
Diana Killian
A literary caper to really sink your teeth into…

Last Seen in Aberdeen
A Sergeant Mornay Mystery
M.G. Kincaid
Detective Mornay must solve a murder while caught between the spotlight of unwanted fame and the shadowy past he'd hoped to forget.

The Kills
Linda Fairstein
Manhattan D.A. Alexandra Cooper becomes involved in a life and death struggle with a violent predator who is determined to silence her forever.

Muletrain to Maggody
An Arly Hanks Mystery
Joan Hess
Away down south in Maggody, Arkansas, Police Chief Arly Hanks must keep the peace when the Civil War—or a darn good replication—masks a modern-day murderer.

Available wherever books are sold.

Cozy up with a good mystery from Pocket Books

PATRICIA HARWIN
Arson and Old Lace
A Far Wychwood Mystery
An American woman. An English town.
A whole lot of trouble.

LAURA BRADLEY
The Brush-Off
A Hair-Raising Mystery
She's a cut above the average sleuth…

LEA WAIT
Shadows on the Coast of Maine
An Antique Print Mystery
Scratch beneath the surface of a small Maine town,
and you'll find murder.

MADDY HUNTER
Pasta Imperfect
A Passport to Peril Mystery
Moonstruck amore…and death al dente.

DIANA KILLIAN
Verse of the Vampyre
A Poetic Death Mystery
A literary caper to sink your teeth into.

Wherever books are sold.

Not sure what to read next?

Visit Pocket Books online at
www.SimonSays.com

Reading suggestions for
you and your reading group

New release news

Author appearances

Online chats with your favorite writers

Special offers

And much, much more!